ROMANCE AT THE EDGE: IN OTHER WORLDS

MaryJanice Davidson
Angela Knight
Camille Anthony

www.loose-id.com

ISBN 1-59632-091-5
ROMANCE AT THE EDGE: IN OTHER WORLDS
Copyright © 2005 by Loose Id, LLC
Cover Art by April Martinez
Edited by: Raven McKnight, Linda Kusiolek, and Maryam Salim

Publisher acknowledges the authors and copyright holders of the individual
works, as follows:
BEGGARMAN, THIEF
Copyright © August 2004 by MaryJanice Davidson
STRANDED
Copyright © July 2004 by Angela Knight
LIGHT ON HER TOES
Copyright © December 2004 by Camille Anthony
Excerpt from *Ontarian Chronicles 1: Taken by the Storm* by Cyndi Friberg
copyright © November 2004 by Cyndi Friberg
Excerpt from *For the Heart of Daria* by Doreen DeSalvo copyright © August
2004 by Doreen DeSalvo

This book is an original publication of Loose Id. Each individual story herein
was previously published in e-book format only by Loose Id and is a work of
fiction. Any similarity to actual persons, events or existing locations is
entirely coincidental.

Printed in the U.S.A. by
Lightning Source, Inc.
1246 Heil Quaker Blvd
La Vergne TN 37086
www.lightningsource.com

Contents

BEGGARMAN, THIEF

MaryJanice Davidson

Dedication

For Karen, who reads everything I ask without complaint...in fact, she does a credible job of feigning interest.

This little story, which has been lurking in the bottom of my heart for several years, would not have been possible without the formation of Loose Id. And so I thank the entire lizard gang, not only for giving me a chance to write about a mutant and a cyborg, but for giving voice to many other authors who might otherwise not have been heard. Thank you.

Prologue

Mitchell Hunter stood at his window and looked out at the city. His city. He owned one third of it. He owned the very hotel he was living in. Top floor. The penthouse.

All his.

He took another swallow of his drink. The sixty-year-old cognac went down like liquid silk. He pulled on the cuff of his shirt. It had been hand-tailored in London. He paced and then sat down on the bed. The sheets were Egyptian cotton, over six thousand dollars per king-sized set, and were laundered in France.

He had taken to tucking thousand-dollar bills into the cups of panhandlers. When the nearby church solicited funds to replace their old stained-glass windows, he gave them a check so large the reverend had to sit down. When one of his employees came to him to resign so she could care for her family while her husband found work in Alaska, he gave her five years' severance. *She* had to sit down, too.

He'd given a ridiculous amount of money to the Independent Party candidate for the presidential election, more out of idle curiosity than anything else. Would the lady win? She had, but it hadn't mattered.

Nothing mattered. He had more money than he could spend in five lifetimes, and it didn't mean a damned thing.

He could see his reflection in the glass, a dark shadow. He looked perfectly normal, which was, of course, a lie. He was as far from normal as you could get. He wasn't even really a man.

Take away the plastic and the metal, and what's left? One third of me. Is that a man?

No more than the metal and glass building he owned made a whole city.

He swallowed the last of the cognac, and crushed the cup— it had been carved out of a single piece of Venutian rock—in one hand. He watched the powder drift to the carpet, and thought again about jumping out the window. He was thirty stories up, but he was afraid it wouldn't kill him. And what would They do? Would They replace *all* of him with metal and plastic? Then what?

He'd volunteered the first time, because he thought he knew what he was getting into. Now he really *did* know. And it wasn't worth it, being stronger and faster and smarter than just about everyone on the planet. It wasn't worth it, because he was alone. There was no one else like him.

He was afraid to die. And he couldn't bear to go on living.

Chapter One

"Say! Is this where Mitchell Hunter lives?"

"Lady, you can't—"

"Because I just wanted to thank him for saving our church."

"Lady—" The petite, gorgeous redhead had walked right up to Harry Gould, barely coming up to his jaw. He'd been on the job a week—night security for HuntCorp—and so far it had been cake. Shooing away reporters—seemed like they all wanted a piece of the boss. Nightly patrols. Escorting the occasional bar drunk back to his (or her) room.

But now here was this teeny redheaded honey with great legs and phenom tits, crowding him in the service entry. How she'd gotten in, he had no clue. And it was tough work, telling her to hit the trail. He'd rather tell her to hit *his* trail. "Lady, you can't—"

"He *saved* it." Her hands knotted together between her breasts, and she blinked up at him like a red-haired Bambi. "All our windows were yucky and we wanted new ones and thanks to him we got a whole new church! And a parish center, too. The bingo committee is thrilled. Where is he?"

Harry cleared his throat. She smelled like lilacs. Lilacs, in March! Shit, in the city at all. "He—he's really busy, ma'am."

"Oh, so he's in town tonight?"

"Ma'am, it's real late. Why don't you come back tomorrow—during business hours—and I'll see if I can get you in to see him." Who knew? Maybe the sight of this fervid cutie would cheer the morbid bastard up. Harry liked his job, and he loved the salary, but Mr. Hunter gave him the creeps. There were livelier statues. "What's your name?"

"Oh, never mind that." She stepped away. "I'll come back tomorrow. Thanks for your help!" She walked away, hips swaying sweetly beneath the black micromini.

Harry watched her go, giving thanks that the miniskirt had been out, then in, then out, and recently in again, with a vengeance. She flipped a wave over her shoulder, shoved open the service door, and stepped out of his life.

* * *

"Well, shit," Jamie Day muttered. Hunter was home! All that research, for squat. Now she'd have to wait until he went to sleep. He only had the Rock in his safe for one night; it was being shipped to the moon tomorrow.

She'd thought Hunter, of all people, would stick to a schedule. And tonight he was scheduled to be in Washington, D.C., at the Inaugural Ball...he had, after all, been a major campaign contributor, and everybody was crapping themselves over the new lady president.

Instead he'd blown it off...why? She'd been watching him for weeks; she knew his habits and schedule as well as he did. Once something was on the Sacred Schedule, he stuck to it. But to blow it off at the last second...

It was almost as if he just couldn't be bothered to take the trip.

Weird.

One way or another, she was getting her hands on the Rock. If he got in her way—well, it wasn't like he could hurt her. He couldn't even stop her. By the time he raised the alarm, she'd be long gone.

Jamie cheered up as she ducked into her car. Fresh plates, clean car, and it'd be in pieces sometime tomorrow. No way to trace it back to her. Not that anybody could trace anything to her anyway—among other things, she didn't leave fingerprints. Ever.

Jamie pulled off the skirt, revealing her thick tights were really thin black leggings. She pulled off the bustier and pulled on a black turtleneck. She reversed her jacket, so the lime green lining was on the inside, and the black was outside. She kicked off the bright yellow pumps and slipped on black ballet slippers, and pulled off the outrageous red wig, revealing her short-cropped, Easter-egg-blue hair. The guard had been so busy staring at her boobs and hair and clashing jacket and shoes, it was doubtful he could place her in a line-up if his life depended on it.

Time to wait. She'd go up around three AM. Pop into the safe. Get the Rock—and any other pretty baubles that caught her attention—and be on her way. She had about a zillion pockets, and each one could hold several diamonds. Or thousand-dollar bills! Hee!

She passed the time by re-reading the King Corporation's latest *(The Shining VI...The Hotel Strikes Back!)* and gobbling Twizzlers.

Chapter Two

Mitchell turned. Something was wrong. Something *had* been wrong for the last few minutes, but he'd been unable to figure out what. At last he had it. The sound, so faint only his cybernetic eardrum could pick it up, was someone breathing, quickly and lightly.

All the lights were off, of course—he could see in the dark like a cat—and he'd been standing before his window for hours. Now, it seemed, he had company.

He stole softly across the carpet, slipped through the bedroom door, into the living area, and saw at once the door to the saferoom was open.

He avoided the furniture, the table, the piles of financial papers, and the squeaky spot by the piano. He paused in the doorway and nearly gasped in surprise.

A woman was working on his safe. *His* safe. Where he kept *his* money. She was short—barely up to his shoulder—with short hair that looked—er, pastel blue—slim limbs, and—and never *mind* what she looked like. How the hell had she gotten in? She'd have had to get past security, multiple alarms, and three locked doors.

He could see she was wearing night goggles. He knew from experience they only weighed about sixteen ounces and looked like regular sunglasses, except for the thick lenses. He closed his natural eye to get a better look—and nearly gasped again.

She'd disappeared.

He opened both eyes. She was back, still working on the safe.

He closed his artificial eye. She was still there.

He closed his natural eye, the better to scan her—and she was gone again.

Interesting. She couldn't be seen by artificial means. His cybereye couldn't see her, nor could the security cameras.

A mutant. He'd read about them but had never met one—not that he knew of.

Fascinating.

Completely, utterly, compellingly *fascinating.*

It had been only a matter of time, the scientists had warned. Thanks to all the nuclear testing, the earth was clicking hot—much hotter than it had been five hundred or even two hundred years ago. And now and again, according to *Scientific World,* a mutant popped up.

The dangerous ones—the ones who couldn't think, but who could set fires when they got angry, or crack cement, or drive others mad with a single touch, had been squirreled away. Most of the time, the flip side of a major mutation was cataclysmic retardation. No one knew why, or where the government put the dangerous ones.

The less dangerous ones kept out of sight, and made darned sure not to do anything extraordinary when people were watching. He'd always assumed they weren't terribly bright— but this one certainly was. She'd picked the right night to rob him, after all.

He watched his thief take a big gasp of breath, and then charge the safe door. Not exactly the door—the crack along the side where the door rested on its hinges. She shoved herself against it, grunting softly, eyes squinched shut. And after a long moment, she started to—to slip through. It was like her molecules had stretched out, or something. Suddenly she was a living ghost, slowly wedging herself through the safe, and after a minute, she popped inside.

Mitchell stared where she had been for a long moment. Then he closed his artificial eye—yes, she was really inside the safe.

Amazing. How did she take her clothes and accessories and goggles with her? Was she able to affect their molecular structure because they were items close to her skin?

Amazing. He had a thousand questions for the blue-haired lady, chief of which: is that hair color natural?

No. Ridiculous.

He didn't care. No, he didn't, not really. She could empty the entire contents and he'd still be a zillionaire. He should just go back to his window and drink some more and let her take what she wanted. Let her leave, never to be seen again. Yes, he should do that. After all, he didn't care. About anything.

* * *

Jamie chortled with glee when she saw the Rock. It looked exactly like it had in the pictures, except a thousand times better. It was as big as her fist—one of the largest diamonds on the planet. And to think it had come from a meteor! Just fell to earth like a present from God. Well, as far as Miss Jamie Day was concerned, that meant it was anybody's game. Just because construction workers from HuntCorp had found it and brought it to Mr. Hunter didn't mean it was *his*.

Besides, it was shiny and she wanted it.

She gathered herself for the arduous trip out of the safe. It was tough work, phasing through solid objects. Took a lot out of her—she supposed molecules weren't meant to be stretched out like that. Well, she'd take a vacation after tonight. Rest up. She just had to get out of the safe (and through all the locked doors), and she could nap for a week.

Jamie took a deep breath...and pushed. And pushed! Cripes, it was like being born. If she was stuck being a mutant, why couldn't she have a power that didn't take it out of her each time?

At last she popped out of the safe and leaned against it, panting. Her nightglasses had slipped, and when she brought up a hand to adjust them, something smacked into the back of her neck, and everything went black.

Chapter Three

"Oh, that's just rotten!" she screamed, sitting bolt upright in bed.

"I—" Mitchell began.

"And sneaky!"

"—have—"

"And *weird,* not to mention depraved."

"—some questions—"

"And you've got a lot of nerve, being home!"

He laughed at her, which shut her up as effectively as if a switch had been thrown. Her blue brows wrinkled in a scowl as he chortled. "Let me see if I understand you correctly. You're angry with me because I'm home?"

"Like I said. Nerve. Lots of nerve." *And by the way, what the hell am I doing in your bed, big boy?* What was that old story she heard when she was a kid? Little Red in the Hood? *My, what big teeth you have, Grandma.*

Never mind. What was the other motto from that other story? *Never let 'em see you sweat.*

She lay back down and twiddled her thumbs on her chest. "I'm waiting for your apology. And make it good."

"I've never met a mutant before."

She sighed. "First of all, that's the worst apology I've ever heard. That's worse than the 'I'm sorry, but...' apologies. You're either sorry or you're not. It's not qualified."

"Fascinating," he said to the air.

"Second, you have no idea if you have or not."

"Have what?"

"Met a mutant. It's not like we walk around with signs taped to our chests. And third, we prefer the term 'interestingly abled.'"

"You do not."

She snickered. "You're right. We don't. Save that PC shit for the twentieth century."

He pulled a chair up beside the bed and sat down. She noticed that the sleeves of his blue dress shirt were rolled up, revealing heavily muscled forearms sprinkled with black hair. Mmmm...hairy...

"How is it that you're...um...that you...er...that is to say..."

"That I don't drool into my cornflakes?" she asked dryly.

He coughed. "Well. I had read—seen on TV—that mutants have—that is to say, they—I don't mean to offend you—although why I'm fretting about that when you were caught breaking and entering—"

"I didn't break shit. I was only entering," she added primly.

He laughed again. She stared at him. Instead of calling the city guard and hauling her off, he was playing Twenty Questions. She wasn't quite sure which one she preferred.

The guard. Definitely.

"Are you stalling me so I don't flee before the guardies get here? I mean, don't you have a board meeting to be in or something?"

"At two o'clock in the morning? No. I really want to know."

"Well, tough." She sat up again and felt the back of her neck. It was sore, but nothing that would kill her. "Do you make a habit of lurking in corners with crowbars?"

"No."

"My throbbing neck says different," she snapped.

"I didn't hit you with anything."

"Well, why did I decide to suddenly take a nap, then? Huh? Why? Huh?"

He grinned at that, then stopped smiling. Too bad. He had a nice smile. For a ghoul who skulked in dark corners. "I asked you a question."

"No, you stammered and mumbled a question. And I asked *you* one."

"All right," he replied calmly. "I'll answer yours if you answer mine."

She thought it over. In the end, she had to know. Everything! How he spotted her, tracked her, nailed her. It hadn't happened since she was too young for training bras. "Okay. The newsies have it wrong. Not all mutes are massively dumb. Only about eighty percent of us are." More like ninety, but *he* didn't know that.

She thought about a girl she'd grown up with in the Districts, a girl who could tell colors by feel. She was blind and deaf and had an I.Q. of twenty-two, but she could tell a red piece of paper from a blue one without any trouble. Or a black marble from a yellow one. Like most mutes, it made for a cute parlor trick that had no actual, real-world application. She had died just before her twenty-first birthday. Also like most mutes.

"The ones of us who *aren't*...let's just say we don't go around advertising the fact."

"I tapped the nerve cluster at the base of your neck."

She made the old-fashioned time-out sign with her hands. Ah, football. Now there was a game. Too bad it had been outlawed in 2052. Too dangerous. But she didn't care if it *was* the national pastime, she wasn't taking up golf. "You want to try that one again, Hunter?"

"Mitchell. There's a nerve cluster at the back of your neck. If you hit it just right, it induces temporary unconsciousness."

"Huh. And don't call me Mitchell. I have to admit, that's a little on the weird side."

"Some people collect recipes," he said, perfectly straight-faced.

"Right," she said, sitting up and swinging her legs over the bed. "Well, since you're here, I shouldn't be here, so I'll just be on my way. It's been just gobs and gobs of fun, but tra-la, and all that."

His fingers settled lightly in the center of her chest and he pushed her back. "Stay a minute," he said, and it wasn't a request. He reached up and felt a bit of her hair. "It's real," he added, visibly surprised.

"Of course it's real. It's part of my mutation, duh."

"Duh?" he echoed, eyebrows arching.

"Enough about my hair." She glared up at him. "Kidnapping! They execute people for that, you know."

"I'm sure the guard will believe you over me," he pointed out.

"Oh, stuff yourself."

"Temper, temper. I take it you were after the Medici Stone?"

"Dumbest name in the world. Worlds, rather. I'm after the shiny moon rock."

"Why?"

"Because it's shiny and I want it."

He blinked. "Well, you can have it."

"Excellent! Gee, I wish I'd known that earlier. Would have saved me gobs of trouble." She narrowed his eyes at him. "What's the catch, Hunter?"

"Mitchell. Stay with me for the next...ah...seventy-two hours. And when you leave, you can take the Medici Stone."

"Hmm. Tempting, but I'll pass. And don't call me Mitchell."

He frowned. "Why?"

"Because it's not my name."

"No, why won't you stay?"

"Because you don't *mean* it," she explained. "It's a trick. It's got to be a trick. Why would someone like *you* want someone like *me* to hang out for the weekend? It doesn't make sense."

"Someone like me?" he asked quietly.

She puzzled over the dark tone in his voice, then shrugged it off. "Yeah. You're rich and tall, and you own half the city and stuff. I'm a mongrel nobody from the Districts. Hell, from C-block!"

"You're interesting."

"You mean I'm a genetic freak."

"I wouldn't put it that way."

"Say it with me, Hunter: juh-net-ick freek."

"Yes, but it's interesting to me."

She rolled her eyes. "Yeesh. Not too terrifying."

"I'd like to find out more about you."

"Suuuuuuure you would."

"No, really."

"I believe you! That's not the problem."

"What is, exactly?"

"Forget it," she snapped.

"Why?" he asked, seeming honestly surprised.

"Because I'm not your fucking science experiment, pal. Now call the guards or let me out of here."

"I think...neither." And he smiled down at her. Weird, how a smile could be so handsome and so scary at the same time.

Chapter Four

"I have to go to the bathroom," she announced.

"No, you don't."

She gasped. "Hunter, you arrogant swine! I think *I* would *know.*"

"Mitchell. It's a ploy to escape me."

"By the way, who talks like that?" she wondered aloud. "And it is not. And I've asked you repeatedly to stop calling me Mitchell."

He leaned over, caught her by the hand, pulled her off the bed, touched her hair again (almost like he couldn't help it, and again, yeesh) and escorted her to a luxuriously appointed bathroom. The place smelled like roses, and Jawheh only knew what it smelled like during, um, other times.

He stood next to her (and the toilet) and waited patiently.

"What?" she asked.

"So. Go."

"I can't do it with you standing right there," she said, shocked.

"I thought you said you grew up in the Districts."

"I grew up poor, not barbaric. I don't know how it is with the country club set, but *we* don't stand around watching each other pee all day. We're a little more preoccupied about not getting evicted, paying the electric bills, boring stuff like that."

He sighed dramatically, then turned his back.

"I don't trust you," she declared. "You'll peek at me."

His back stiffened and he turned around. "I will not!"

"All right, all right, don't yell." She was looking around for something to hit him over the head with. Maybe she could bind him up like a mummy with toilet paper? "Turn back around. And don't listen, either."

"How can I not listen?" he asked the wall.

"Oh, stuff yourself. Hey, you got any aspirin or something? You're giving me a splitting headache." She eased open the medicine cabinet door, keeping a wary eye on his back at the same time. Success! An old-fashioned straight razor nestled in its case...*who* shaves with straight razors? What year was this? Yeesh.

Never mind. Focus! Jamie silently manipulated the blade open and, quick as a flash, had seized the back of his thick black hair and whipped the blade around, under his chin.

He yawned.

"All right, buddy-punk. You're gonna walk me out of this place, or I'm gonna fingerpaint with what's in your jugular."

He yawned harder and stretched, causing her to lean away from his long, windmilling arms. "I mean it! Now march! No time for a nap now."

"Are you done going to the bathroom?" he asked politely.

"Am I—what's *wrong* with you? Do you think I won't cut your throat? Because it's not really a problem for me, I can assure you!"

"Really?" he asked, sounding interested. "Why not?"

"Because—because I'm a cold-blooded killer, and you're between me and what I want and—and I'm just a scumskank from C-block with nothing to lose and—and I'll do it!"

He laughed again, more a soft chuckle this time. "You're a thief. And your mutation allows you to ply your trade with minimal confrontation. So I would imagine you go out of your way to avoid just this sort of thing."

"Where I grew up, it was kill or be stomped! Or however the saying goes."

"Have you ever killed anyone in your life?"

"Gobs of them," she replied, wondering exactly when she'd lost the upper hand. She had the sneaking suspicion she'd never had it. "Tons of them. Metric tons. Now—don't do that!"

He'd jerked his head to the side, forcing the blade to slit his throat open. The cold-blooded action made her scream and scream. The sound bounced crazily off the marble walls. She didn't think she'd ever be finished screaming.

"—all right?"

"—gggggggggggggggghhhhhhhhhhhhhhhhhhhhhhhh...what?"

He looked at her, concerned, while clutching his throat. "I said are you all right? You look like you're going to lose your feet any minute."

"And *you* look like you're going to *die!* Any minute! Jesus Christ on a jumped-up Gilligan's Island!"

"It's touching," he commented, "that you appear to be concerned."

She slapped his hand away, already flinching, expecting to be drowned in a bucket of blood. "Call the hospital guard—you can do that from up here, right? Fuckit, *I'll* do it. Got any bandages? We can use toilet paper," she said, grabbing blindly. "Oh, good, it's tri-ply. It's—um—" She was staring at his throat, which was winking at her.

Well, no. It wasn't exactly winking at her. The light in the bathroom was bouncing off the wires and circuitry sticking out of his neck, making it seemed like there were lights in there and they were—were flashing. There was some blood, yes, but not very much, and it seemed to be seeping like a slow leak of oil.

"Uh—you're not going—uh—to—to bleed to death, are you?"

"Not today," he said, with something very close to cheer.

"But you're not like me." That had come out tentatively, but she thought about it and her voice was firmer. "You're not a mutant. You can say anything you want about us mutes—"

"Can I? Thanks."

"—but we're all one-hundred-percent organic. We're not—y'know—enhanced by science or whatever."

He quirked an eyebrow at her. "Is that what I am? Enhanced by science?"

"Well. *Aren't* you?"

She took a wad of tri-ply toilet paper and dabbed ineffectually at his bloody throat. He took her hands and held them. "I don't know what I am," he said quietly, looking down into her eyes. "I've never known. But I know what I like. And I like you. If you promise to cease and desist all throat-cutting activities, if you promise to stay the weekend, I'll give you whatever you want when it's time to leave."

Whatever...? She wanted the moon rock, for sure, but he had a few other baubles in his collection she'd been dying to get a look at...and now he was offering them to her on a plate!

"How your eyes gleam," he commented, "when you're contemplating theft."

"Shut up," she said automatically. And...she had to admit...she was curious. She'd never met anyone like this guy. And she'd thought that before she sliced him up.

"You're gonna have to change your shirt," she told him, then flushed the bloody toilet paper down the toilet.

Chapter Five

He took her quickly, almost as if he wanted to get "that" out of the way. They were both products of the looser sexual mores of the latter half of the twenty-first century, so there was no virginal squeamishness, no "let's have a drink and get to know each other" bushwah.

No, he pulled her clothes off and stripped and pushed her down on the bed, worked her with his fingers until she was gasping and squirming and ready for him, then took her until she had had enough, took her until orgasms were bursting within her like fireworks, took her until she begged him to come.

And afterward, he asked her questions.

"Can't we at least get something to eat first?" she griped, coming out of the bathroom, freshly showered. "And maybe some clothes? Or am I supposed to scamper around naked all weekend?"

"As you wish," he replied, and favored her with a rare grin. "But if not, help yourself."

She did, stepping into a pair of dark blue boxer shorts and buttoning up one of his dress shirts. Then she flopped onto the bed and wouldn't say a word until he ordered up a steak from room service.

"That's better," she said with her mouth full. "I was starving."

He looked concerned, or as concerned as anyone could look while sniffing a brandy glass. "Is food a—um—an issue where you live?"

"You mean, am I malnourished because I'm poor? No. This is America. They make it easy for you to eat...as long as you don't mind eating crap. This—" she gestured to her steak and salad— "this is much better. By the way, you are *excellent* in the sack."

"In the what?"

"In bed. How shall I put this so a man of your sensibilities can understand?" Her eyes tipped up, and then she said, "You fuck good."

"Thank you so much. Likewise. I must say, I've never seen dark blue pubic hair before."

"Don't start on my hair again." But she was blushing. "Of course it's dark...it doesn't get much sun. I was thinking of dying it in red and white strips for the Fourth of July, but never got around to it."

"Fascinating. Would you like another supper? Some dessert, maybe?"

"What is this, like a *Pretty Woman* thing going on?"

"What?"

"Never mind." He was smart and rich and all, but she doubted he was into classic twentieth-century movies like she was. "So what's your deal, Daddy-o?"

He barely concealed a shudder. *He* hadn't bothered to get dressed again, she couldn't help but noticing, and it was distracting beyond belief. There wasn't a spare millimeter of fat on the man. He was all long legs, flat stomach, and, not to put too fine a point on it, big cock. And his throat...his throat had healed completely. When had *that* happened? Did he call a mechanic and somehow she missed it?

"First off, please don't call me that again. Second, I don't have a deal."

"Right. You convince strange women to spend the weekend with you so you can play Twenty Questions."

He shrugged. "You're interesting. I confess I've never met anyone like you before."

"And never will again, Daddy-o," she said, satisfied.

"Oh, my. The ego on you."

"Hey, if you're not going to toot your own horn, who's gonna do it for you?"

"Toot your what?"

"Never mind. And pass the salt."

Chapter Six

"I want to see it," he said as she was polishing off her second bowl of peach ice cream.

Jamie laughed. "You didn't get enough half an hour ago?"

"No, I mean...I want to see you do what you do. Again."

Her smile disappeared. "This isn't a peepshow, chum."

"Now, now," he said gently. "A deal is a deal."

"Yeah, well, I thought you meant sex. If I spent the weekend, I figured we'd be doing it 'til we were sore."

"Well, that, too."

She ignored his teasing. "That's fine. I don't mind the sex. Gods, I haven't gotten laid in...ugh, I don't want to think about it. Anyway, having some naked fun with you, no problem."

"That's something else I wish to discuss," he said quietly.

"What? Why?"

"I'm just...curious. Curious and gratified. That you would consent to letting me...touch you. After what you saw."

"Well, you *do* have an unnaturally clean bathroom," she said, understanding mixing with a little pity. Big, strong badass, and he looked like he was going to bolt from the room any second if she so much as laughed at him or asked where he kept the spare oil can. "I admit, that was a little off-putting. Who dusts their toilet paper? As for the rest of it..." She shrugged. "Who am I to judge? I'm a *genetic* freak. You're the way you are because it was your—your will, I guess. I mean, something happened, right?"

"...right..."

"And you could have died, or you could have let...whoever...fix you. So you paid the price, but I bet you did it on your own terms. I think that's pretty stokey, y'know?"

There was a long pause, and then he sat on the bed beside her and said, "Something did happen. A crash. And they fixed me. But nothing is free."

"You're telling that to a thief? Mitchell, I *know* nothing's free. Not even these days, when the government's regulating every damn thing they can get their hands on."

"Ah." He looked gratified. "I knew I could get you to call me by my first name. Eventually."

"Well, hooray for you. Okay, fine. But this is a one-time-only thing. And for the record, I *never* do this." She squinched her eyes shut and held her breath, and wriggled her shoulders, and the last things she saw before she disappeared through the bed were his dark brows, arching in surprise.

She hit the floor beneath the bed with a thump. "There," she said, coughing on the dust bunnies. "You happy?"

"Amazing!" he cried. She felt him grope under the bed, grab her by the ankle, and haul her out. "Can you go through anything?"

"Sure."

"Rocks? Cement?"

"Sure."

"Doesn't it—ah—tire you?"

"Sure."

"Would you..." He seemed to reconsider what he was about to say, because he cleared his throat and said, "Would you like more ice cream?"

"Sure!"

Chapter Seven

She was awake in the dark, and wondered why in the world she was still there.

Because it was nice. It was nice to be here in Mitchell's bed, cuddled into his side, listening to his deep breathing. It was comfortable and warm, and her life had had few moments of comfort and warmth. As for men, there hadn't been many over the years...and there was no one like Mitchell. She suspected that would be true even if he wasn't—how had he put it, and with such a sarcastic smile, a smile it hurt to look at? "Half man, half machine."

The only reason she had agreed to stay was because she knew she could slip out anytime. Piece of cake...phase through the bed, the floor if she had to, all the way down to the lobby, and out the door.

So why was she still there?

Good damn question. She should have phased out two hours ago, instead of watching him sleep, big gooshy softy that she was.

Okay. So, fix it. Go now.

Okay.

She eased away from him, intent on the door and moving noiselessly, when his hand shot out and seized her elbow, which startled the shit out of her.

"Forget something?"

"Aaaiiggghhh! Don't *do* that!" In retaliation, her own hand shot out and closed around...his dick.

"Don't do *that,*" he retorted. "Where do you think you're going?"

"Well, I was escaping," she said reasonably.

He snorted. "I didn't expect you to admit it. Going back on our deal already?"

"Sure. Me, thief. You, amoral zillionaire. My conscience—"

"Such as it is!"

"—is clear."

"Well, too bad. You can't sneak out on *me*, dear. I hear like a bat. My...enhancements...are good for more than scaring you in bathrooms."

"Well, hip-hip-hor-fucking-ray." Disgruntled, she sat and thought. She could still make a break for it. She didn't think he could stop her...no one had ever been able to stop her.

Trouble was, she didn't especially want to. Except for the small matter of Brennan and fellows, to whom she owed the moon rock. They'd be expecting her. In fact, she was late already. Then there was the—

"Dear, what are you doing?"

"I'm thinking."

"Well, can you—ah—loosen your grip a little while you ruminate?"

"Oh." She realized she had a vise-like grip on his dick, and loosened accordingly. "Sorry."

"Not that I mind. Much. Ah, Jamie, while you're down there..."

"Pig," she said automatically. Although it *would* be fun. Escape or blowjob? Escape or blowjob? A question for the ages...

"Jamie? Are you still with me, dear?"

"Shut your pudding hole—I'm thinking."

He snorted again in the dark. "You know, most people in this situation would assume I have the upper hand..."

"Sure, sure. Most people couldn't phase your dick into the comforter and let go."

"Ouch," he said respectfully.

"Oh, the hell with it," she sighed, and yanked the covers out of the way, and covered his dick with feathery kisses. He grew beneath her lips in an amazingly short time, and she licked his hot, hard length, pulling the velvety head into her mouth and sucking and even (very gently) nibbling around the tip. His hands were buried in her hair, and he was groaning and thrusting his hips against her face. She cuddled his plum-sized balls with her hands and gently stroked while she licked and sucked.

"Oh, Christ," he rasped in the dark. "That's amazing. You're amazing. Don't—don't stop, I'm going to—to—"

Then he was pulsing in her mouth, and when he was finished, she bounded off the bed, found the bathroom, and spat in the toilet. The taste of him hadn't been unpleasant, but strong and metallic.

"Yech!" she called cheerfully. *"What* have you been *eating?"*

He laughed so hard, she heard the thump as he fell off the bed.

Chapter Eight

"So, what do you do, Mitch? Besides kidnap women and make them hang out with you?"

"More like apprehend thieves," he corrected her dryly. "How many pancakes are you going to eat?"

"As many as I want, pal. You can't get stuff like this at McBurgerKing. So what are you going to do this weekend? It's only Saturday."

"Oh, you know. Seduce, betray, impregnate." He looked at her through narrowed eyes. "The usual."

"Yech. Forget it, I'm on city water."

"So am I," he admitted. In 2047, the city had voted to spike the drinking supply with contraceptives. If you wanted to have a baby, you certainly could, but first you had to see the doctor to get a prescription for daily medication to counteract the effect. And you could only get that prescription if you passed the physical, the I.Q., and the light battery of psychological tests.

"I'd never pass it, anyway," Jamie admitted.

"Because you're…"

"A genetic freak."

"I was going to say," he corrected gently, "special."

"Six of one, pal." She shrugged bravely. "What would I do with a baby, anyway?"

"I could pull some strings. If you wanted a baby."

She looked down at her plate. "It'd be…just another mouth to feed."

He didn't say anything.

"You're out of syrup," she informed him.

"Mmmmm. I'll call room service."

"Then I'll have to take a bath," she called after him as he went to the phone. "I'm all sticky. Pervert," she muttered, as he flashed a diabolical grin over his shoulder.

* * *

"Look, having sex in a bathtub—even one the size of my living room—doesn't work."

"You just have to be committed."

"Seriously," she gasped as his fingers disappeared beneath the bubbles and stroked her. "It looks great in the movies and—ah!—and all—uh—but it doesn't—ooooh—doesn't—it's just not that easy."

"I'm sure we have the fortitude for the task. I'll be back." Then he took a deep breath and disappeared beneath the water. She felt him spread her knees apart, and then his tongue was lapping at her, licking her, spreading her lower lips apart and stroking. She let her head fall back and nearly drowned—it was a *big* tub. Instead, she clung as best she could to the sides while he brought her body to wracking orgasm.

He popped up, gasping, and she said (gasping a bit herself), "How did you *do* that?"

"My cybernetic enhancements are superior at extracting oxygen from their—"

"Yeah, way to kill the mood, Science Boy. So you can hold your breath for, like, five minutes?"

"More like ten," he said, leaning in and kissing her deeply. "Or fifteen. But who's counting?"

"I still say this won't work," she said, as he gripped her hips and positioned her exactly the way he wanted her. "But hell. I'll give it a shot. By the way, you have a *devilish* mouth."

"Yes," he said smugly, and she bit him on the ear, hard. Then groaned as she felt him pulling her onto him, impaling her like one of those old-time bugs you used to be able to see in the country—a butterfly! He pulled her to him and she wrapped her legs around his waist. It was a tight fight, unbelievably tight, but mind-numbing in its intensity, the pure goodness of how it felt.

"Oh," she sighed, resting her head against his shoulder.

"Told you," he said smugly, if slightly out of breath. He pushed her onto him and pulled her back, again and again, forcing her to be the friction, the force bringing them together, the force bringing her to orgasm again, so hard she saw black roses when she closed her eyes. And at the last, he pulled her onto him so hard her hips went numb from the pressure of his fingers. Then he was shuddering so hard, water splashed over the sides, and then he was relaxing, falling away from her and slipping under the water.

"Hey!" she shouted at the bubbles. "Get back up here! What, that's it? You come and, what, go swimming? No pillow talk? Are you listening? You can hear me, you cybernetically enhanced prick."

He popped up, laughing, and she brushed bubbles out of his eyes, and complained when he snatched her to him for a friendly squeeze, but she didn't really mean any of it. And for some reason, that was the scariest thing that had happened to her so far that weekend.

Chapter Nine

"I think you should stay longer," Mitchell said, rubbing more vanilla-scented oil into her shoulders.

"Why?" She groaned, as he worked his talented fingers into her knotted shoulders.

"My goodness, for such a laid-back individual, for someone who can never get caught, you're tremendously tense."

"Rich people have no idea," she said, grumpy.

"Oh, hush up. Try managing a coup without anyone tumbling to what you're up to sometime. That'll knock the needles on a stress machine."

"Yeah, yeah, cry me a fucking river, RoboBoy."

He groaned. *"Please* don't call me that. Unless you'd like to be called Blue."

She shivered. "Sorry. And why should I stay here? Why the hell would someone like *you* want someone like *me* hanging around?"

"Well," he said reasonably, pounding the kink out of her left shoulder, "why wouldn't I?"

"Um, because we're totally different and we'd drive each other insane?"

"Besides that."

"That's not *enough?* Ooh, don't stop."

"Ah," he said. "If only I had a ten-dollar bill for every time I heard a woman say that. Oh, wait. I do."

"Shut up," she snapped. "Pervert. Look, I'm out of here tomorrow…with any piece of your collection I want. You promised, right?"

"…right."

"Well, I'd think you'd be glad to see the ass end of me," she pointed out reasonably.

"Ah, your ass."

"Seriously, that's what I think."

"You shouldn't think," he said sweetly. "You're too pretty."

Quick as a flash, she phased through the table, then grabbed his ankles and yanked as hard as she could. He went flying, the vanilla oil went flying, and he was flat on his back in the suite.

"Served you right!" she crowed, then tried to crawl away, but he pounced on her. A minute later, they were both exhausted from the impromptu tickle fight, and he was complaining about the oil stains on his shirt.

* * *

"I want you to stay with me," he said quietly in the dark.

They had just finished another bout of lovemaking, this one less energetic and more tender. She was curled into his side, her hands on his ribs, listening to his soft breathing in the dark. When he had been inside her, his breathing had been harsh, almost like panting, and then stopped altogether for a long moment, and then he was soft inside her, soft and slipping out, and she shuddered all over from the pure sweetness of it.

"Mitchell, I'm really flattered. But I have responsibilities. I can't just—"

"And I have a checkbook. If you're looking after a family, I can take care of them. If—"

"But see, you don't even know. For all you know, I'm married with six kids."

"It's against the law to have more than three," he said automatically. "And you're not wearing a ring."

"Still."

"And I don't think you could be...like that...with me. If you had a husband."

"Well, okay, as it happens, I'm not married. But my point is, we don't know much about each other."

"You know my greatest secret," he said quietly.

"Well, yeah."

"And you stayed anyway."

"The food's great."

"Jamie."

"Yeah." She sighed. "I stayed anyway."

"That meant...everything. Everything."

"Look, Mitchell, I like you, okay? I really do. And not because you're fucking phenomenal in bed, no pun intended.

You're a smart guy; I can talk to you. And I'll admit it, there's attraction in the fact that you didn't run out of the room screaming when you saw what a blue-haired freak I was."

"Jamie, I wish you wouldn't refer to yourself as—"

"But," she continued, cutting him off, "there's got to be more to it than that. Right?"

"Well," he said reasonably, "stay. And find out. You can still leave whenever you wish. But this sort of thing... I've had women up here before—"

"Oink!"

"—but none of them knew my secret, and I never wanted any of them to linger in the morning. You're *different.* This is *different.*"

A line from an old, old movie popped into her head: *This is true love. You think this happens every day?*

"Okay," she said, kissing his shoulder. "I'll stay. I've got some stuff to take care of—"

"I'll help you," he said quickly.

"—but then I'm all yours, as they say." Her hand slid down his flat stomach and found him, already hardening. "Oh, my, what have we here?"

"I'm happy to see you," he said, and giggled.

Giggled!

She climbed on top of him, felt him slide inside her, slick and sweet on the juices they had already made together, and did some giggling herself as she bounced up and down, as his big hands reached up and found her breasts and played with them, as she arched her back and stared at the ceiling and felt her uterus clench around him, as she shook from coming and coming and coming once more. She collapsed over him, panting.

"Did you...?" she gasped. She'd been having so much fun, she honestly hadn't noticed.

"Oh, yes," he groaned, stroking her back.

"That's all right, then," she said, and climbed off.

"That's not the only thing," he replied, and walked her to the bathroom, and cleaned her with a warm washcloth, and his lips, and his tongue.

Chapter Ten

Mitchell woke up and reached for Jamie who, to his surprise, wasn't in his bed.

An immediate scan showed she wasn't in the bedroom. Or the bathroom. Or the hot tub room. Or the floor.

Or the building.

Cursing, he tossed the blankets back.

* * *

"We don't have an explanation, sir. The moon rock was just…gone. No alarms were tripped, and look." The security guard gestured to the large monitor taking up most of the wall. "On the *screen,* it's still there. But if you go into the vault, it's gone. We're going crazy trying to figure out what—"

"Don't bother," he said curtly. "I know what happened. And I know where it is. I'll be back with the rock, and the perpetrator. Have a cell ready, I'll want h—the thief transferred to state custody by the end of the day."

"Uh…yes, sir." The guard watched nervously as Mitchell stomped out, then wiped his damp brow.

* * *

Fool, fool, a thousand times a fool! He'd been tricked by a pretty face and a sympathetic ear and a fascinating mutant talent. And she certainly had his number, the whore. A little sympathy, a little bedroom gymnastics, and he'd found himself thinking he wanted her around for—for—well, forever. Idiot!

She'd clearly never forgotten her initial mission: to steal The Rock. Never mind that he promised it to her by the end of the weekend. She'd obviously been scared off by his whole "stay with me" nonsense and fled the moment she could.

And he…he had thought…thought she would…and so he had slept. Deeply, and for the first time, and never noticed her slipping through the walls like a deceitful ghost.

Well. She wasn't the only deceitful one. He could track her down—there were only so many places one could take The Rock for quick cash. He had resources all over the city…the county, state, and world, quite frankly. When you were sinfully rich, you could find anyone, given enough time. And he would find his little ghost.

Find her. And make her pay.

Chapter Eleven

A lot of people think being slapped in the face is the worst thing someone can do to you. Robs you of your dignity, a direct affront, an insult, blahdy-blah.

The truth is, Jamie would take a slap in the face any day (and twice on Sundays) over a gut punch. *Those* were the worst. They were so bad that for a second, she didn't feel any pain. She always had time to think, "That wasn't so—" and then found herself bent over, sobbing for breath and trying very hard not to puke. It got worse, too, hard as that was to believe: a sickening wave spread from her stomach to her neck, and that wave clogged her throat. She'd get goosebumps, and the corners of the room would go dark.

What was worse, a gut punch doesn't hurt the guy punching at all. At least if he went for the jaw, he might crack a knuckle or two and lose his taste.

No, a truly dedicated asshole could gut punch all day.

She'd known all this by her tenth birthday, and spent the following fourteen years trying hard not to learn any more about it.

Not today, though.

"What did I say, Jamie? Huh? Did you turn stupid like the other mutes and forget English?"

She opened her mouth, but all the air in her lungs had taken a quick vacation, and she had no breath for words.

"Because I thought it was pretty simple. I want the moon rock. I work for people who want the moon rock. So who did I come to? I came to the best mute on my C-block, the one who can get the job done."

"I got the job done," she whispered.

Brennan ignored her, pacing around her like a broad-shouldered moon. "And then what? You disappear for three days, and I'm left with my dick in my hand. You know how that looks?"

She didn't want to even *think* about his dick. "Bad?" she ventured.

"Yeah. Bad."

She straightened painfully. "Well. You got it now."

"Yeah, my buyers are out of town now. I can track them down, but I've lost face. You know about that?"

Jamie rubbed her throbbing stomach and didn't say anything. She was wondering how she could get the watch off Brennan's wrist. Among other things, Brennan had contacts in the military, which were always interested in the question of mutes: could they serve their country? Could they be a weapon? And, most important, could they be neutralized? The president of the United States, who was a very savvy lady, was rabid on the subject of mutes: They Must Be Stopped. Never mind that most of them couldn't remember which shoe went on which foot.

So, there was an inhibitor chip in Brennan's wristwatch. A gift from his military pals. Poor Brennan, always hanging around D-Block and C-Block uptown. You never knew what kind of scum he might have to come across. Better keep all the bases covered, yep yep.

As long as she was in the room with him, she couldn't phase. This was alarming, for several reasons. Brennan was a jerk whose mother had never let him breastfeed. He liked to use his hands. He liked to hurt people. And she hated getting hit. Managed to avoid it most of her life, in fact, thanks to her handy dandy powers, which were on coffee break until she could smash that watch.

"So," Brennan was concluding cheerfully, "I think the best way to go about it is, beat the living shit out of you. I mean, just beat you until you can't see, walk, stand, move, or eat. I'll feel better. Like, it'll be closure, y'know? Then I'll take your rock—finally! Bet you won't be late again, eh?—and hunt down my buyers."

"Maybe you should get to the buyers first," she suggested.

He considered for a moment, his large, bullet-shaped head tilting as he thought. The fluorescent lights bounced off his shaved skull, making Jamie wince. "No, that won't work. I'll be distracted the whole time. Thinking about how you kept me waiting. Thinking about how embarrassing it was, not having the rock when they wanted it. Thinking about you walking, standing, moving, or eating. No," he said regretfully, shrugging out of his overcoat, "I really have to get this off my chest. Then we can move on."

"Uh-huh." *Note to self: stop taking freelance jobs from crazy people.* "You touch me again, and I'm warning you...I'm gonna bleed all over you. You'll never get the stains out of that shirt."

"I'll risk it," he said, and his big fist looped through the air, straight for her face. She side-stepped and slashed out. She wasn't a fighter, didn't know a single self-defense move, so when her hand blurred out, it was pure instinct. She didn't realize she'd pulled her fingers into claws until she heard Brennan's shriek of surprised agony, and saw the furrows on his cheek fill with blood.

"Whoa," she said, backing up.

"You—you—" Blood dripped off his jaw and he touched one of the scratches, winced, and showed her the tip of his bloody finger, looking amazed and horrified. "You—you *did* that. You *hurt* me! You..."

Like any deviant sociopath, Brennan loved dishing out the pain, but practically had a breakdown if he was hurt himself. Torture, beatings, the occasional rape...those were all fine and dandy. Those were his to do because he took by force, and what he reached out and took, he deserved to have. But *he* could never...EVER...be hurt. It was...it was beyond an outrage. It was...sacrilegious. Yes. That's what it was. Sacrilege.

"I have to admit," Jamie said, "that went a lot better than I expectedaaaarrrrrgggggggggggggghhhhhh!" She bent double as Brennan's fist once again buried itself in her stomach. *Oh, you're gonna pay for that one, Jamie my girl,* she thought, and would have groaned if she hadn't been so busy throwing up. *And it's almost worth the beating you'll get. The look on his face when he saw he was bleeding. Yep, almost worth it.*

Then the door banged open so hard it actually cracked down the middle when it hit the wall and rebounded. Which was crazy, because that would mean somebody—cop?—had gotten past the six or seven goons Brennan usually kept around him. And who'd come around C-block unless they absolutely had to?

Whoever it was kicked the door open again and stepped into the room.

She wiped her mouth and climbed to her feet. "Hi, Mitch. What's new with you?"

"Fuck off," Brennan replied, less warmly. "I'm working here."

Mitchell took it all in…the bloody scratches, the way Jamie was hunched over, the vomit on the floor, the watch. Which, among other things, had a tracking device. Brennan's military buddies (who really weren't his buddies, but that is a story for another time) had neglected to mention it. They did not, however, hesitate to mention it to the richest man in the country.

"If you touch her again," Mitchell said, speaking slowly and carefully, "I will break your neck."

"And then he'll *really* go to work on you," Jamie wheezed cheerfully. Maybe it was silly romanticism, but she sure felt a lot better now that Mitchell was here. Or maybe it was the internal bleeding. Either way, she was glad to see him.

"You're out of your neighborhood, Rich Guy," Brennan said. "Go back to your skyscraper."

"Indeed. But not alone, I think. Actually, my large, ugly friend," he said, looking down at Jamie with narrowed eyes, then back up at Brennan, "I might break your neck just on general principles."

"Well, in that case, what have I got to lo—" That was it. "Lose" would have been his last word, except while Brennan was reaching for Jamie, Mitchell walked up to him, cupped Brennan's chin in the heel of his hand, braced his *other* hand on the back of Brennan's head, and twisted. It had taken about half a second, and the ensuing sound, Jamie thought, was a lot like the noise you heard when you were twisting the leg off a piece of fried chicken, sort of a cartilage-grinding snapping sound, and really, it was all just so—

"Gross," she managed, and then passed out.

Chapter Twelve

"I am so furious with you right now," he told her when she opened her eyes.

She groaned. "Be furious later. Can I have a glass of w—"

He carefully helped her sit up, and held a glass of water to her lips. "Where to begin."

She gulped. It was cool and good. "Please don't."

"Waking up alone...bad. Finding out you were consorting with a city crime lord...bad. Finding out he appears to be interested in beating you to death...bad. Oh, and you stole my rock. Bad."

"It's *my* rock," she hissed. "I spent the weekend for it, and I fucking *bled* for it."

"You did not spend the weekend—"

"I left after midnight. Learn to tell time, Captain Neckbreak. Ohhhhhh, my head...my stomach..."

"When you are recovered," he said through tight lips, "we will discuss your...infractions...in detail."

"Who...talks...like that? Fuck you, I had a job to do. I couldn't stay with you until the job was done. Shit, I was two days late and look what happened! Imagine if I'd never come back! We'd have spent our lives looking over our shoulders. No, thanks."

His face was like granite, so terribly immobile, like he was afraid it would crack if he showed emotion. Weirdo. "You left...to protect me?"

"No, I left because the room service sucked," she snapped. "Jesus, Mitchell, OF COURSE I left to protect you. What's the matter with you? You *saw* that guy, right? You think I wanted him showing up here? I couldn't let him hurt you because of choices I made. I figured I'd get him the rock, then slip back to bed and be here when you woke up."

"Ah, but your little plan failed when he commenced—"

"Beating the snot out of me. Yes, well, the plan needed some modifications," she admitted. "Okay, so, I should have figured he'd be mad. In fact, I *did* figure he'd be mad. But I figured I could smooth him down. Stupid, stupid. Thanks for showing up in the nick of time, by the way." She said it casually, but she had never meant anything so fundamentally, so deeply. He had come into the room like one of the Knights of the Round Table. She had never been so glad to see anyone in her life. The scary part was, it didn't have much to do with what he could do for her. It was enough that he was there. That she wouldn't have bled to death alone in a filthy warehouse office on C-block.

"I—I didn't come to save you."

"News flash! You *did* save me. And on behalf of all my bones, none of which are broken, thank you."

"I came to arrest you."

"That's so romantic! But you're not a cop."

"I've been granted certain privileges by state government. And I thought—when I woke up and you were gone—and the rock was gone—"

"So, what's your point? Next time leave a note?"

"I didn't realize you had...you had responsibilities. I was focused on how I could keep you in my world, and I arrogantly and stupidly thought it would be as easy as gaining your agreement." He shook his head. "I have been a bigger fool than I thought."

"Well, cheer up. Nobody's perfect, RoboBoy."

He shuddered. "You must never call me that again."

"And can we get some room service up here? If I eat, I'll puke—again—but I sure could go for a margarita. Or five."

He stared at her. "You seem...oddly cheerful."

"Are you kidding? Brennan's dead!" She happily kicked her feet, dislodging the covers. "And even if he wasn't, I did what I said I would do. Now I'm free lak ze baird, and I'm lovin' it." She snuggled up to him on the bed. "And I'm lovin' how you rode in to rescue me like the Lone Ranger on Silver."

"Like the what on who?"

"Never mind."

His arms tightened around her, and he rested his face against the side of her neck. "I was so angry...and then, when I saw him...saw you...I was so frightened..."

"You didn't seem frightened," she said. "You seemed mildly annoyed, like we were making you late for a business meeting."

"Well, you were."

"I hope you know what this means, Mitch."

"That I have to keep a constant close eye on you?"

"Ugh, creepy, *no.* It means now I can stay. You'll never be rid of me," she said gleefully.

"I guess that's a nicer way of looking at it than what I had in mind," he admitted, "which is, 'you'll never escape me again.'"

"Aw. That's a little romantic. Okay, not really." She kissed him. "We'll work on it."

MaryJanice Davidson

MaryJanice Davidson is the best-selling author of several books, most recently *Undead and Unappreciated* (May 2005) from Berkley, and *Hello Gorgeous* from Brava. She currently writes for Loose Id, Kensington, and Berkley, and has ten releases scheduled for 2005. She lives in Minneapolis with her husband and two children, and is currently working on her next book. You can visit her at www.maryjanicedavidson.net or e-mail her at maryjanice@comcast.net.

~*~

Other titles by MaryJanice Davidson currently available from Loose Id:

Beggarman, Thief (e-book novella)

"Santa Claws" in *Nicely Naughty* with Lani Aames and Treva Harte (e-book only)

"Savage Scavenge" in *Charming the Snake* with Camille Anthony and Melissa Schroeder (soon to be released in e-book and print formats, Spring 2005)

STRANDED

Angela Knight

Dedication

This one is dedicated to my wonderful SPs, who buy and read my stuff so loyally. And of course, it's dedicated to my wonderful crit partner, Diane Whiteside, who keeps me from doing stupid stuff.

And last but not least, it's for Treva and Allie, who wanted it!

Chapter One

Alexandria Kenyon lay staring up at the ceiling fan circling lazily over her bed. Each moonlit rotation sent shadows spinning across the cherry colonial furniture, but she was far more interested in the erotic images flickering through her own mind. Her nipples rose hard and hungry under the lace of her camisole, and she ran her fingers over them, sighing in pleasure.

Closing her eyes, Alex pictured a man, broad shouldered and blond and feral, with broad, hard hands and a long, hungry cock. And a cruel mouth that rasped erotic orders.

He'd taken her prisoner. Now she lay on his immense bed looking up at him, bound and naked and breathless. He stood there with muscled legs braced wide, surveying her with a conqueror's smile, his cock jutting in cruel anticipation of his pleasure. "You're mine now, sweet. You challenged me and lost, and now I'll take you. Every way that pleases me."

Imagining the lust and triumph in her dream lover's gaze, she licked her lips and slid her other hand down the waistband of her little lace panties. *Bad Alex,* she thought as she stroked between the soft, creamy lips. *Not politically correct, Counselor.*

She didn't care. Bob had moved out a year ago, and she hadn't wanted to get anywhere near a man after what he'd done to her. Now her libido was gnawing holes in her self-control. Yet cruising singles bars wasn't the kind of thing an Atlanta prosecutor could afford to do.

God, she needed a man. A bad man. A wicked dominant who'd grin in anticipation when he discovered the submissive streak she hid under the persona of ass-kicking prosecution lawyer. Brass-balled bitch by day, bound and gagged by night.

Oh, yeah. She slid a finger between her dewing lips. *Fuck me, Master.*

Yeah. Like she'd ever call any man master. She'd spent the first twenty years of her life trying to get out from under Daddy's suffocating protection. And he'd been trying to get her back under it ever since she'd moved out nine years ago.

Which was *not* a thought conducive to orgasm.

She added a second finger and slid it deep inside her pussy. Kneading her nipple with the other hand, Alex hummed at the lazy swirl of pleasure.

He slid one brawny knee onto the bed as she gazed up at him, quivering in a combination of arousal and fear. "I'm going to fuck you, sweet," he rumbled. "I'm going to suck those pretty pink nipples until you stop struggling and start begging. I'm going to get you hot and creamy enough that when I drive my big cock into that tiny cunt, you'll hardly scream at all."

"No," she moaned, as his big body mantled hers. "You can't do this to me. I don't want this."

"Don't lie to me." He lowered his head to one bare breast. "I'll have to punish you."

"If you release me, my father will pay you well!"

"It's not money I'm interested in." He gave the desperately hard nipple a slow lick. Pleasure sizzled through her. "It's you." Another slow, swirling lick. "Your pretty tits. Your tight aristocratic pussy." He switched his attention to her other breast, considered the impudent point. Raked it gently with his teeth. "I'm going to tame you, Alexandria. I want to see you on your knees, that lush mouth sucking my cock like the slave you are."

"No! I'll never yield to you! I'm of royal blood!"

His gaze shot to her face and hardened. "No more. I rule now. I conquered your lands as I'm going to conquer your body. You'll fall to me just as your castle did."

He slid a hand between her spread legs. She groaned in shame and pleasure as he found her wet and ready for him. Triumph shone in his eyes. "And something tells me my conquest won't take long at all."

As pleasure swirled around her masturbating fingers, Alex shuttered her lids and grinned at the fantasy she'd conjured. *I really should be ashamed of myself.* Two fingers stroked deep. *But I'm not.*

So she had a kinky streak. After twenty-nine years of playing by the rules, she was entitled to...

Blinding light exploded across the room, jarring her out of her sensual preoccupation. Alex jerked her head up and yelped in shock. The ceiling fan had disappeared, replaced by a glowing, six-foot hole. "What the...?"

Something jerked her up off her bed and sucked her right into the blazing opening. She didn't even have time to scream.

* * *

"All right, dammit," John Hawke growled as he floated in the Caribbean blue water. "I'm here. Give me whatever it is so I can go home."

Overhead, the tell-tale ring of clouds remained open. And stubbornly empty.

A bumblebee circled his head. He swatted it aside absently as he glared up at the clouds. Maybe they were finally going to send him that axe he'd been doggedly visualizing for the past month. If he thought about something long enough, sometimes the Bastards would send it to him.

Last time the gift had been a waterproof bag that turned out to contain five pounds of iodized salt. It had been more than welcome, since the mineral was otherwise unavailable on the artificial world of the Goldfish Bowl, with its freshwater sea and tropical temperatures. He'd have died of a fatal electrolyte imbalance without it.

Over the past year, he'd found the Bastards sent him whatever he couldn't catch, scrounge or make for himself, dropping it from the cloud ring they used as a sign. Of course, immediately afterward they'd send something that would try to kill him, so he never felt grateful.

He'd tried to ignore the ring this time, sick of playing their sadistic little game, but the Bastards had promptly triggered a migraine so severe, he'd had no choice but to swim out and wait. As usual, the headache had disappeared as soon as he'd obeyed.

There was a reason he called them the Bastards.

As he watched, the cloud ring began to sink toward him. Treading water, Hawke blinked at the sky. It had never done that before. Usually they just dropped the gift and let him dive after it.

The ring kept descending until it was about six meters over his head. Despite himself, he felt a sudden spurt of hope. Was it descending to scoop him up? Back in Afghanistan, the damn thing had just sucked him right off his feet, pack, body armor, and all. He'd almost drowned when he'd hit the water before he managed to cut his way loose from his own gear. So what were the Bastards up to now?

Something too big to be an axe plummeted out of the ring, falling right toward him. A piercing female shriek rang out.

Sweet Jesus, it was a woman!

SPLASH! Water flew skyward as she hit.

Hawke sucked in a deep breath and dove, afraid she'd drown. A trail of bubbles led him to her in the blessedly clear water. He could tell by the way she writhed that she was disoriented, not sure which way was up. Without his help, she didn't have a prayer.

He clamped a hand on her wrist and hauled her up until he could grab her shoulders from behind. Then, holding her pinned against his body despite her panicked struggles, he kicked toward the shimmering light above them with everything he had.

She broke the surface choking and fighting in animal panic, flailing arms and kicking legs battering at him. Luckily, Hawke had anticipated that, which was why he'd grabbed her from behind. Now his greater strength kept her from drowning them both. "Lady, you're all right!" he shouted over her sputters as he began a one-armed stroke toward shore. "I've got you!"

Long, wet fingers clamped around his wrist in a death grip, but she had the sense to quit fighting. "What's going on?" She spat out another mouthful of water so violently she narrowly missed the bumblebee that lazily circled them. "Where the hell am I?"

"God alone knows, sweetheart," he told her grimly. "I sure don't."

It took only a couple dozen strokes to reach the artificial shallows, since what passed for ocean floor in the Goldfish Bowl resembled the bottom of a swimming pool more than anything else. When his bare feet hit the fine sand, Hawke waded up onto the beach, half-carrying his wet, trembling gift. The minute he let her go, she collapsed into a panting tangle of slender limbs and long hair.

"You okay?" He crouched beside her.

"I don't... I don't know." Blinking, she stared wildly at the beach around them, visibly bewildered by her close brush with death. "I don't understand any of this."

Finally getting a good look at her, Hawke whistled silently. Even half-drowned, she looked like every wet dream he'd had for the past two years.

Hell, she looked like every wet dream he'd had since puberty.

She wore a pair of tiny panties that barely covered the shadow of her bush, and her soaked shirt was some kind of silk and lace thing that had gone perfectly transparent, revealing round, pert tits with hard little nipples. Hawke couldn't tell what color her wet hair was, but there was a lot of it, falling in tangled strands over that centerfold body.

When she looked around at him again, her gaze was sharp and considering. She recovered fast, he'd give her that. "You saved my life. I thought I was dead." Her eyes were a clear, crystalline blue, even more vivid than the Goldfish Bowl's ocean. Her nose was straight and narrow in her elegant, long-boned face, and her mouth—damn, those were definitely dick lips. Full and soft and lush, the kind a man wanted to see wrapped around his cock. They made quite a contrast to that blue-blood diva face. She sat up, raking her hands through her hair, unconsciously trying to set herself to rights. "Thank you."

Hawke was rock hard behind his loin cloth. "Believe me, it's my pleasure."

But even as he imagined everything he was going to do to her, he wondered what the Bastards would do to make him pay.

* * *

She'd been rescued by Tarzan.

Alex blinked up at her savior, who wore only a strip of brown hide around his narrow hips. Luckily, he had the kind of body that could pull off an outfit like that. Shoulders easily twice the width of hers, biceps the size of coconuts, and a six pack that made her want to purr, *It's Miller Time!* His legs were long and muscular, giving her the impression he'd easily catch anything dumb enough to run away.

Not that she had any intention whatsoever of going anywhere.

And his face—well, he definitely didn't look anything like the parade of pretty boys Mama assembled for her approval every time she went back home. First, of course, there was the long, blond hair that lay in wet tangles across those quarterback shoulders. Daddy wouldn't have let him in the house with that hair. Yet he was intensely masculine, with a regally Roman nose and broad, high cheekbones. A broad jaw and square chin gave him the look of a heavyweight boxer, though a sensual, well-shaped mouth and smoky gray eyes saved his face from outright brutality. Judging by the hungry heat in his gaze, it was for damn sure he wasn't gay. That wasn't always a given with Mama's dinner guests, whether Virginia Kenyon realized it or not.

The question was, how the hell had she gotten from her bed to the feet of a sex god, with a dunk in the ocean in between? "Who *are* you?"

"John Hawke. And who are you?"

"Alex. Alex Kenyon."

"Nice to meet you, Alex Kenyon." Reaching out, he cupped her chin in long, strong fingers, tilted her head up, and leaned in close. "Very, very nice."

Even as her inner Southern Belle squealed in offended shock, his mouth closed over hers in a warm, wet slide.

Her heart, just beginning to slow its frantic beat after her brush with death, lunged back into a gallop. Automatically, she started to pull back in surprise, but his callused fingers tightened, holding her in place. His tongue stroked boldly between her lips as he kissed her with a rough, predatory hunger that made her nipples peak. She really should knock him on his backside for his gall, but God, it had been so long. And maybe he deserved a kiss for saving her life.

So Alex closed her eyes and kissed him back.

Then a wet hand boldly cupped her breast. The big opportunist was *groping* her! "What are you doing?" She jerked back, outraged. "A kiss is one thing, but saving my life doesn't entitle you to paw me."

Tarzan's luscious mouth curled into a dark smile. "Look around, Dorothy. You're not in Kansas anymore. This is the Goldfish Bowl, and I make my own rules."

He had a point about the Kansas thing. She'd already noticed it was broad daylight, which was pretty damn weird considering the moon had been shining just a minute ago.

And then there was the beach. She lived in Atlanta, hundreds of miles from the ocean, so how had she got to the seashore?

Frowning, she turned to look out to sea. And stared. She sure wasn't in Georgia anymore. She wasn't even in Miami, despite the stretch of pristine white sand underfoot and the clusters of big palm trees inland.

For one thing, the horizon was far too close. It was almost as if they were an immense, round room—if a room could be ten or fifteen miles across. And the sky… Alex tilted her head back and stared upward. It had an odd, milky quality, painted in swirls of iridescence—not clouds, but patterns of moving light, something like the Aurora Borealis. She couldn't see the sun at all, yet the light was as bright as noon. "Where *are* we?"

Hawke rose to his considerable height. "Like I said, I call it the Goldfish Bowl."

"I can see why." It felt odd lying at his feet, so she scrambled up too, noting absently that he didn't offer her a hand. To her annoyance, her legs trembled. She stiffened them as he strode to a pile of equipment on the sand. "What are you doing?"

"I've got a bad feeling we're about to get a guest a lot less pleasant than you." He crouched and started picking through the gear.

"What kind of guest? And what makes you think that?"

"It's the pattern. They send me something, and then something worse shows up." Hoisting a pouched belt that reminded her of something solders wore, he buckled it around his narrow waist with the grim air of a man expecting eminent attack.

She propped her fists on her hips and frowned at him. "What do you mean, worse?"

"As in 'kill it before it kills you' worse." Next, he strapped a short, sheathed knife to his ankle. Tarzan evidently had access to Velcro.

Then he picked up something she first took for a stick and some kind of belt. As he swung it across one shoulder, she got a better look. "Is that a *sword?*"

"Yep." He belted the thick leather strap diagonally across his torso. The sheathed sword it supported was easily three and a half feet long, not counting the two-handed hilt.

He wasn't Tarzan, he was Conan the Barbarian.

Hawke turned toward her, settling the blade into place with a shrug of those Olympian shoulders. "When I was first snatched, this weapon was an M-16. By the time I arrived here, it had morphed into this. Evidently the Bastards didn't want me having access to firepower."

"I have no idea what you're talking about. Could you please quit being mysterious and tell me what's going on? Who are the Bastards?" She was getting thoroughly fed up. "And how did I get here?"

He lifted his head suddenly and turned to stare off into the trees, his expression alert. "Same way I did, I'd imagine," he said absently. "You were abducted by aliens. And I think you're about to find out why I call them the Bastards."

Aliens? Good God, she was stranded with a lunatic. "Is this some kind of joke? Because it's really not funny."

"Shut up."

Anger zapped her appreciation of his amazing butt as he turned his back on her. Nobody talked to a Kenyon that way. "Who do you think you are?"

He closed a hand around the hilt of his sword and levered the big blade out of its scabbard. "I said *shut up.* Something's coming."

Before she could tell him off, the bushes rattled. A roar split the air, loud enough to make her jump.

Something burst from the trees in an explosion of scales and teeth. Alex screamed like a fire siren as it lunged right at Hawke, snapping massive jaws.

"Get back!" he bellowed, running to meet the monster. Even as it tensed to spring, he swung his sword. Blade bit into scaly hide. The monster howled and reared, slashing at him with knifelike front claws. Hawke leaped back and circled. It turned with him, snapping.

Good God, it had six legs!

It scuttled on four of them while it tried to rake him with long, thin forearms, snapping and roaring like a nightmare cross between a Tyrannosaurus Rex and a scorpion. It was easily the size of a horse.

Alex wanted to run. She wanted to help him. But she couldn't do either, because she couldn't move. Her body was completely frozen with terror as he hacked at the monstrosity slashing and snapping at him like something out of *Alien.*

I've got to do something! It's going to kill him!

Chapter Two

Hawke grunted in pain as the thing raked claws across his thigh.

Jolted out of her shock, Alex looked desperately around for a stick, a rock. Anything. She had to get her hands on a weapon.

At her feet lay what looked like a misshapen conch shell. She snatched it up in a sweaty hand and started toward them even as her every instinct howled at her to run away. She couldn't just stand around while a monster chowed down on the man who'd saved her life.

But before she could take another step, the thing screeched, took a step, and toppled into the sand. Alex had no idea what Hawke had done, and he didn't give her time to figure it out. The minute the monster was down, he pounced and started chopping. Purple blood flew. The thing roared and flailed, but he ignored its claws and kept hacking with grim intensity.

"Jesus," Alex whispered as the shell dropped from her lax fingers. *Note to self. Never piss off Hawke.*

Finally the thing's struggles subsided. Hawke's Ginsu imitation slowed. Finally, with one last chop for good measure, he rose from the twitching corpse. The only sounds were his harsh breathing and the lazy buzz of bumblebees.

Edging closer, Alex looked down at the thing. He'd cut off its head and one foreleg. The rest of it looked like it had been put through a Cuisinart.

It had six eyes.

This thing couldn't be real. Yet indisputably, it was. Just as indisputably, it hadn't evolved on Earth. Everything from the color of its blood to the weird structure of its muscles told her that. "Is this the alien that abducted us?" Alex whispered. She was shaking.

"This?" He wiped purple blood from his forehead and snorted. "Not likely. This thing is dumb as a post."

"It tried to eat us." She felt numb.

"We'd have given it a belly ache." Hawke turned to look down at her with a euphoric grin, visibly high on his dangerous victory. "I tried meat from one once. Gave me the runs like you would not believe."

Alex stared at him. "You *ate* one of these things?"

"A piece of it. Seemed only fair." He pulled a piece of leather from a belt pouch and started cleaning the blood off his sword. "It would have eaten me."

Suddenly she realized some of the blood running down his thigh was red. "You're hurt!"

He looked down at the gash cutting across one thigh and shrugged. "It's already healing."

"But it..." Alex broke off. As she watched, the wound narrowed, sealing over like a special effect in a werewolf movie. But that was impossible.

She stepped back, keenly aware of what he'd done to the alien lizard. No ordinary man could have done that much damage with nothing more than a glorified machete. "You're not human."

Hawke rolled his eyes. "Oh, give me a break."

"Your strength—the way you heal. You're not from Earth any more than that...thing is!"

"I was born in Virginia." Glaring at her, he sheathed his sword with a slither of steel on leather. "It's just that ever since the Bastards took me, I've gotten stronger and harder to kill. Which is a damn good thing, or we'd both be monster chow by now."

She winced, suddenly feeling like a paranoid bitch. "You've got a point. Sorry. I guess this whole situation is just making me a little nuts."

"Tell me about it." Hawke slumped, suddenly looking weary as all the anger ran out of him. "Look, I'm going to wash this shit off. It stings. Wait here." Turning, he strode toward the ocean, stripping off his gear as he went.

"Wait!" Alex called, shooting a hunted look at the trees. "What if another one of these things come along?"

Hawke glanced back at her. "It won't. The Bastards never send more than one WTF at a time."

With one last uneasy glance at the cooling corpse, she hurried after him. "WTF? What does that stand for?"

"'What The Fuck.' It seems to fit."

"Guess it does, at that." As Alex watched, he crouched and began to splash the blood off. Seawater turned pink as it ran in glistening trails down the ridges of his body. "Doesn't the salt sting?"

"There is no salt. This is more big-ass lake than anything else."

He was right, she realized, looking out to sea. There was almost no wave action at all, unlike every ocean she'd ever seen back home. "It's almost as though it's man-made."

"More like alien-made."

Alex wrapped both arms around her body. A cool breeze blew into her face, smelling of flowers and monster blood. She shivered, though her body had almost dried from its dunking. "I don't understand any of this."

"Join the club." He rose from the water, slicking his wet hair back from his head. "You know, I haven't had to shave once the entire time I've been here. My hair grows, but not my beard. I'm not sure why, but that bothers me almost more than anything else. Why do aliens care if I get stubble? Doesn't make sense."

"Why should it? Apparently nothing else does."

"Good point." Hawke waded back toward her. Cool gray eyes studied her with approval. "So, Alexandria Kenyon. What do you do back home?"

She forced herself to straighten up and stop huddling as he stepped out of the water. "I'm an attorney."

For a moment something flickered in his eyes. Then it was gone. "Yeah? I was a Marine. The aliens abducted me from the middle of a battle in Afghanistan. Must have been a year ago now. What day was it when they took you?"

Alex blinked, watching the water sluice down his magnificent body. It suddenly hit that she was completely alone with him on this planet, or space ship, or whatever the hell it was. God knew how far away Earth was. "July 7, 2004."

That stopped him in his tracks. "2004?" He frowned. "I've been here more than two years? That can't be right. It was March 2, 2002 when they took me, and only three hundred and sixty-seven days have passed since then. I've kept track."

So he was snatched during the war in Afghanistan, just a few months after September 11. "Could the days be longer here?"

"Not according to my watch." Hawke picked up his belt and buckled it around his lean waist, then collected the rest of his weapons. "It's broken now, but the first couple of weeks, it worked fine. The Goldfish Bowl is on a twenty-four hour cycle." Fastening the sword belt across his torso, he shook his head and dismissed the question. "Never mind, it doesn't matter. I'm not a Marine any more."

Gray eyes lifted to meet hers. She felt her mouth go dry at the heat that flared in them. He started toward her in a long, sensuous pace, like a tiger stalking something slow and delicious. "And you're not a lawyer," he continued in a deep, velvet voice. "There is no law here."

That did not sound good, especially given what he was capable of. She looked him right in the eye anyway. "Wherever there are people, there are laws."

He lifted a blond brow as he stepped up to her, muscle sliding under tanned skin. A lot of tanned skin. "Sure of that, are you?"

"Absolutely."

"In that case, I guess that makes me the law." Hawke's gray eyes searched her face with predatory intensity. "At least as far as you're concerned."

Her mouth went dry, but Alex knew she didn't dare back down. She couldn't let him think he could bully her. "Just exactly what do you mean?"

"At least once every couple of days, sometimes more often, something's going to attack us. It may another WTF, like our scaly friend over there, or it may be a lot of small, ravenous things, or it may be something even I have never seen before. But whatever it is, I'm going to have to defend us both." His gray gaze intensified. "I'm going to bleed for you, Alex. I already have."

He had a damn good point, but she had no intention of admitting it. "I'm not helpless."

"Aren't you?"

She tilted her chin at him. "Maybe I'll get superpowers too."

"Maybe. But maybe you won't." He straightened his brawny shoulders, silently drawing attention to his size. He was a good eight inches taller than she was. "And even if you do, somehow I get the feeling I'll still be stronger."

"So, what? That gives you the right to order me around?" She attempted a scornful laugh. A husky note spoiled the effect.

"Yes, actually. It does."

"I don't think so."

"You'd better. Our toothy friend is just a sample of what I've faced on this rock every single day for the past year. I've had to work my ass off to stay alive. Now I'm going to have to work twice as hard keeping you breathing too."

"I'll do my part."

"Yes. You will."

Damn, why did she have the feeling she'd just fallen into a trap?

And why, she wondered, staring up into his brutal face, were her nipples getting hard?

"Sometimes the Bastards send a deer, and I have to hunt it." He took a step forward. Alex took another step back. "I kill it, skin it and butcher it. I tan its hide to make leather for what clothes I have. I carve its hooves and horns into tools. When there's no meat, I harvest the local plants and berries."

"I can do that. I'm not afraid of work."

"I'm relieved to hear it." His gaze bored into hers. "And you'll do everything else I tell you to do, too."

"Or what?"

"Or I'll..." His sensuous mouth curled into a smile "...persuade you."

"I'll bet." Alex gave him her best regal glare. She'd learned the fine art of putting a man in his place from Virginia Kenyon, and she was willing to bet her mother's techniques would work just as well on Conan the Sex God. "What's your first order—Master?"

The cold mockery in her voice would have made most men back off in a hurry, but Hawke didn't even blink. "Suck my cock."

She didn't even wonder what her mother would have done. She just bared her teeth. "Go to hell, Conan."

His gray eyes crinkled at the corners, amused rather than threatening. Was this was some kind of test? "That's no way to talk to your lord and master."

"I won't be bullied into sex." But despite her anger, despite her offended dignity, something in her responded to his outrageous demand. Her nipples ached as they contracted even further into tight, ready peaks.

He glanced down, as if his attention had been drawn by the subtle movement of those hardening tips. "When I give you an order, I expect you to obey it," he said, still watching her breasts. "If you make me stand around arguing, we're both going to end up dead."

She fought the impulse to cover herself and silently cursed her randy libido. "Not when the argument involves sex."

"I just saved your ass. Twice, come to think of it."

"Thank you." Her heart was pounding. This shouldn't be turning her on, no matter how big, bad and gorgeous he was. "I'm willing to concede all that might deserve a gratitude hummer, but I won't be forced."

"So why am I getting the distinct impression you'd like to be?"

Heat poured into her cheeks. On top of everything else, she was blushing. Fantastic. "Now you're just being insulting."

"Am I?" Hawke broke into a feral grin. In one smooth motion, he reached back and drew his sword. It hissed as it emerged from its scabbard in an endless length of gleaming steel. Biceps rippled as he placed the sharp edge just under her chin. "Get on your knees."

She swallowed, looking from the glittering blade to his hot, aroused gaze. "You do know the definition of rape, right?"

"Yeah. This isn't it. On your knees."

Had she misjudged him? Was she stuck on this island with an abusive superhuman creep?

Testing, Alex stared hard into Hawke's eyes. There was heat there, true, a hint of dark pleasure in what he was doing. But there was humor too. Like a kid playing a game.

A really big kid playing a really kinky game.

She relaxed slightly. Sword or not, she could sense he wouldn't hurt her. Dominate the hell out of her, yes. But he wouldn't hurt her.

Besides, wouldn't it feel good to just *play* for once? There was nobody here to judge her, nobody to find her a disappointment. Nobody to remind her of her responsibilities as a Kenyon. For once, she could be herself. She could act out her kinky dreams without fear. Hawke would be delighted to help.

"Alex." He said her name gently, with just a hint of artistic male menace. "I gave you an order."

Looking into his hard, deeply masculine face, she felt fine inner muscles clench and heat. Slowly, she dropped to her knees in the sand at his big feet.

Chapter Three

"That's better," Hawke purred, lowering the sword to reach for his loin cloth with one hand. He tugged the flap of leather out of his waistband and dropped it with a wet plop.

Alex sucked in a breath as his cock spilled out at her. It was beautiful—a long, smooth column of hard flesh, flushed with lust, invitingly thick. Imagining how it would feel pushing its way into her aching core, she had to fight back a moan.

"Put it in your mouth."

She shot a look up at him. He was watching her, gray eyes narrow, sensual lips parted. She knew she should make some kind of effort to let him know he hadn't intimidated her. That she wasn't falling for the act.

Instead she caught his cock in one hand, leaned forward and gave it one teasing lick of her tongue.

Hawke stiffened, sucking in a hard breath. Despite all his rough orders, she suspected she'd surprised him.

"How long has it been, Hawke?" Alex asked, caressing his thick length. She wanted to suck him, yes, but first she'd damn well let him know she wasn't a doormat. "At least a year, right? Probably longer, if you were at war before that."

"About…eighteen months." He stood rigid, as if he didn't trust himself to move. She wondered what he was afraid he'd do to her.

Cupping his heavy balls with her free hand, she gave him a gentle squeeze. "A long time without a woman."

"Yeah. I want your mouth, Alex. Now."

Smiling at the rough hunger in his voice, she leaned forward until her mouth was a bare half-inch from the flushed head of his cock. But instead of engulfing him, she blew gently.

"You'd be wise not to tease me." There it was again—that hot male rumble that never failed to send cream trickling into her core.

Gently, she closed her teeth over his cockhead and raked them across the flushed knob, drawing back until they clicked closed. "Or what?"

"Or I'll take you over my knee and beat that pretty ass until you squeal." His hand threaded through her drying hair to curve around the base of her skull. Not quite dragging her onto his cock, but close.

A glistening bead of pre-cum emerged from the flushed head. Alex licked the drop away with a flick of her tongue. The hard muscles of his belly laced. "Do I look like your slave?"

He laughed, the sound rough with need. "Half naked, on your knees in front of my cock? Yeah, as a matter of fact, you do."

She gave him another teasing nibble. God, she loved this. Loved the idea of taunting this powerful man until he was helpless with need. "Well, I'm not."

"Baby, I could change that by nightfall."

"I doubt that." The wildfire racing through her veins made her want to stroke herself.

Why not?

She released her hold on his cock and balls and caught her breasts in both hands. Cupping the full globes through the lace of her camisole, she squeezed her nipples and tilted her head up to meet his gaze. "But I'll bet I could enslave you."

Long fingers tightened around the base of her skull, reminding her he still held her. "Honey, you don't have the slightest interest in enslaving me." The corner of his mouth curled up. "Your eyes light up too much whenever I order you around."

She stiffened. That hit a little too close to home. "Bull."

He grinned darkly. "I'd bet a month's pay you're slick as melted butter between those pretty thighs."

"You'd lose."

"No I wouldn't." He lifted the sword. Before she could jerk away, he rested the cool edge of the blade against the side of her neck. "Open wide, honey. I want to find out if you can do something with that mouth besides tease." The hand around her head pulled her closer to his jutting cock.

She resisted more for form's sake than anything else. Then, with a hungry moan, she opened her mouth and sucked the big head inside.

"Mmmm. More." He arched his back, gently forcing another inch of his shaft between her lips. She sucked him so hungrily, her cheeks hollowed. "Oh, yeah, that's right. Nice and obedient. I always wanted a slave girl."

Alex tightened her jaws, not quite biting down on his cock, but making sure he got the threat.

He chuckled, a dark rumble. "You're bucking for that spanking, sweetheart. Deeper."

She drew back to pull in a breath, then leaned forward and slid his cock so far into her throat, she gagged.

"Swallow it," he rasped. "You can take more when you swallow."

Obeying, Alex realized he was right. Pulling back to steal another breath, she tried again and worked him further down. He rewarded her by tightening his grip on her hair.

Then, slowly, carefully, he began fucking her mouth.

* * *

Hawke threw back his head and groaned helplessly at the raw pleasure of Alex's lips around his cock. He'd had kinky dreams like this, but even back on Earth, he'd never expected to live any of them out. Hell, there'd been a time when a woman like her was a lot more likely to throw him in jail than suck him off.

Slowly, he stroked back into her mouth, fighting desperately not to come. He wanted to make this last as long as he could. He could feel her hot little tongue swirling around the crown of his shaft as she gave him sweet, rippling suction like a burning gift.

He looked down, watching hungrily. She'd wrapped one slender arm around his hip as she held his shaft with the other hand. Those luscious lips pouted as they surrendered his cock. Shuddering, he carefully pushed back inside, then pulled out again, trying to moderate his strokes and give her plenty of time to breathe. Self-control wasn't easy with the ferocious climax building in his balls.

Particularly since a woman like Alex wouldn't have given him the time of day back on Earth.

But he could have her here. She wanted him. He knew that from the way her eyes glittered with arousal even as she bitched about his dominant bastard act. Why else would she blow him with a hot enthusiasm that was almost enough to make him come all by itself?

He was just enough his old man's son to take advantage of her hunger.

Hawke thrust into her mouth again, using the slightest bit more force than he needed, knowing it would make her hotter. Sure enough, she gave his cock a sucking pull so hard, it was all he could do not to spill on the spot.

Oh, yeah. She liked this game.

And he was more than happy to play it however she wanted. He'd pretend to be Master Bastard for her, and he'd fuck her any way she'd let him. But he'd make damn sure she never guessed where he came from.

Panting, he tipped his head back and listened to the delicious sounds of her mouth working his cock. A bee flew around his head, but he barely noticed, all his attention focused on the shimmering pleasure. With a strangled shout, he drove his cock hard into her mouth and let himself pump. "Drink it!" he growled. "Swallow my cum. Now!"

She made an odd sound, a delicious little moan. And then she did exactly what he'd told her to do. The ripple of her throat sent his orgasm blazing up like pure oxygen on a forest fire. He roared.

Oh, yeah. He was going to take everything she let him have.

He just had to make sure she didn't get too much of him.

Chapter Four

Hawke pulled his softening shaft out of Alex's mouth and sheathed his sword. "That was…nice." His voice was hoarse. He stopped and cleared his throat. "Come on, I'll show you the cave."

Still on her knees, a storm of heat rioting in her blood, she stared at him. "Nice? It was *nice?*"

"What, you want an Academy Award for best Blowjob of 2003?"

"2004. And no, what I want is for you to return the favor!" Alex gritted her teeth against the need to jump the arrogant bastard, kick his feet out from under him, and ride his cock all the way down.

He smirked. "We can't hang on the beach having sex all day. Something'll eat us."

She rose to her feet and glowered at him as she dusted the sand off her shins. "I thought you said we'd hit our monster quota for the day."

Hawke shrugged brawny shoulders. "They could always change the pattern. I don't call 'em the Bastards for nothing."

"They're not the only bastards around here," Alex muttered.

Starting off toward the trees, he glanced back, a devilish glint in his eyes. "Now, is that any way to talk to your lord and master?"

"You want to know where you can sheath that sword, Conan?"

"You're just begging for a spanking."

"You and what army?"

"I'm a Marine. I'm an army all by myself."

"You do have enough ego for a platoon." She stalked into the trees after his broad back.

"I'm really going to enjoy turning that pretty little ass pink." Pushing a low hanging branch aside so she could pass, he grinned wickedly. "'Course, once I've got you bent over, who knows what I'll do next?"

Her unruly libido purred. Trying to ignore it, Alex glared at him as she ducked past. "Yeah, and once I find out where you sleep, who knows what *I'll* do next?"

"Fall asleep bound and gagged, with a pink, aching butt. Have I mentioned I like anal sex?"

She choked and stopped dead to stare. "You're not serious."

His grin was slow and lethal enough to make her heart pound—and not with fear. "I just love forcing my cock into a tight little asshole and listening to the squeals."

Alex swallowed as he sauntered past her and reached for another low-hanging frond. Determined to fight her perverse arousal, she managed a sneer. "And here I thought you were straight."

He curled a lip and pushed the limb aside for her. "I'm not even going to dignify that with a response."

"Probably best. Don't ask, don't tell."

Hawke let the frond go to smack her lightly in the face. Over her yelp, he growled, "I'm straight."

"Sure you are." Alex batted the frond aside and grinned. God, she loved irritating him. It was like teasing the Big Bad Wolf. Sooner or later, she was going to get eaten.

She was hoping for sooner.

* * *

Hawke actually liked her, dammit.

He had not expected that. Oh, he'd known she'd be bright—attorneys were rarely dumb—but he hadn't anticipated her wicked sense of humor.

Then, of course, there was her sassy courage. After witnessing what he'd done to the WTF, most women would probably have hesitated to give him this much hell.

Don't ask, don't tell, my butt. She really did need that spanking. And he was looking forward to giving it to her, too.

Hawke glanced over his shoulder as they approached his cave. She was watching his backside. "Enjoying the view?"

Alex jerked her gaze up to meet his. To his delight, she blushed bright red. "Well, the way it's just kind of hanging out there, bare and flexing, it's tough to miss. What, didn't you have a bigger piece of leather?"

"You saying I've got a broad ass?"

"No, actually it reminds me of a pair of cantaloupes." She winced. "God, did I just say that?"

Hawke couldn't help himself. He roared with laughter.

"Oh, shut up. Me and my mouth. My mother would be mortified."

"Actually, you have a very nice mouth. Given a little training..."

"A little *training?*" She stopped at the foot of the cliff to glare. "You rat, see if you ever get another Lewinsky from me."

"If it's any comfort, you obviously have natural talent. Surprising, given your background." He leaned a shoulder against the cliff and settled back to enjoy her reaction.

Alex gave him a suspicious, narrow-eyed stare. "Now, what do you mean by that crack?"

He hadn't had this much fun in two years. "Blue-blood Southern Belles usually aren't hummer artists. And with that accent, I'd bet a month's pay you're FFV." "First Families of Virginia" was a very old term for the state's very old money— people who could trace their ancestry back to the early colonial period.

She curled a lip, outraged. "Accent? I don't have an accent." There was a definite drawl in those A's.

"Forgive me, Scarlett. What *was* ah thinkin'?"

"Oh, kiss my ass." She huffed, then reluctantly admitted, "Okay, yeah, I'm one of *those* Kenyons. My father's Harold Kenyon."

He started, straightening away from the cliff. "Judge Kenyon?"

Delicate brows lifted. "Why, Hawke—have you had professional dealings with Daddy?"

As a matter of fact, he had. Not that he had any intentions whatsoever of telling her that. "I was stationed in Norfolk for a couple of years. He made the papers about once a month." But Hawke had actually met the judge years earlier, at the Old Man's trial. Hangin' Harry was an intimidating bastard, particularly to a seventeen-year old kid who was scared he was seeing a sneak preview of his own future. After watching Harry rip a strip off Tom Hawke at the sentencing, Hawke had decided the only way to avoid following in his father's bloody footsteps was to enlist in the Marines.

Good God. He'd just shot his wad in Judge Kenyon's daughter's mouth. Hangin' Harry would have a stroke.

Hawke was still contemplating that appalling thought when, like the Southern girl she was, Alex asked the question he dreaded. "So what'd your folks do?"

Well, Dad knocked over convenience stores until he killed a clerk, and Mom was a drunk who moonlighted as a stripper. Hawke was the first male in his family in three generations to avoid jail time. "This and that." He gestured at the rocks overhead. "The cave's up that way. 'Fraid you're going to have to climb."

The distraction worked. She looked up the cliff face, an expression of dismay growing on her pretty face. "Up there?" Then she processed what he said. *"Cave?"*

"WTFs don't like to climb either, sweetheart."

"Good point." Alex contemplated the cliff, visibly appalled. "So how do I get from here to there?"

"Grab a rock and start pulling yourself up. Don't worry, I'll be right behind you." Watching her pick out an outcropping to use as a handhold, Hawke smiled a little grimly. At least he'd distracted her from probing his background.

Because there was a fine old Southern phrase for his family too, and it sure as hell wasn't FFV.

White Trash.

* * *

"Damn, Conan, you sure don't mind working." Alex stared around the cave in admiration.

He snorted. "Well, it's not like I can lie around all day watching TV and playing video games."

"Guess not." She'd expected cramped, damp and dirty, but the cave was really quite spacious, with a high ceiling, curving rock walls, and a hard-packed sandy floor. Her eyes were drawn to the back of the cavern, where a surprisingly big bed stood. The frame was made of thick bamboo lashed together with white nylon cords Hawke must have brought with him. To make a mattress, he'd sewn together a couple of blankets. The result looked fat and inviting. "What'd you stuff the mattress with?" she asked, moving over to get a closer look.

He shrugged. "Leaves, grass. Whatever was handy. I strung parachute cord across the bed frame to give it some support."

Alex nodded and kept exploring. A couple of clay oil lamps hung from the ceiling, supplying a flickering light. Several spears leaned together in the corner. The walls were lined with clay pots, hide bags, and baskets he'd woven out of vines. There were even a couple of military canteens wrapped in desert camouflage. She nodded at the containers. "What's in those?"

"Oil. Fruit. A few vegetables. Smoked meat. I fill the canteens with water twice a day."

Alex nodded. She'd seen the fire pit he used to smoke the food just outside, to one side of the cave. He'd also built bamboo drying racks that currently held several hides he was in the process of curing in the sun.

She squinted, her attention caught by what appeared to be a bamboo platform leaning against the back wall. He'd tied the thick bamboo together with lengths of vine. Two wooden oars lay on the floor in front of it. "Is that a raft?"

"Yep." He started taking off his weapons to stow them neatly beside the bed. "Built it not long after I got here. Used it to paddle out to the barrier."

Interested, she turned toward him, absently waving aside a cruising bumblebee. "What barrier?"

"There's some kind of force field or something surrounding us. It's what holds in the water and atmosphere, just like a goldfish bowl." He pulled out a cloth and sat down on the edge of the bed as he drew his sword from its sheath.

Alex frowned. "What's beyond it?"

He shrugged, wiping down the weapon. "I couldn't tell. You can't see through it. It glows with a milky light during the day that's blinding close up. Apparently, it's the only source of light in here, since we don't have a sun."

She leaned against the cave wall. "Did you try getting through it?"

Hawke shook his head. "Pounded my fists against it so hard I capsized the raft. Didn't do a damn bit of good."

Alex frowned, considering the implications. "Weren't you afraid it would burn you, if it's glowing like that?"

"It wasn't radiating heat." He shot her a look. "Besides, it's not like I had a hell of a lot to lose."

She nibbled a thumbnail. "So if the walls aren't hot, and there's no sun, why is it warm in here?"

"I'm just a poor, dumb Marine, Alex. I don't know these things."

"Dumb, my ass. You seemed to have coped with plunging back into the Stone Age pretty damn well."

"I haven't had a whole lot of choice." He sheathed the sword and put it on the floor beside the bed, within easy reach. "And I've had a great deal of time to figure out how to make what I needed." Rising from the bed, he gave her a wicked grin. "In between jerking off, that is." As her head snapped up in astonishment, he sauntered across the cave toward her. "Fortunately, now I've got you."

"You do know how to sweet talk a girl."

"Hearts and flowers have never been my thing."

She backed up a cautious pace. "I did pick up on that, now that you mention it."

"I knew you were a clever woman. Take off your clothes."

"I beg your pardon?"

There were an awful lot of white teeth in his smile. "I suddenly realized I haven't seen you naked."

She folded her arms and glared at him. "So therefore I should strip."

"It *would* help."

"Forget it, Conan."

"You've seen me naked."

"Only because you made me give you a blow job."

"Would have been tough to do otherwise. Besides, I thought you wanted me to return the favor." He tilted his head, long blond hair sliding over his brawny shoulders. "Licking those pretty little nipples won't be nearly as satisfying with them all covered up."

Alex's heart began pounding again. His blunt orders had a way of turning her on even as they rubbed her the wrong way. Besides, he looked so damn luscious. She'd never had a lover that damn big, and she yearned to touch him. Then, too, there was something about teasing Hawke that never failed to get her motor running.

"Weeeelll... Okay." She smoothed her palms down the front of her camisole. "If you insist."

He grinned wolfishly. "I do."

The fabric had dried from the heat of her body, and now the lace was just slightly stiff. Lifting the hem an inch, she watched Hawke's gaze sizzle.

Oh, this was going to be fun.

Chapter Five

Hawke watched her lift the lace hem of that camisole with his heart pounding and his dick pressing into his loin cloth. Inch by taunting inch, she showed him her taut, tanned little belly, the curve of her waist, the rise of her rib cage—and the sweet, full contours of her lower breasts.

As he caught his breath, willing her to lift the hem further, she purred, "Like what you see?"

Little tease. "Almost as much as I'm going to enjoy watching your ass turn pink," he growled.

"That's no way to talk." She dropped the camisole back over her centerfold body and gave him a smirk that was pure naughty little girl.

He almost snarled in frustration. "Take off that shirt."

"Make me."

"Don't tempt me."

"Judging by that hard-on, I'd say I already am."

Hawke gave her his best menacing smirk. "Your asshole is going to feel really good stretching around my cock."

She turned her back on him and huffed. "Bully."

"I've always wanted to ream a blue-blood belle. I hope you're a virgin."

Alex snatched the camisole off in one movement and threw it aside. "There. Satisfied?"

Hawke drank in the sight of her long, deliciously bare back. Her round little butt cheeks flexed each time she shifted her feet, bisected by the tiny lace thong that was more enticement than anything else. He reached for her. "No, but I'm going to be."

She yelped as he grabbed her by one forearm and hauled her toward the bed. "What the hell do you think you're doing?"

"I seem to recall promising you a spanking." Hawke dropped onto the bed and jerked her down across his thighs.

"What?" Alex tried to rear up, but he planted a hand across her back and kept her there. Her skin felt silken under his palm. Her pretty breasts were so warm and soft pressing against his thighs, it was all he could do not to moan in pleasure. "Stop that!"

"Not a chance." He let his free hand stroke boldly over the round, smooth cheeks of her bottom. She squirmed, but he held her still with no effort at all. She was completely at his mercy.

Hawke let the idea sink in for both of them as he caressed her creamy little backside.

"I'm warning you," Alex said breathlessly. "Don't even think it."

"Or what?" He traced a finger up the cleavage between her pretty haunches.

"Or..." She broke off as he reached the waistband of her thong. He wrapped his fingers around it. "Don't you dare!"

Hawke jerked. The string snapped. "You were saying?"

"Jackass!"

"That's no way to talk to your lord and master." He gave her butt a light swat. She bucked, screeching more in outrage than pain as she snapped her head around to glare at him. Despite the anger, there was even more arousal sizzling in her eyes. "I know where you sleep, you big jerk."

"Oh, come on, Alex." He reached down between her thighs to find the soft, furry lips of her labia. "A spanking can be sexy." Dipping a finger between them, he found her slick and snug enough to make his dick twitch in anticipation. He grinned. "And I'm not the only one who thinks so."

* * *

Dammit, he was right.

She'd had fantasies just like this—being draped across some big sex god's thighs while he got ready to paddle her butt. And the reality was even hotter than her kinky daydreams.

Hawke slid that big finger inside her again in one long, seductive stroke that made her squirm. Alex gave him another testing buck, but he held her still without effort. She was completely at his mercy.

And God help her, she liked it.

"I think I need to repeat the new ground rules," he told her in that rumbling purr of his as he withdrew his finger from her body. "Rule one—I am the master." That broad palm landed with a *SMACK!* Alex jumped and gasped, though the blow produced more noise than pain. "Rule two—*you* are the sex slave."

"You are sooo full of…"

SMACK!

"Rule three—you'll do exactly what I tell you to do." *SMACK!* That one was a little harder. She panted as her arousal grew. "Because otherwise, something's going to eat us." *SMACK!* He paused for another leisurely exploration of her pussy, which, shamelessly, had grown even wetter. "Why, Alex—I do believe you're starting to enjoy this."

"Don't…" she broke off to moan as he added a second finger, "…don't flatter yourself.

He yanked his fingers out. *SMACK!* "Don't lie to the lord and master, Alex." *SMACK SMACK SMACK!*

Her yelp was genuine this time as her backside heated under the rain of burning slaps. "I'll 'lord and master' you, you big…"

Smack! "I can keep this up all day, babe. How about you?"

Blood rushed into her stinging cheeks, and her tingling labia swelled. Every time he'd spanked her, he'd given her clit a little jolt. "Bully." The word emerged as a moan.

"Feeling abused, sweetheart?" Big fingers stroked over her blazing flesh. She squirmed. "Damn, that's a pretty pink. I do believe it's giving me an appetite." Before she quite knew what hit her, he tossed her lightly on the bed and knelt beside it. Alex lifted her head, dazed, as he hauled her thighs over his brawny shoulders. His smoke-gray eyes focused hungrily on her pussy. "And I know just the perfect appetizer."

That wicked mouth fastened directly over her sex, tongue stabbing right between her lips. His first lick pulled her back into a bow. "Jesus, Hawke!"

His only reply was a hungry hum as he went to work, flicking his tongue up and down over her opening, each pass catching her clit. Simultaneously, he reached up to capture her breasts. Long, strong fingers stroked her nipples, squeezing and plucking until she squirmed. "Oh, God!" she gasped, writhing. The extravagant pleasure made a deliciously arousing contrast to the sting of her paddled ass.

He licked. He suckled. He kneaded and twisted. Alex, her thighs draped over shoulders, arched her back and clawed at the grass-filled mattress. It was as if he'd pulled her favorite fantasy right out of her head and brought it to life. Groaning with maddened pleasure, she ground her pussy against his face. Obligingly, he closed his mouth over her clit and sucked hard. His tongue made a single searing pass over the little nubbin…

Alex screeched as her climax boiled up out of nowhere and drowned her in fire. Bucking mindlessly, she rode the molten wave home.

It hadn't even crested yet when he jerked his face away from her, grabbed her thighs, bent them up and back, and crammed the entire meaty length of his cock inside her. "Oh, yeah," he growled over her yelp, hauling her closer, working the thick shaft even deeper. "That's what I want!"

Stunned by the deliciously erotic violence of his entry, Alex could only blink at him. Hawke rose over her, his hard face brutal with hunger, his eyes glittering, both her knees cupped in his hands.

"Now," he said, giving her a feral grin. "Let's fuck."

He pulled out slowly. Heat skittered along her nerves at the sensation of his thick shaft withdrawing. The tip of him actually left her body. He leaned forward again. Her slick, tight flesh twisted as his length slid back inside. Fire curled into a hot ball low in her womb. "God, that feels good," Alex gasped.

"Mmmm," he agreed, and pulled out. Satin thickness caressed her sensitive inner core. Looking down between her thighs, she watched his abdominal muscles ripple as he pushed deep. "Oh, yeah. My own little sex slave," he rumbled, watching her face with hungry intensity. "So sweet and slick and hot. Mine to fuck however I want."

"Nooo," she groaned, not meaning the refusal.

"Yeeah." He drew out. "Oh yeah. I think I'll tie you up next. Maybe grease up that little ass and..." He slammed deep, making her yowl in a combination of pleasure and torment as her entire nervous system lit up like Christmas tree.

"Forget it," she gasped, writhing at the starburst sensations. "You're not putting that thing in my..."

Hawke laughed and began to pump in long, ruthless strokes. "Babe, once I've got you bound and gagged, you're not going to have much say in which little hole I bang."

Alex cried out, her climax cresting hot again. He was right. He was so damn strong, he could do whatever he wanted with her.

At that thought, the orgasm he'd been stoking with every stroke of his cock launched up her spine like the Space Shuttle. She convulsed, helpless in his grip as his broad shaft worked in and out of her creamy sex. That was when she knew—Hawke was the man of her dreams.

Every last kinky one of them.

* * *

He threw back his head and fought for control. It wasn't easy, given the sweet pull of Alex's hot inner muscles milking his cock. It had been so damn long since he'd ridden a woman. Even then, it hadn't been anything like this.

Hawke could still taste her on his tongue, salt and vinegar and musk. Her cunt clung and gripped him with every hard stroke as her lovely little breasts bounced. Her blue eyes glittered as her little pink tongue flicked out over her lips. Long hair the color of honey tumbled across the bed he'd never expected to see a woman in.

Sucking in a breath as pleasure clawed at him, Hawke thought about everything he'd ever imagined doing to a woman. Imagined tying her up. Imagined the tight, slick grip of her asshole as he gave it the fucking he'd been threatening her with.

She was his. Hangin' Harry's blue-blood daughter was his, and he could have her however he wanted. And the thought obviously turned her on just as much as it did him.

Hawke threw back his head and gritted his teeth as the fire clamped hot claws around his balls. He felt a wave of it rolling up his cock. "I'm coming!" he gasped.

"Hawke!" She arched, eyes squeezing shut, pretty lips gasping. Her tiny inner muscles clamped and pulled at his cock in yet another climax. He roared, coming like a freight train in a blaze of heat.

His last thought before the fire took him was that he'd never had a woman like her.

And now that he had her, he was damned if he'd let her go.

Chapter Six

With a sense of regret, Alex felt his softening cock slide from her body. Hawke collapsed beside her with a heartfelt groan. "You okay?" He was panting.

She whimpered, not quite up to speech.

He reared up on one elbow, concern in those smoke gray eyes as he examined her face. "Alex? Did I hurt you?" A tight little line grew between his thick eyebrows.

He was really worried. The thought sent a bubble of pleased warmth rising in her. "I'm fine," she managed.

"Are you sure? I'm a lot stronger than I used to be, and I got a little carried away." He caught her by one hip and rolled her over to examine her backside. "I don't think there's any bruising."

"Hawke…"

"I really did pull those swats."

She grinned back over her shoulder at him. "Hawke, I'm fine. You didn't hurt me. As much as I hate admit it, I enjoyed every minute of it, including the spanking."

He searched her face. "You sure?"

"You know, you're completely ruining your image as a dominant asshole."

"*That* was a game." His sudden grin was wicked. "Mostly."

Enjoying herself, she asked, "How mostly?"

Hawke sobered, his gray eyes going serious. "When something's getting ready to eat us and I give you an order, I don't want an argument. I realize you argue for a living, but whenever I'm fighting a WTF is not the time."

Alex snorted. "Give me credit for a little sense, Hawke. The only creature I want eating me around here is you."

He laughed. "I can't tell you how gratified I am to hear it."

"Gratified." Deciding it was time to start teasing him again, she stuck her tongue in one cheek. "That's a really big word for you, isn't it? I'm so proud."

"Smartass. You want *another* spanking?"

"Only if you promise to kiss it and make it well."

The humor drained from his eyes as he leaned down and tilted her chin in one big hand. "Love to."

Hawke's kiss was slow and sensual, his lips moving over hers in a silken possession that made her toes curl. His warm tongue slipped between her lips in a gentle mating stroke that made her sigh. When he finally lifted his head, she whispered, "You're really good at that."

"I'm really good at a lot of things... Ow! You bit me!"

"Oh, that was just a little nip, you big baby."

"I'll *give* you baby, wench!" Long, merciless fingers went for her ribs.

She shouted in laughter and kicked at him. "Get off me, you brute!"

"Watch where you put those bony little feet. Or..." He grabbed an ankle and wiggled the fingers of the other hand menacingly above her sole.

"Don't you *dare* tickle me!"

"Or what?"

"Or I'll..." She lunged for his ribs.

He convulsed with a booming laugh and let her go to fend off her hands. "Cut that out!"

"Ha! Conan is ticklish!"

"I'll give you ticklish!" The mattress rustled as they wrestled, laughing and panting.

* * *

Alex lay draped over Hawke's bare chest, listening to his heartbeat settle into the slow rhythm of sleep. Poor guy. Between fighting the WTF, banging her brains out, and having his secret ticklish spot discovered, he was worn out.

She yawned so hard her jaws creaked. Okay, so he wasn't the only one.

Alex settled her head more comfortably in the hollow between his shoulder and the swell of his right pectoral, smiling sleepily. She really should be more upset about this. She'd been abducted by aliens, for God's sake. She had court next week. Guilty pleas alone would take two days.

Grimacing, Alex pictured the long lines of drunks, petty drug dealers, and car-breakers who'd assemble in the courtroom Monday, waiting to plead guilty. Most of them would get probation, though a few would do time. Hours and hours listening to bullshit excuses. "I lost my job, Your Honor. That's why I had to steal my neighbor's stereo to buy crack." Yeah, right.

She released another huge yawn and hooked her arm around Hawke's broad ribcage. His skin still felt a little sweaty from their play.

A movement in the corner of her eye attracted her attention. She looked down to watch his thick cock slide into full erection. She blinked at it, remembering what it had felt like thrusting deep into her eager sex...

A loud, rattling sound brought her head up.

Hawke was snoring.

Alex buried her head against his chest and giggled softly. Maybe being abducted by aliens wasn't really so bad after all.

* * *

One Month Later

Concentration fierce in her eyes, Alex drew back the spear, her body silhouetted against the vivid blue of the Goldfish Bowl's ocean. The wind whipped the dark honey hair she wore tied up in a long ponytail. She wore only three strategically placed bits of leather and just enough cord to support them.

Hawke's cock thoroughly approved.

A drop of water rolled down one perfect breast. He gave serious thought to licking it off, but decided she wouldn't appreciate being interrupted. At least this minute. He'd learned over the past weeks that Alex was ferociously driven; once she'd attained her goal, she'd be more than happy to celebrate.

He watched her brows draw down as her eyes narrowed. Her little pink tongue stole out to the corner of her mouth, a measure of her concentration. Hawke felt his heart roll over in his chest.

She was just so damned adorable.

"Hah!" Alex drove the spear ferociously downward, her entire body surging with effort. The weapon bit into something below the water. She leaned into the shaft with her full weight, grinding down as whatever it was kicked up spray around her.

Finally the splashing stopped. Bumblebees buzzed lazily. He watched her rise on her toes to get a better look at her catch. "Yes!" Alex crowed, and levered the spear up. A bass flailed weakly on its flint point. "Look at that! By God, I did it!"

Hawke grinned, unable to resist her incandescent joy. "You certainly did."

She waded toward shore with her catch. "You get to clean this one."

"Sure do." He followed her, watching her delightful ass, clad only in a couple of bits of string he fully intended to snap. "A deal's a deal."

"I told you I could do it!"

"I never doubted you."

Alex lowered the struggling fish to the sand. "Uh, could you...?"

Drawing his knife with a wry grin, he crouched to finish the fish off. She couldn't stand to see anything suffer. Hawke had only persuaded her to try spear fishing by offering to give her a pass from her usual fish-cleaning duties. He'd figured it was an important skill she needed to know. She had to be able to fend for herself if something happened to him.

Now, there was a thought to kill a good mood. The idea of Alex going up against a WTF or any of the Bastards' other nasty pets chilled him right to the marrow. Particularly since, unlike him, she'd never acquired superhuman strength.

Thing was, it did sound like something the Bastards would do—take him out of the picture and leave her defenseless. Oh, Hawke knew she'd rise to the occasion—there was some serious steel hidden under all that pretty fluff—but he hated the thought of the fear and grief she'd feel if something happened to him. They'd gotten close over the past month.

Close, my ass, he thought dryly, watching her do an impromptu victory dance on the sand around her catch. *I'm head over heels in love with her.*

That thought would have scared the shit out of him if they'd been back home. The more Alex talked about her blue-blood family—her fiercely protective judge daddy and matchmaking mama—the more obvious it was they'd hate him with a passion. Hawke might have enough medals for a platoon in his footlocker, he might have worked his way up from lowly private to lieutenant in the Marine Corps, but he'd still be trailer trash to them. Which was why he'd never let her worm the truth of his background out of him.

Oh, he'd learned enough over the past month to know Alex herself wouldn't care. She knew he'd worked his ass off to get where he was—he'd told her that much—and that was all she'd care about. To her, the fact that his daddy and brother were doing time would be irrelevant in the equation of what Hawke himself had accomplished. That ferocious sense of justice was one of the things he adored about her.

That, and those lovely tits. Among other things.

Oh, yeah. He had it bad. So bad, he was no longer all that sure he wanted to go home. Back home, the fact that he'd grown up in a seedy trailer park would matter. Back home, it wouldn't take Alex long to discover his mama drank most of the take-home pay he sent her.

Hawke knew he was probably enabling the old lady's drinking problem, but he just couldn't stand the thought of his mother going hungry. And she did occasionally buy food, at least between pints of Mad Dog 20/20.

Okay, so he was a sucker.

But in the Goldfish Bowl, he could keep Alex in happy ignorance while screwing her brilliant brains out. Here he could slay all her monsters and bask in the adoration in her eyes. His mother would still be taken care of, since he'd be listed as Missing In Action and the Marines would continue to send her his pay.

Of course, the trick was, he had to keep killing the monsters. If one of them actually got him, Alex was fucked.

So he'd just damn well make sure none of them got him.

"I think I'm going to try to catch another one," Alex announced, wading back into the water.

"Good idea." Hawke trailed her happily. Walking a pace behind Alexandria Kenyon was no hardship; her ass was a thing of beauty. "We can smoke whatever we don't eat tonight."

"Oh, yeah. Or I could try to whip up a nice fish stew. A few potatoes, some carrots…" They tended his garden on a daily basis. Even weeding was more fun with Alex beside him.

No doubt about it. He had it bad.

Hawke watched her draw back the spear and go still in the water as she waited for her prey to swim by. From the corner of one eye, he spotted a ripple in the water. Something was definitely headed their way.

He frowned. Damn big ripple. Too big for a…

A head the height of his body rose from the water on a long, snaking neck. As they gaped at it, the thing roared, revealing a mouthful of shark teeth.

"Oh, shit," Hawke breathed, and grabbed her arm. "Run!"

Chapter Seven

"Faster!" Hawke roared, hauling her across the beach with running strides so long she could barely keep up. "A thing that size is not going to want to leave the water! If we can get inland, we're safe!"

But if we can't, we're toast, Alex realized grimly as she poured everything she had in pelting over the sand at his heels. She didn't dare take time even to drop her spear.

Slap! Something cold and wet wrapped around her left ankle. The sand came up and slammed into her chest, ripping her hand out of his and knocking the spear from her grip. Instinctively, Alex tried to scramble back to her feet. She heard Hawke's bellow of horror at the same time she realized she was caught. Twisting around, she saw what had her and screamed.

A thick, meaty tentacle had wrapped around her bare ankle, suckers gripping her flesh. As she stared at it in frozen horror, it jerked, hauling her over the sand, back toward the edge of the water where the thing's head towered over the water. The arm had to be a good thirty feet long and thick as a python. "Fuck!" she screamed. "Haaawke!"

He lunged past her to pounce on the tentacle with a roar of fury. His sword caught the light as he lifted it and chopped down on the thick limb just beyond where it wrapped around her foot. Orange slime flew through the air, and the tentacle's grip convulsed. Alex shrieked as what felt like a dozen needles sank into her skin. "Hawke, its suckers have *spines!* Oh, *damn,* that hurts!"

He didn't look around, just held on and hacked as the tentacle dragged them toward its horrific owner. A second tentacle lifted out of the water and plunged toward them. "Look out!"

Hawke threw a quick look over his shoulder at the whipping arm, but instead of letting her go, he gave the tentacle another vicious chop, hacking right through the end that held Alex.

Despite the biting pain from the spines, she struggled to her feet as he jumped up. The second tentacle whipped down at him, but he ducked aside and slashed at it.

"There's another one!" she yelled, seeing a third arm rise from the water. "How many tentacles does that thing have?"

"Run!" Hawke bellowed, dancing around the flailing arm. "I'll distract it!"

"But...!"

"Goddammit, I said *go!"* He chopped. Orange blood flew.

Just as the third tentacle snapped around his waist. "Shit!" he bellowed, and twisted around to attack the arm with his sword. That sounded like a cry of pain; it must be digging into him with those spines. "Let go, you bastard!"

A weapon! She needed a weapon! Desperately, Alex whirled, looking around for her fallen spear. There! She spotted the long wooden shaft lying on the sand where she'd dropped it. She raced to pick it up.

But by the time she turned around with it, the thing had wrapped still another tentacle around Hawke's sword arm as it hauled him toward its fanged head. He wasn't making it easy; he'd managed to get his legs braced in front of him to resist its pull. His feet dug furrows in the sand, cords standing out on the side of his neck as he strained, face going bright red.

With a desperate scream, Alex lunged toward the tentacle holding Hawke's sword arm and drove the spear into it with every ounce of her strength. Both tentacles convulsed, coiling like snakes. Hawke cursed viciously as they dragged at him. Bright red blood snaked down his bunched biceps. The spines must be tearing the hell out of his skin.

She jerked the spear out and looked for another spot to jab.

"Look out!" Hawke roared. "There comes another one!"

Alex whirled, saw the meaty arm shooting right for her face, and ducked. She gave it a savage jab when it feinted at her, dancing out of its path. Shooting a look at Hawke, she tried to decide whether she could get in another shot at the ones holding him. He'd twisted his sword around and jammed the weapon into one of the tentacles, all the way up to the hilt.

"What the hell do you think you're doing?" he bellowed. "Get the fuck inland!"

"And leave you?" She danced and jabbed with her spear. "I don't think so."

The fourth tentacle suddenly whipped around to catch his left leg. It jerked him right off his feet. He cursed savagely.

She screamed as the monster lifted him off the ground and carried him toward its open jaws. "Alex, get clear!" he roared. His face was as white as parchment.

"Fuck that!" It was going to eat him!

The sheer blazing panic of that thought swamped every other consideration. Alex took off running straight for the thing's head. She had to get there before he did. Luckily, the thing wasn't lifting very fast, probably because Hawke was fighting for everything he was worth.

"Go back!" he bellowed.

The creature's massive head whipped around to stare at her with malevolent interest, but it had its tentacles full with Hawke. Membranes snapped back and forth across its huge yellow eyes. It plunged toward her, jaws gaping wide.

Moving faster than she'd ever moved in her life, Alex jumped aside. It missed.

"Hey, ugly!" Hawke yelled. "Over here, you slimy motherfucker!" He'd cut off the tentacle around his sword arm, and now he jabbed his blade savagely into the one that circled his waist. He bore down, twisting the sword.

The thing's head reared up with a shrill, ringing cry of pain. It whipped around and started hauling him toward its open mouth. Alex saw her own reflection in one huge, yellow eye...

And stabbed her spear right into it with the entire weight of her body behind the blow.

The thing howled like a banshee. Its massive head whipped toward her as it lashed in agony. She tried to duck, but it clipped her shoulder. She went flying like a Mark McGwire home run.

The sand came up at her face...

* * *

Hawk shouted as Alex hit the ground and tumbled like a rag doll, but there wasn't one damn thing he could do about it. The remaining tentacles that held him lashed back and forth with the creature's death throes, threatening to tear him apart. Its spines ripped his skin in white-hot agony. He kicked, felt the one around his ankle tear away, but he was still trapped in the arm that held his waist. It flailed, flinging him upward. His stomach somersaulted as he shot skyward, flew twenty feet, then plunged down again.

The ocean shot up toward his face. *Fuck!* He sucked in a breath.

It was like slamming into a brick wall at thirty miles an hour. Cold and pressure rammed his face. And then he was underwater, being dragged relentlessly downward as the creature sank. Tendrils of red blood snaked past his eyes, mixed with streamers of orange. Huge bubbles rolled up.

The need to breathe clawed at his chest, but he fought it, sensing the tentacle was losing its grip. Black spots floated in front of his eyes, and he knew he was on the verge of losing consciousness. For a moment, it seemed easier...

And then a thought pierced his stunned brain.

Alex! Fuck, he had to get loose. She was up there hurt. He had to get free!

He shoved free of the tentacle and kicked, clawing and fighting toward the light he could see over his head. Too far off. He was never going to make it.

He had to. She'd risked her life to save his ass; he couldn't do less for her. Lips sealed and eyes burning, he kicked hard, driving for the surface.

His head exploded into air and blinding light. Hawke sucked in a desperate, furious breath. His body felt like solid lead, but he ignored his exhaustion and turned in the water, searching for the beach.

He spotted it. And there, lying on the sand, was a small, crumpled figure.

Alex. Goddamn her, she'd better not have gotten herself killed.

Hawke flung himself toward shore in what had to have been the ugliest swimming stroke he'd ever performed. Finally his feet hit sand, and he staggered up the beach to collapse beside her.

"Alex?" He turned her over awkwardly, ignoring the vicious stinging pain in his biceps from the thing's spines. "Alex, baby, be alive." His voice choked. "You'd better not be dead, you hear me?" He dropped his head on her chest and listened.

For a moment, he heard nothing but the buzzing of those damn bees, and his own heart stopped. Then...

Thump. Thump. Thump.

"Oh, Christ!" His eyes filled with tears. "Thank you, Jesus." He straightened and began carefully examining the woman he loved.

* * *

The first thing Alex heard was her lover's deep sensual growl. "I am going to kick your ass unless you talk to me right now."

With considerable difficulty, she managed to pry her lids open. His face loomed over hers, dripping water onto her chest.

There was a marked gray cast to his skin, and his eyes looked wild. She coughed. Everything hurt. "Is that any..." She had to stop to pant. "...any way to talk to the woman who saved your life?"

A broad, relieved grin broke over his face. "Saved it, hell. You damn near gave me a heart attack."

"Ingrate." She rolled over onto her side and groaned.

"You okay?" Tenderly, he ran a hand over her back.

"Everything hurts." Alex frowned, and cautiously rolled over onto her hands and knees. "But I think it all works. You?"

He sat back on his haunches and looked down at his flat, muscled belly. A set of horrific punctures marked his skin as if he'd be run over by a spiked tire, but the openings were already closing. "Motherfuckin' monster made hamburger out of everything it grabbed, but I'm already starting to heal."

With a sigh, she staggered upright. "I should be so lucky." Then, aiming a frown down at her ankle, she saw the puncture wounds there were indeed beginning to heal. "And apparently I am."

"Good." He clambered to his feet and stood there swaying as he glowered down at her. "I want you in perfect shape when I wallop that disobedient little ass."

"What?" She glared at him in outrage.

Gray eyes blazed. "I told you to leave, dammit! You disobeyed me! It almost *ate* you!"

"Well, if I had obeyed, it would have eaten *you!*"

"So?"

"So I love you, you big dumbass! You're not becoming monster chow as long as I'm around to do something about it!"

For a moment, incredulous joy flooded his gaze. Then it vanished into a snarl as he poked a finger toward her chest. "Sorry, you're not distracting me that easily. The point is, when I give you an order, you do what I tell you to do!"

"Yeah?" Furious, fighting mad, she sneered at him. "Well, here's an order for you—kiss my ass!" Snarling, she whirled around and stomped back toward the cave.

The next monster that came along could eat him with her blessings!

Chapter Eight

She loved him. The thought filled Hawke with giddy joy.

Which he had no intention whatsoever of letting her see. Alex had almost gotten herself killed, dammit. Trying to save him, true—and he had to admit there was a good chance he'd be dead now if she hadn't. But when he'd looked around and seen her flying at that monster with that silly toothpick of a spear, he'd damn near had a heart attack right then. He'd thought the thing was going to eat her on the spot.

When Hawke remembered the monster's long, snakelike neck, all those teeth, how fast the fucker moved—it made him sick. He couldn't let her do that again. He'd rather die himself than watch something take a bite out of her. He had to make damn sure that the next time he gave her an order, she obeyed it.

Striding along behind her as she stalked toward the cave, Hawke eyed her round little ass, just barely clad in a tiny triangle of leather. A wave of violent lust rolled over him. He recognized it as the flipside of terror; he always got horny as hell right after a battle. He'd bet a month's pay Alex felt the same, no matter how pissed she was.

Suddenly he knew just what he was going to do to make sure she never took a chance like that again.

* * *

Dammit, all the little hairs were standing up on the back of her neck. Hawke was projecting hot male menace at her so hard, he was damn near giving her radiation burns.

Perversely, Alex felt her nipples peak. He was probably going to spank her again before screwing her brains out. The thought turned her on even as it ticked her off. It was just not fair. Nothing she'd ever experienced made her as hot as John Hawke being a dominant asshole. He was so gorgeous; it wasn't as if he needed any other unfair advantages.

She stomped up the winding path toward the cave, acutely aware of the rustle of bushes behind her as Hawke stalked her. Rivulets of warm cream slid into her cunt with every step she took. Any minute now, he was going to grab her, rip her clothes off, and beat her butt. Then he'd slide that humongous cock into her aching pussy and fuck her until she saw stars.

She really should put up a fight. Just on general principles. She'd saved his life, dammit. Where did he get off being such a prick about it?

And to make matters worse, she'd blurted out that she loved him. Like he needed any other ammunition.

He hadn't told her he loved her back, either.

Alex brooded about that thought as she climbed the cliff up to the cave. She never found it an enjoyable trip anyway, and it was even worse now, with all the aches, bruises and puncture wounds she'd managed to collect during the fight. She was healing fast, but not that fast.

And horny on top of all that. It just wasn't fair.

After an interminable climb—feeling Hawke's gaze burning her ass the whole way—Alex scrambled into the cave. She'd really like to collapse, but that blazing glare was making her far too jumpy. Instead, she made for one of the canteens and slugged down half its contents.

When she was done, she wiped her chin and turned to look at him as he bent to dig through one of the leather bags. "Oh, hell," she said, grimacing as realization hit. "We forgot the fish."

Hawke shrugged. "Something else has probably eaten it by now."

"Guess it's veggies and fruit tonight."

He pulled a handful of cords out of the bag and turned toward her. "Actually, I had something else in mind."

Her heart gave an enthusiastic little jump. She backed up a pace anyway. "Like what?"

Hawke gave her a grin that was all teeth. "Like an in-depth discussion of why you're going to fucking *obey* me the next time I give you an order."

"Oh, come on, Hawke! It was going to kill you!"

"That's not the issue."

"Oh, hell yes, it is! If you think I'm just going to stand by and... Hey!" He grabbed her by one arm, kicked her feet out from under her, and pushed her down onto a fur pelt on the dirt floor.

The next thing she knew, he'd flipped her over on her belly, grabbed one wrist, and started whipping the cord around it. "You'll do what I tell you to do," he told her grimly.

"What the hell do you think you're doing?"

"Guess." He grabbed the other wrist and bound the first to it with a couple of ruthless loops.

"Hey!" Alex tried to flip over, but he dropped a knee in the small of her back and pinned her in place. Finished, he released her wrists. They dropped to the pelt over her head. "Cut it out!"

"Oh, no." Steel slithered as he drew his knife. She felt the cool brush of the blade against her waist as he cut the cord waistband of her leather thong.

"Let me guess," she snarled, frustrated and turned on as he sliced her clothes off her. "You're going to beat my ass again, right?"

"No," he drawled lazily, rising to his feet and tossing her bra and thong aside. "Actually, I've got something else in mind."

"What?" She twisted around on the pelt and glared as he went to the collection of clay jars against one wall of the cave. "What the hell are you doing?"

"Looking for the animal fat." Picking a jar up, he uncorked it, took a sniff, then capped it and put it down again. He chose another, opened it, and nodded in satisfaction. "There it is."

"What do you need animal fat for?" Alex watched as he headed back toward with the jar in one big hand.

Her heart began to pound. She knew damn well what he needed it for.

With a nasty grin, he bounced the jar in his palm and confirmed her fears. "Greasing your tight little asshole."

"Oh, no. Forget it." She tried to flip over, but he dropped to his knees and slapped a big hand in the center of her back to shove her flat. Before she could rear up again, he turned around and half sat on her facing her backside.

She heard the clink as he pulled the clay cork off the pot. "I'm afraid this is not a topic for debate."

"You'd rape me?" Alex flinched as he used the other hand to part her butt cheeks.

"It won't be rape." Warm fingers stroked between her cheeks, seeking the little puckered opening. "I'll make sure you're nice and hot before I start your punishment."

She caught her breath as Hawke's long, thick finger found her asshole and began to push. He entered slowly, the penetration both a bit painful and shockingly erotic. Despite herself, she felt a hot, scandalized arousal growing as he probed her. "You can't do this!"

"Sweetheart, I can do any damn thing I want to with you. You're the one who's tied up, remember?" The dark purr in his voice made her heart pound. "Oh, yeah. You're definitely a virgin there, aren't you? Nice and tight."

She swallowed as he drew his finger out of her and delved into the pot again. Her voice cracked. "I hope that's not what you use to cook with."

"Don't be disgusting. I whipped this up especially with you in mind."

"Well, that's a…" She squeaked. He was using two fingers this time, and the slow penetration stretched her brutally. "Dammit, that hurts!"

"Good. It'll hurt even more when it's my cock." He rotated those long fingers, and she caught her breath. "Oh, I'm gonna enjoy this. There's nothing quite as hot as working my dick into a pretty little sub's tight asshole."

Alex was feeling distinctly lightheaded as every bit of blood she had headed straight for her pussy. "I'm not a sub."

"Yeah?" He slid the forefinger of the other hand into her pussy. She caught her breath in agonized pleasure as he stretched both tight channels. "You're pretty damn creamy for somebody who's not a sub. Especially considering what I'm getting ready to do to your virgin ass."

She really ought to tell him off, but the sensation of his big fingers working her pussy and anus was just too overwhelming. Dropping her forehead to the pelt under her, Alex sobbed in a breath.

"I'm gonna fuck your little butt real slow," he purred in the menacing rumble that could make her cream even when he wasn't strumming her clit and fingering both holes. "Long, deeeeep thrusts. It's gonna hurt, but this is a punishment, so I don't have to be gentle."

"Bastard!" She shuddered, ferociously aroused.

"You bet. That's why you don't want to piss me off."

"I saved your life, you prick!"

"And I gave you an order you disobeyed." He jerked his fingers out of her, grabbed her hip, and flipped her over on her back. Then he moved around to kneel between her spread thighs. "Luckily for you, I think you need to be a little hotter before I start your punishment."

She watched breathlessly as he spread her lips, lowered his head and extended his pointed pink tongue. Its first pass over her clit sent a sizzle through her that made her back arch. Then, as she writhed, he started eating her out. A moment later, two of those big fingers went back up her ass.

* * *

Hawke danced his tongue around Alex's hard little clit, enjoying the way she twisted against his mouth. Simultaneously, he fingerfucked her, in all the way to the knuckles. Her backside gripped him like a fist. Imagining what it would feel like to force his cock into that little hole, he growled in pleasure against her cunt.

Oh, yeah. He was going to give her a reaming she'd never forget.

And judging by her panting groans, she loved every minute of the preparations. He'd suspected Alex had a masochistic streak, but she was even more responsive than he'd hoped.

Which meant he could give her the truly brutal assfuck he'd been dreaming of for weeks now. By the time he was done with her rectum, she'd never dream of disobeying another order.

Yeah, it was highhanded. Yeah, he should be ashamed of himself. But he really didn't give a damn. If being a prick was what it took to make sure she never again risked herself like she had today, he was more than happy to play sadistic bastard.

Particularly since he was so hard, he could drive nails with his cock.

She was grinding her wet little cunt against his face now, savaging her own backside with his fingers, on the verge of an explosion.

Hawke jerked his hand out of her butt and sat up, licking her hot juices off his lips. "Sorry, babe," he told her, watching the shocked fury roll over her face. "You don't get to come. This is a punishment, remember?"

Her eyes narrowed as her pretty mouth curled into a snarl. "You asshole!"

He grinned. "No. Yours."

Reaching for his loincloth, he jerked it away, freeing his aching cock.

Chapter Nine

Her heart pounding with a potent combination of arousal and fear, Alex watched Hawke grease his cock. He took his time, scooping out a dollop of the animal fat and stroking it up and down the jutting shaft, his gaze never leaving hers. His smoke-gray eyes seemed to smolder.

"You're going to want to fight it at first," he told her in a velvet rumble that made her nipples ache. "But your best bet is to push out with those little muscles while I force it in."

Licking her dry lips, she stared at the massive rod, hypnotized by the way it bobbed under his stroking hand. She was acutely aware of her bound wrists.

"Feeling helpless?" he purred. "You look it. Tied up and ready to take my cock up your virgin ass. All pretty tits and long legs and anxious eyes." Hawke grinned. "It's no wonder I'm hard as a rock."

"You do realize you're being a bastard?" She sounded breathless, dammit.

"Oh, yeah." He caught her under one knee and lifted her hips off the pelt. The movement spread her wide. With the other hand, he reached between her cheeks, parted her. His glittering eyes studied her, his angular face sharp with hunger. "What a pretty little rosebud asshole." He let go of her backside to grab his massive cock, simultaneously dragging her close with the other hand. "Don't worry, baby, I'm not really going to split it open." His teeth flashed. She felt something smooth and hot press against the delicate flesh. "It's just going to feel that way."

Alex's eyes widened as she felt the crown of his cock pressing against her anus in a savage demand for entry. The tiny opening reluctantly spread, admitting the knob a fraction. "Hawke!" she gasped. "That hurts!"

His eyes blazed up as he grinned. "I know." Another flaming inch slid inside. "This is what happens when you don't mind the big, nasty Marine." He licked his lips and grabbed her other hip, pulling her closer, slowly impaling her. His face tightened with voluptuous pleasure. "He ties you up and helps himself to your anal cherry."

Alex groaned, tossing her head as she tried to adjust to his relentless entry. His cock felt like a red-hot baseball bat.

"Push, babe," he growled. "Let me in."

Desperate to relieve the pressure, she obeyed. As the grip of her muscles eased, he sank deeper and deeper. Finally her butt was snug against his washboard belly. He released her hips and came down on top of her, big hands braced beside her shoulders. He gave her a conqueror's grin. "Mmmmm. Finally. Balls deep in your ass. I think I like it here."

"Oh, God." It felt like he'd shoved a burning torch up her butt. "Hurry up and get off already, you sadistic son of a bitch!"

"Not so fast. Here comes the good part." Slowly, he began to pull out.

She gasped. He wasn't kidding. The sensation was dark and exotic and really kinky, and it went on and on as he withdrew his big cock. Alex squirmed, catching her breath.

"Told you you'd like it." Hawke smiled smugly. "Now…" He thrust. Another wave of dark, hot pain. Then he pulled out again, very slowly, sending pleasure snaking along every nerve ending she had.

"I think you're beginning to get it," he rumbled. "Let's pick up the pace a little…"

Oh, God.

* * *

Pleasure wrapped around Hawke's balls like wet silk as he fucked Alex Kenyon up her deliciously tight ass. It wasn't the first time he'd tied up a pretty submissive for a thorough rectum reaming, but it had never been this hot.

She'd pissed him off, of course—that was part of it—and then there was the wicked kink of butt-banging Judge Kenyon's virgin baby. But most of it was just the searing response she gave him every time he shoved his cock up that butter-slick channel and felt her squirm in painful pleasure.

Sweet Alex had a masochistic streak that brought his inner sadistic bastard roaring to the surface.

Not that it had ever been all that deeply buried to begin with.

Hawke drew out, listening to her conquered moan of delight. He pushed inside. She twisted, her tight, well-greased flesh gripping his cock. As he felt the little hole strain to take his invading width, she whimpered, a tiny, helpless sound that made his dick twitch in sadistic pleasure.

Oh, yeah. He was giving poor little Alex a very hard time. And damned if she didn't love it almost as much as he did.

Taking pity on her, he reached down and stroked his thumb over her clit as he forced his shaft in. She jerked and moaned.

"Like that?" he drew out, circling and strumming her clit.

Alex groaned, throwing back her head and arching her spine until her pretty nipples pointed at the ceiling. "Oh, God! Yes!"

"More?"

She panted. "Oh. Oh, yeah!"

Hawke gave her a dark smile. "Here it comes then."

Then he started fucking her—long, hard strokes that tore a scream of tormented ecstasy from her mouth. He gave her no mercy at all beyond the thumb that stroked her clit as he rammed her ass.

"Hawke!" she gasped, writhing under his hard strokes. "Sweet God, I'm coming!" Tiny inner muscles clamped over his cock, pulsed as she convulsed in her bonds.

He'd never seen anything as hot in his life as the sight of Alex climaxing as he fucked her tight, virginal ass.

Hot Roman candle bursts of pleasure began to shoot up his spine. With a roar of savage joy, he drove to the hilt and threw back his head, pumping Alex full of hot cum.

* * *

Hawke collapsed against her, all hot, sweaty muscle and delicious male weight. She groaned in pleasure even as her violated ass ached in protest. He'd sodomized her without any compassion whatsoever, yet she'd never experienced anything so utterly arousing. Her climax had lit her entire nervous system up like an overloaded Christmas tree.

"Damn, Hawke," she wheezed. "That was rude, crude and socially unacceptable."

"Yeah." He sounded distinctly smug. "Wanna do it again?"

"Give me a week to recover, and I'll think about it."

"Glad you approve." He reached for her bound wrists, grabbed the knife, and freed her with a single pass of the blade. She let her arms fall, but before she could get comfortable, he scooped her off the floor and carried her to the bed.

After laying her down on the thick mattress, Hawke went to rummage among the supplies against the wall. He returned with a wet cloth he put to use cleaning her well-fucked backside. She sank into a pleasant lassitude as he busied himself again before sliding into bed next to her.

As Hawke wrapped brawny arms around her, Alex nestled her head into the hollow of his shoulder and sighed in pleasure. "That was really hot."

"Oh, yeah."

"You're not a nice man."

"Nope."

"But if you think I'm going to just stand by the next time something tries to eat you, you're out of your ever-lovin' mind."

Hawke sighed.

* * *

Alex came awake slowly to the sound of a low buzzing. She opened her eyes and saw one of the ever-present bumblebees hovering over her head. She frowned. It seemed to be watching her.

She swatted at the thing. It ducked aside like a tiny helicopter, but it didn't buzz off. Instead it returned to hovering over her and Hawke. It still seemed to be watching her.

Come to think of it, those damn bees always seemed to be watching her.

And what the hell were they anyway? Narrow-eyed, she considered the insect. Now that she looked more closely, she saw that though it did sound like a bumblebee, it was matte black instead of striped. Too, its anatomy was wrong, with an oddly shaped head that was much bigger than a normal insect's in proportion to its size. Too, rather than multifaceted eyes like a real bee, it had single-faceted ones set on the front of its "face," rather than on the sides of its head.

All of the bumble-things behaved strangely too. Instead of buzzing around the local fruit and plant life like real bees, they seemed to have a real affinity for her and Hawke. But they never seemed to bite, so they weren't bloodsuckers like mosquitoes.

Suspicion tugged at her. "Hey, Hawke."

"Hmm?"

"What are those things?"

He opened one eye and followed her pointing finger. "It's a bumblebee, Alex."

"No, it's not. Look at it."

Hawke groaned. "Alex, baby, I don't give a damn."

"No, think about it. This is a man-made—or alien-made—environment. Everything in it was added for us to eat, use or run from. So what are the bugs for?"

Hawke's eyes narrowed. Suddenly his big hand flashed upward and two fingers snapped closed, right over the bumble-thing.

"Damn, you're quick."

"I try." She scrambled onto her knees as he sat up. His eyes narrowed, and he squeezed so hard his fingertips turned white. His brows flew up and he opened his opened his fingers.

The bumble-thing took off, obviously unhurt by his attempt to crush it.

"You losing your touch, Hawke?"

He snorted as he eyed the circling bug. "Hardly. I don't know what that thing is, but it's no insect. I'd have crushed it otherwise."

Alex glared, suspicions confirmed. "I'll be damned. It may not be an insect..."

"But it's definitely a bug." He glared at it. "I'd bet a month's pay that thing is the alien equivalent of a camera."

"That's why they're always around, especially when we're fighting something." The bumble-things had been all over the place when she and Hawke had battled the tentacle thing. She just hadn't registered them at the time.

"They seem to love it when we have sex, too." His jaw line was tight with fury.

She snarled. "Peeping toms. Where's a fly swatter? I say we start eliminating a few winged spies."

A strange male voice spoke. "I suppose that's my cue."

With a muffled shriek, Alex jumped for the nearest pelt as Hawke lunged for the sword he'd left lying beside the bed. "Who the hell are you?" he roared at the tall, slim man who sauntered casually into their cave.

"I am Nathaniel Oritz Krikor," the man said, sweeping them a theatrical bow, arms spread wide. "Your humble host."

Whipping the pelt around her body, Alex glared at their visitor. He had an inch or two on Hawke himself, but if he weighed more than a hundred and fifty pounds, she'd be surprised. He wore a white linen suit that looked like it cost a grand or so, and his hair was a blond so pale, it matched the suit. So did the elegant leather loafers on his narrow feet. His irises were a strange, iridescent shade that shifted color every time he moved his head, from blue to purple to red to yellow, then back to blue again.

"What are you, the Good Humor Man?" Hawke snarled.

Studying the invader's narrow, too-handsome face, Alex added, "Or an alien?"

Krikor threw back his head in a laugh that showed every perfect tooth in his head. It still sounded far too practiced for genuine humor. "An alien? Me? No, Ms. Kenyon, I'm afraid you and Lieutenant Hawke here have jumped to the wrong conclusions." He aimed a wide, bright smile at them, but there was something malicious in his eyes. "You weren't abducted by aliens. Believe me, aliens have no interest in our little Earth whatsoever. At least, not during your time."

Alex's jaw dropped. "But they do in *yours?*"

"Just what is your time, mister?" Hawke lifted his sword, rage in his eyes.

Krikor backed up a cautious step, smiling even more broadly. "Now, there's no need for violence here, Lieutenant."

"I strongly suggest you tell me what the *fuck* is going on, or you're going to encounter more violence than you know what to do with." Each word dripped icy menace.

Now Krikor's artificial smile looked distinctly panicked. He shot a look at one of the hovering camera bees, then straightened his shoulders. "What you don't realize, Lieutenant, is that over the past year, you've become a hero to billions of humans. Many of them routinely check your data stream dozens of times a day to see how you're coping with the challenges of the Bubble."

"Billions of people?" Alex whispered. "Bubble?"

"Data stream?" She'd never seen Hawke so furious. He took a step toward Krikor. "What fucking *year* is it, asshole?"

The slender man blinked and licked his lips, his gaze flicking to Hawke's sword. "Using your calendar, it would be May 25, 2443."

Chapter Ten

Alex's legs went weak. She sank down on the bed, clutching her pelt. "Four hundred and thirty-nine years. We've come four hundred and thirty-nine years. Into the future."

"That's right." Evidently realizing he'd rendered them too stunned to attack him, Krikor straightened and fingered the elegant lapels of his suit. It must be some kind of costume; it was doubtful even menswear would remain that static for four centuries.

For that matter— "How come you speak English?"

Krikor shrugged. "I have a translator, of course. So does everyone else. Otherwise you wouldn't be so hugely popular." His iridescent eyes lit with greed. "And you are. Huge. We've made billions, just on merchandising alone."

It was impossible to take in. "You took us from our own time," she said blankly. "Aren't you afraid of, I don't know, changing history or something?"

Krikor laughed lightly. "My dear, one can't change history. It's already happened."

Alex looked at Hawke, feeling helpless and overwhelmed. "Do you understand any of this?"

Their host ignored the question. "At any rate, I'm here to tell you it's time for you to return to the twenty-first century. The Lieutenant's visa has expired and..."

"Visa?" Hawke demanded.

Krikor nodded. "Your time travel visa. Of course, that's not the actual term, but the concept is close enough. Now." He rubbed his thin hands together. "I'm pleased to inform you we have some very nice cash prizes waiting for you back home..."

"Prizes." Hawke's lips pulled back from his teeth. "This has all been some kind of fucking reality show. Only instead of eating bugs, I got to fight monsters!" Stiff legged, he began to stalk Krikor, whose expression shifted from smug to panicked with every step Hawke took. "What would you have done if one of those things had eaten me, you son of a bitch?"

The man cringed. "We'd have stopped it before you were really hurt."

"Yeah?" He jerked a thumb at Alex, who was crowding at his heels, steaming with fury. "What about her? Why'd you pull her into it?"

"Well, just watching you fight *C'kici* and *varitakor* had gotten a little dry. We decided you needed a love interest."

"But why kidnap *us?*" Alex exploded. "Aren't there people in your own time that would have played your stupid game?"

Krikor blinked at her. "Oh, we couldn't use anyone from the present. Not anymore. *Everybody's* heard of the Bubble. They all know the rules, so there's no fear. And if the contestants aren't afraid, there's no drama. Besides, you two are..."

Hawke's fist slammed into his face before he could finish the sentence. Krikor went down like a sack of cement as the big man threw his sword aside and lunged for his throat.

Alex flung herself on her lover as he grabbed the man's skinny neck and began to squeeze. "Hawke, no! Please! Let him go!"

He threw her a wild-eyed look over his shoulder. "He's not going to just get away with this!"

Softly, Alex said, "But Hawke, you can't do this. Let him go."

He looked down at Krikor's purpling face, his expression twisted with rage. Slowly, the fury faded. He released his hold and straightened off his gasping victim. "Yeah. I guess you're right. I can't just kill him."

"No." Alex calmly stepped around him, drew back her foot, and rammed her bare heel right into Krikor's balls. As the skinny little creep curled into a gagging ball, she gave Hawke an angelic smile. "Not until I got in my shot, anyway."

His answering grin was savage. "That's my girl. Let's…"

White light exploded over their heads from the glowing hole that had opened in the ceiling of the cave. Alex and Hawke stared up at it in horror. "Oh, sh—"

They were sucked off their feet before he could finish the curse.

* * *

"—it!" Hawke spat, just as his booted feet hit the ground in the pitch dark. Gunfire exploded around him. He hit the dirt more by instinct than anything else as the enemy fired wildly, probably reacting to the hole of light that had spit him out.

Hawke curled instinctively into a ball, his hands over his helmeted head.

Helmeted?

In the darkness, his hands explored his body, discovered familiar cloth where he'd been almost naked before. Holy crap, he was wearing his uniform again—apparently the same uniform that had long since been reduced to rags by alien fangs.

It couldn't be! And yet, it was. The show's bastard producers must have somehow duplicated all his gear. Including—thank you, Jesus—his M-16. He pulled the rifle off his shoulder and began firing it in the direction of the enemy. Somebody screamed.

Everything went quiet.

"Lieutenant!" Sergeant Ron Jacobs bellowed from somewhere nearby. "Lieutenant, what the hell was that light?"

Hawke took a deep breath and lied. "I haven't the faintest idea, Sergeant."

The Bastards had returned him to the exact moment he'd left—two full years before they would abduct Alex from her bed. She didn't even know him yet, much less love him.

Why should she? He was just the Jarhead son of trailer trash. And she was Alexandria Kenyon, blue-blood Southern Belle.

Way out of his league.

* * *

Alex yelped as she fell out of the light, hit something soft, and bounced. "Oh, hell. Hawke?"

She blinked at the moonlight-washed furniture around her, then reached for the crystalline lamp gleaming in the dimness. A moment's fumbling turned it on.

Stunned, Alex stared at her surroundings. She was back in her own bed. And... She looked down at her chest. She was wearing the same camisole she'd had on when they'd snatched her a month ago.

It was as if none of it had ever happened.

A sense of hollow emptiness washed over her. Hawke. God, Hawke. If they'd sent her back to the moment she'd left, they'd sent him back too—straight into the middle of the war in Afghanistan.

Two years ago.

Feeling sick, she rolled out of bed. He might be dead now. And even if he wasn't, how the hell was she going to find him?

But she had to. Somehow. She loved him, dammit. She wasn't about to lose him after everything she'd done to keep him alive. She'd fought a monster for him, for God's sake.

Think, Alex. What did she know? She knew his name. She knew he was a lieutenant in the Marine Corps. Her father had connections. Surely she could convince him to...

The doorbell rang.

Alex shot a glance at the clock. It was the middle of the night. Who would...?

She was running downstairs before she even had time to complete the thought. Hope swelled in her chest as she skidded to a halt in the foyer, flipped the porch light on and snatched the door open. "Hawke?"

The tall man on the other side wore a Marine dress uniform and a chest full of ribbons. Her heart skipped in anguish. *He's come to tell me Hawke's dead...*

Then Alex registered the hard, handsome face under the shining black bill of his uniform cap. His blond hair was cut so painfully short, she hadn't even recognized him. "Hawke?" Her voice broke. "Hawke?"

Then she was in his arms.

They both started babbling at the same time. "I thought I'd lost you..."

"Jesus, I've been waiting so long..."

"What have you been...?"

"I couldn't stay away any longer."

Alex grabbed his strong arms and dragged him inside, banging the door shut. "They just sent me back. How did you know?"

Hawke studied her face, his gaze fierce and hungry. "You'd told me it was 2004 when they took you. I served out the rest of my tour while I waited until the Corps transferred me back to the States. A month ago I managed to track you down, but I didn't dare approach you, because I knew you wouldn't know who I was yet."

She closed her eyes, imagining it. "Oh, Hawke."

"Then today I went to the ATM, and there was ten million dollars in my bank account that just appeared out of nowhere. I knew it was the prize money. I figured that must mean you were on your way. So I pulled up outside your house and waited until I saw the flash."

Alex blinked. "Ten million? Hell of a prize. How are you going to explain it?"

"According to the bank and a lawyer or two, I've developed a rich relative." A faint smile curled his mouth. "Think Judge Kenyon would mind a wealthy son-in-law—even if he did come from trailer trash?"

"What?"

Right there in her foyer, he swept his hat off, dropped to one blue-clad knee on the marble floor, and took her hand. "Alexandria Kenyon, will you marry me?"

She sucked in a gasp as joyous tears prickled her eyes. "Oh, God, Hawke, do you really have to ask? Yes. Oh, yes."

"John." His gaze searched hers. "My given name is John."

The tears swelled hotter. "I love you, John."

He grinned. "Even though I'm a dominant asshole?"

Alex pounced on him, knocking him onto his back. His medals pricked her breasts as she dove in for the kiss. "Since I'm incredibly kinky—oh, yeah."

His mouth tasted of mint as his lips moved hungrily against hers. She slid both hands up into his short-cropped hair as his own went to her ass and pulled her astride him. His fingers felt deliciously warm on her spine.

By the time they both came up for air, Hawke's eyes were smoky with passion and growing heat. Alex pushed herself up to straddle him and contemplate the best way to get his uniform off.

Cupping one of her breasts through her camisole, he grinned. "Oh, I remember this. I considered ripping it off you."

Starting work on his intricate gold buttons, she narrowed her eyes. "Lieutenant John Hawke, don't you dare."

A big, warm hand slid under the lace hem and went looking for bare flesh. "I'm going to have to teach you to read Marine command insignia. I'm a captain now. God, I've missed these breasts."

She closed her eyes as his clever fingers did wonderful things to a nipple. "And they've missed you."

"Oh, come on. We'd just made love when the asshole showed up."

"You mean you'd just banged me up the backside playing Master Bastard."

He winced. "Sorry about that."

"No, you're not. And neither am I." She managed to drag another button from its buttonhole, exposing a tempting sliver of abdominal muscles. "You Marines sure wear a lot of clothes, Captain."

Hawke laughed and reached for one of the hooks holding his tunic neck closed. "Let me help you with that."

"Thank you." She rose off him to stand astride his hips, pulling her camisole over her head. "By the way, I am not making love to you on this cold floor when there's a perfectly good mattress upstairs. Which doesn't crackle, rustle or sag, unlike the last one we played on."

"Have I mentioned you have the most gorgeous tits I've ever seen?"

"Yeah? Maybe I'll let you kiss them." Alex turned with a teasing roll of her ass. "If you can catch me." She sprinted for the stairs.

Hawke caught her before she got four more steps. She rode up the stairs across his brawny shoulder.

Five minutes later they were naked in her bed, and Hawke was demonstrating exactly how much he'd missed her nipples. Each long, wet stroke of his tongue made her squirm, while the big hand exploring between her thighs sent sweet pleasure sizzling through her body.

For her part, Alex caressed the hard ripples of muscle sheathed in satin skin. Being back in civilization hadn't made him go soft—in any sense of the word, judging by the warm, thick cock nestled against her hip.

She wrapped her fingers around it and smiled lazily as he gasped.

"You're distracting me," he protested over her nipple, his free hand gently cupping her other breast.

"Good." Alex stroked the length of the bobbing shaft. "I'd hate to think I was losing my touch."

"Noo." His voice sounded distinctly strangled as she brushed her thumb over a bead of pre-cum. "You're definitely in no danger of that."

"Good." She grinned impishly. "'Cause, you know, I was getting worried. I mean, you've been here thirty whole minutes, and you haven't tied me up yet."

Hawke lifted his head. Smoky gray eyes sizzled over his feral smile. "Are you disappointed?"

"Who, me?"

"Alex, love, are we getting bored with foreplay?"

She wriggled under him. "Well, I *am* really, really wet..."

With a low, menacing growl, he reared back onto his haunches between her thighs, grabbed her knees, and spread her wide. She yelped as his thick cock speared into her in one hard thrust.

Hawke grinned down into her startled eyes. "In that case, it has been an awfully, long..." he drove in all the way to the balls "...long..." pulled out and jammed in again "...*long* time."

Her entire nervous system jolting with each thrust, Alex wrapped her calves around his back. "Tell me about it."

As his massive shaft worked in and out of her creamy sex, she grinned happily. *One thing's for sure—Mrs. Alexandria Hawke will never, ever be bored.*

Epilogue

They were married a year later, after twelve months of living in glorious, engaged sin. Hangin' Harry gave his daughter away with a proud smile in a church ceremony that was the biggest social event of the year. He hadn't even flinched when Hawke had told him about his father. To the old man's credit, his new son-in-law's status as a war hero seemed to weigh more than the millions he'd won in that mythical lotto.

He and Virginia were already hinting broadly about their yen for grandchildren.

Hawke and Alex had every intention of obliging them—and enjoying the process thoroughly.

Angela Knight

Angela Knight's first book was written in pencil and illustrated in crayon; she was nine years old at the time. But her mother was enthralled, and Angela was hooked.

Whatever success she has enjoyed would be hollow without the love of her husband, Michael, and her son, Anthony. Her parents, Gayle and Paul, have been unfailing in their support and encouragement. Her sister Angela, whose name she adopted, was her first and most helpful editor.

Hot Blooded, a Jove anthology featuring Angela Knight, Christine Feehan, Maggie Shayne and Emma Holly, hit #31 on the New York Times' extended bestseller list. *Bite*, another Jove anthology featuring Angela Knight, along with authors Laurell K. Hamilton, MaryJanice Davidson, Charlaine Harris and Vickie Taylor, made #23 on the New York Times' bestseller list its first week out. Other popular books by Angela Knight include *The Forever Kiss* (Red Sage), *Master of the Night* and *Jane's Warlord* (Berkley Sensation).

You can visit her on the Web at www.angelasknights.com or email her at angelanight2002@bellsouth.net.

~*~

Other titles by Angela Knight currently available from Loose Id:

Stranded (e-book novella written as Victoria Michaels)

"Hero Sandwich in *Hard Candy* with Sheri Gilmore and Morgan Hawke (e-book only)

LIGHT ON HER TOES

Camille Anthony

Dedication

To my Wild, Wacky, Wonderful "big" little sister, Jackie, who breathed life into Dohsan.

Little sisters should NOT be taller than their elders, nor more savvy about life!

Prologue

Princess Dohsan 'abret Glenbrevchanka stared off into the distance, scouting for a first glimpse of her brothers' approaching vehicle, one slim strong hand shading her lime-yellow eyes. No sign, yet, of her brothers' arrival...

In three directions before her, the starkly beautiful Jakwylla Mountain range stretched as far as the eye could see. Heat waves dancing above ground level caused the scene to ripple and waver, skewed visual judgment, making a true measurement of distances almost impossible.

This high up the barren mountainside scant vegetation grew, but a thousand feet below, lush maroon brush blossomed in the verdant valley and deep-hued purple grasses waved under the influence of an ever present breeze.

Dohsan sighed in wondering awe and appreciation. Every day she found new discoveries to marvel over, intriguing facets of her new planetary home. She doubted she would ever grow tired of this fascinating world. It held much she wanted to familiarize herself with, much she wished to explore.

How wildly the temperature fluctuates and changes in this relatively small region, she mused, eyes sweeping the vast expanse. *The extreme climatic deviation within such narrow spatial parameters is spectacularly different from anything I've ever known on Mars.*

A movement out of the corner of her eye distracted her. She glanced up, caught the flutter of wings as a *spratot* plummeted down to snatch unsuspecting prey. Hand shielding her eyes, she followed the raptor's upward surge as it arrowed toward the heights, prairie beast tucked close to its lower body.

As she turned, following the aviator's path, her present home came into view. Attention snagged, arrested by the sheer overwhelming magnitude of the rock-hewn buildings, she stared, entranced, a smile widening her generous mouth.

The massive, ancient stone Citadel of the vaShafaran Priestesshood reared above the forbidding mountainous terrain nestled on the highest peak. Hewn from slabs of solid rock— each taller than the height of three *qarm*—the structures of the final sanctuary of Fem Domination on planet Rb'qarm had survived the corrosion and wear of centuries. Many believed it to be the oldest *qarm*-made dwelling on the planet.

It was here in the southern province of her sister Nnora's new homeworld, among fem who honored the ancient ways instilled in her by their traditionalist father, that Dohsan came closest to finding serenity.

Usually, this place bathed her senses in peacefulness and calm. Lately, she'd found no measure of lasting tranquility and she greatly feared the fault lay with her inability to forget the man she'd fallen in love with as an immature *'tweener.*

She had pretty much acknowledged she'd never win the heart of the *qarm* who had claimed her adolescent first love.

That knowledge didn't seem to make a difference to her unruly emotions. Knowing he was no good for her, understanding that their lives traveled along widely differing paths didn't matter an iota. Despite all her efforts to the contrary, she still ached, still hungered…still lusted after him.

Because of her lingering feelings for *him*, true peace continued to elude her. Lately, she'd come to the realization it always would. She would never be able to take the irrevocable life vows of the vaShafaran—until and unless she confronted the looming obstacle blocking her path.

Her sister acolytes and the other residents of the Citadel believed she dutifully departed today at her elder sister's command. In reality, though Nnora had indeed summoned all the Mars Colony fem to her, Dohsan had already made up her mind to withdraw from the vaShafaran retreat—at least, for now.

Refusing to leave the compound without acknowledging her true intentions to the venerated head of her sect, Dohsan had requested an audience with GlenEleth 'abret GlenTamin, ruling mother of the vaShafarans.

How was she to justify her choice to the ancient one when she had yet to find a way to make sense of it herself?

The decision hadn't been an easy one for her. She'd worried at it—picked at each possibility, each choice as a child picked at a scab, driven to explore the small addictive pain—repeatedly going back over old ground.

Should she stay and bond with one of the *qarms* in the Citadel, knowing she would never love him as she loved the other?

Should she leave and find the *qarm* that plagued her, try to win the mate of her heart, regardless of the incompatibility of lifestyles that separated them?

She felt torn and tugged in two different directions. One moment she wished for nothing more than to remain here in the mountains, take as mates the multiple husbands due her rank and rule her household with tolerance and tenderness. The next moment, she battled the insidious urge, the cycles-long need to rush down the mountainside, jet over to the capital city of Rb'qarm and hogtie a certain arrogant commander.

She longed to bring him home draped over her shoulder. Like a woman of ancient times, she'd lock him away in her private harem and fuck all thoughts of *qarm* superiority out of his fevered mind.

The dust of an approaching vehicle swirled on the heated air, drawing Dohsan's attention away from her ongoing internal conflict. Narrowing her eyes, she squinted into the light, glad to identify her elder brother's *Lorme*.

Anticipation swirled in the pit of her stomach, threatening to unwind the tight knot of need that had kept her muscles clenched for ages. The boys' arrival meant her departure crept that much closer.

Very soon, she would come face to face with 'Dari.

At that exciting thought, biting hunger exploded in her *pava*. She rubbed her thighs together in an effort to ease the sudden need, but slippery juice slicked her mound and ran down her thighs as her body refused to obey her will.

Fighting for control, Dohsan rode the heated wave until it crested. When it finally receded, she lifted a trembling hand, wiped the sweat from her upper lip and swallowed back a despairing moan.

The onset of her *pava* cycle had only recently begun and had yet to normalize, surging and waning erratically. During the surges, she suffered from a magnitude of need the likes she'd never encountered, never dreamed possible.

She dreaded the time when her *pava* would kick in totally. This bad now, what would it be like when she flowered continuously?

The scrabbling of rocks rattling over loose sand tore her mind from her troubles. Twisting in alarm, she dropped into a defensive crouch from sheer force of habit. Even as she tensed, she realized only one person could have approached her solitary retreat without tripping her inner alarms earlier.

Relaxing, Dohsan watched the elderly fem gingerly picking her way toward her rocky alcove. She rushed to offer her hand, helped steady the ancient crone, as she stiffly settled onto the chair-shaped rock hewn by nature over relentless millennia.

She bowed with respect. "Welcome, Mother. Thank you for agreeing to see me."

A gentle smile crossed the fem's face. "One does not lightly ignore the request of a ruler's heir, Dohsan. We are no different here in that respect."

Dohsan frowned, the old priestess's words stirring her ire. She fidgeted uneasily, debated blurting out her concerns.

"Mother, I would hope it is my convictions and actions, not my royal status, which gained me acceptance and honors here."

A mottled hand waved impatiently, halting her stiff words. Aged eyes shot her a disgruntled look as the old fem shifted into a more comfortable position. "Do not be childish or so quick to take offense, 'abret Glenbrevchanka. Your place among us never rested on your birth, but on your destiny. I have made no secret of the fact I wish you to rule this community after me."

The Reverend's revelation didn't quite come as a shock. As the daughter of a royal line, trained to lead, ruling came naturally. Supremely confident in her abilities, Dohsan didn't doubt she could carry that load. Her recent decision had changed all that. She felt led to explore a different life path. "I would have been honored to serve in your stead, Mother, however—"

A quieting hand halted her interruption. "Others feel the same as I. You have the makings of a fine leader, Dohsan. You have matured much over the cycles you have been with us." She sighed. "If only you would consent to take one of our *qarm* as first-mate. Many fem have approached me with petitions to advance the offer of a lover or mate for your consideration. They would welcome any alliance with you through their sons or brothers."

"I wish it were so easy. I don't think I can settle here without first proving to myself that I have tried everything in my power to gain that which I have desired for several cycles."

"What drives you into the shadows, child of the sun? What has darkened your brightness and dulled your joy?"

Dohsan hesitated, fidgeted nervously under the patient, knowing gaze of her mentor. Of all people, she trusted this fem implicitly, yet she balked at sharing her innermost thoughts. Naturally inclined toward self-sufficiency, she warred with herself over revealing such an intimate glimpse of her pain and hope.

"There is this *qarm*, Mother... When I am near him, he drives me insane with anger and frustration, yet, once parted from him, my mind cannot cease replaying his image."

"Come." The matriarch beckoned, indicated a place at her feet. "Sit and tell me why this should trouble you so much."

Dohsan plopped down onto the warm slab of rock that formed the platform for the rock chair. "I am troubled because I cannot control how I feel."

"And that bothers you, of course." The Mother chuckled. Her infectious giggle made her seem eons younger. "You are determined to master your surroundings and it irks you that you cannot even master yourself."

Dohsan laid her head in the elder's lap. "My ears echo with every word he has spoken to me. My *pava* burns and weeps for want of him. He lit these flames in me long ago, even before my *pava* began. I greatly fear no other *qarm* can cool them."

"Ah," the matriarch nodded sagely, stroking the flame-bright locks of Dohsan's hair, "the fires of youth, once lit burn hotly. The newness of your *pava* is taking its toll. Trust me when I say you will eventually come to terms with it. It is not, 'abret Glenbrevchanka, something to be conquered. Rather, it is a glorious flame. Surrender to it, fling yourself into the furnace and be reborn!"

"If only it were so easy—" Dohsan's teeth worried her bottom lip— "I would have taken a mate and cooled this heat. My mind wants only him. My body melts only for that one particular *qarm*."

GlenEleth tilted her head, wrinkled her brow thoughtfully. "I take it this *qarm* is resistant to the lifestyle espoused here in our mountain hold." She gestured toward the compound behind them.

The wide central square had begun to fill with people. Stirred from their caverns, roused from the lazy afternoon *doniom*, slumberous males herded still-sleepy children toward the public caverns. Fresh springs, sheltered from the high temperatures caused by the dual suns' rays, lay cool and inviting, awaiting the influx of happy youngsters. The afternoon swimming sessions—one of the new programs Dohsan had instigated since coming here—had gained favor quickly. The children loved exercising in the shadowed depths of the secluded pools instead of under the broiling heat of the afternoon suns.

"That would be an understatement. He is the commander of the *Chyya's* guard—personal bodyguard to the queen."

That information arrested even the Mother for a moment. She straightened in her seat. "I—*see.*"

"Do you?" Dohsan asked, strangely angry and antsy. She jumped to her feet and paced back and forth. "Then perhaps you could tell me what's wrong with me. How could I want a *qarm* so diametrically opposed to what I believe, what I need?"

"Is he worthy? Is he honorable?"

Dohsan didn't even need to think on her answer. "He is all that and more. Nevertheless, how could I want a male who feels nothing but disdain for me, who still sees me as a pre-*pava* child? Can you tell me that, Mother? For I cannot for the life of me figure out why I am plagued with such idiocy."

"Child, the heart loves where it will, and is not subject to reason or logic. It is unruly and wayward, yet have I found that often, the heart sees clearer than do our two eyes. What does your heart tell you, 'abret Glenbrevchanka?"

Dohsan returned and stood at the matriarch's feet, gazed down at her with lemony eyes wide and a mouth grim and tight. "My heart tells me to take what is mine! To claim and bind the *qarm* who is my *va'pava.*"

Chuckles shook the wizened frame of the old fem. "Now, *that* is something that can be achieved. Good *qarms* are few and rare these days. Acquiring a worthy mate is a quest requiring one's total commitment. Go, then, and obtain your *qarm*. Fix your mind only on this goal. Your destiny will wait."

The fierce fem disappeared, leaving behind the youngling hovering on the edge of adulthood. Dohsan mangled her lower lip, uncertain how to ask her next question. *Oh, the hell with it!*

"What do I do if I cannot convince him to return with me? Which should I give up...my destiny or the *qarm*?"

The matriarch's gentle smile stretched her wrinkled face. Her wisdom shone brightly, illuminating her eyes. "Perhaps you will find that the *qarm is* your destiny, perhaps not. Seeking, you will find. Finding, you will know."

"*Mother*," she wailed, sounding like any *'tweener*. "What kind of answer is that?"

"Go, 'abret Glenbrevchanka." An unsympathetic laugh and an impatient hand shooed her away. "The vaShafaran way is not confined to a place, but is a way of life. We have been here for millennia. We will be here when and if you return. If not, then perhaps it will be time for the headquarters of the discipline to relocate."

"*Move*, 'abret GlenTamin?" The idea shocked her. The Citadel seemed ageless and timeless...unchangeable. She couldn't imagine it ever being different.

The matriarch laughed joyously. "Why not? We have not resided in these mountains for all eternity. Stop stalling and go!"

Dohsan bowed in respect before turning and striding away. She'd best hurry. The boys would be here any minute and she still had to finish packing.

She'd never been a neat packer and didn't plan to change her habits today. Quickly bundling everything up in a haphazard mass, she stuffed it all into her carrier, abandoning what wouldn't fit.

Done, she placed her hands on the small of her back and stretched. Absently rubbing at a tight muscle, she surveyed the stripped room. Her eyes clouded with moisture as she fondly recalled the time she had spent here.

She would miss this place, these people, but her heart drove her relentlessly and would not keep silent. It cried out for its mate, for the only *qarm* to pierce her thick, self-protective shields. It demanded she claim GanR'dari 'abri GlenglanR'on.

Once, cycles ago, in a moment of adolescent anger, she had arrogantly warned a man she would one day rock his world. The time had come to redeem her promise.

* * *

How much longer before we reach Father's palace?

Dohsan fidgeted in her seat, one foot tapping an impatient tattoo. She leaned forward, twisted her neck for a better view out the *Lorme* viewing panel and gaped at the scenes flashing by.

GlenFaren, the capitol city of Rb'qarm, teemed with people. To her unease, the majority were large groups of *qarm*. As the Lorme passed along the fashionable streets, she caught glimpses of suspicious activity in quiet, shadowed corners—saw what looked like gangs of *qarm* preying on lone fem.

"Stop the *Lorme!* Back up!" Dohsan thumped the back of Puorgkrow's seat to get his attention. "There are *qarms* accosting a fem in that alley back there. Kardenez, pass me my sword!"

Her older brother shook his head. "Puorgkrow, don't you dare stop," he snapped when their younger brother started to slow and turn the responsive vehicle.

"But Dohsan said—"

"I don't care what she said. Yes, she's the fem here, but she doesn't know about what's been happening in the cities. I do not intend to bleed today. Drive on. You know those *qarm* won't hurt that fem."

Heart pounding, Dohsan glared at her brothers. "Are you insane? Has my mother raised cowards? If so, I'll deal with that disappointment later. For now, I've given you an order. Stop the *Lorme* and give me my weapon."

Kardenez sighed. "We're not cowards, nor are we insane. And, no, Dohsan, I won't pass you your sword. You will only cause someone to be hurt, maybe killed. If that person turns out to be you, I, for one, don't want to be the one having to report to Mom or Dad."

"But the fem…those *qarm*…"

"They are testing her. When they see she is infertile, they will let her go."

"Leaving her with what damage, what emotional injuries? How can you know what is happening and not do something about it?"

Kardenez sighed, his young face drawn in lines of bitter helplessness. "What would you have us do? We don't run in the packs. We would never treat a fem like that, but if we interfere, that mob will kill us. After all, we are only two males in competition for the small supply of viable fem. As royals, we have a better chance at actually being able to mate with a flowering fem. That alone—that unfair advantage—would condemn us in the eyes of those desperate, hopeless *qarm*. They'd gladly eliminate two rivals."

"This is horrendous. To accost a fem in the public street...bare her *tlinis*...force *terat*-play..." She shook her head. "How long has this 'testing' been going on? Are Nnora and Dev aware of what goes on in their capital?"

Puorgkrow glanced over his shoulder. The look in his young eyes hurt Dohsan's heart. No youngling should have such cynicism staring out the windows of his soul. "I am too young to be allowed in the councils, but I'm not too young to see what goes on around me."

"No, you're not." Dohsan murmured agreement with his sentiments. She'd run up against the same age prejudice a few years back. The boy had a valid point. He'd lived through war, had experienced more than the average run of youngling and usually had a firm grasp on current events. "Tell me what's going on."

"The city warriors are called out daily to fight the growing gangs. The *qarm* are growing angrier. Having the colony fem here is worse than having no viable fem at all. At least, when there were none, all the *qarm* banded together since they were in the same hopeless situation. Then we Colonists came along and suddenly one or two *qarm* get mates. Now they have fertile fem walking the streets. The *qarm* can smell them, almost taste them, but they still can't touch or have. That's bitter...very bitter."

"You sound as if you are personally affected by this, Puorgkrow."

The boy grimaced. "Well, I am! You know, the colony was better than this. On Mars, I had *terat*-play with loads of fem, whenever I wanted. Here, I can't even be in the same room with one without a companion. I thought our freedoms were restricted back home, but GlenFaren is sick with violence and no one can risk traveling alone. I wish I was back on Mars."

"Oh, honey, I promise it will get better. Nnora, Lori and I are working on finding a solution. I swear we'll find a way to make sure you have a mate."

Puorgkrow met her eyes in the rearview mirror and nodded. "If anyone can do it, you three will. Just—could you hurry? I'm not getting any younger."

She laughed, then sobered. "None of us are."

Dejection swamping her, Dohsan slumped against her seat, leaned her head back and wearily closed her eyes, wondering how in hell they were going to deal with this latest detestable development. She *had* to do something, because she could not allow this heinous behavior to continue.

"What's that smell?"

Opening her eyes, she saw Kardenez stiffen in the front seat. He glanced back at Dohsan and she saw his eyes widen in alarm. He exchanged a lightning glance with his younger brother.

"Oh, hell, Dohsan, you're flowering. Quick, Puor, shutter the windows. If anyone catches a whiff of her, they'll mob the *Lorme.*"

Puorgkrow hit the buttons that raised the windows, eyes wide and frantic, responding to the panicked note in his brother's voice. "Yeah, I got you. We're heading home. Hope nothing gets in my way. I'm not slowing down for anything."

"What are you guys going on about? My *pava* just started recently. It's not stable yet. Usually, it remains dormant unless strong emotion triggers it."

Kardenez angled his body so he could talk to Dohsan without twisting his neck. "Word to the wise, sister dear— better not risk going out on the streets. Period. When we told you the gangs wouldn't harm that fem, we didn't know you'd started flowering. They wouldn't hurt her because she's infertile and their *terat* won't soften, but, if they find *you*, they'll gang rape you; they'll seat your nipples between each *qarm's* usage to keep you generating gift. You wouldn't survive being taken by that many *qarm*!"

Ice slid down her spine. Her fear lessoned the sharp sweet tang of her flowering. "Frazing Hell! Has it gotten that bad?"

"Weren't you listening to what Puorgkrow said? Multiply that by a thousand."

Heaven above, the situation had worsened much faster than any of them had anticipated. This was probably why Nnora had called an emergency meeting of the Viables, as they called themselves. Their crippled society was barreling toward a *mr'nok* of immense proportions.

As the Lorme sped through the city, shielded against the bright afternoon light of the twin suns, Dohsan contemplated what more she could do to relieve some of the pressure of this building powder keg.

Chapter One

GanR'dari 'abri GlenglanR'on surreptitiously shifted from foot to foot, seeking a more comfortable position. His feet hurt and his back ached. Every inch of his body throbbed with tiredness after standing at attention for hours in his official capacity as bodyguard to the *Chyya'va*.

Inwardly seething, he gnashed his teeth in growing ire, had to school himself to maintain an outward show of objectivity while on duty. With difficulty, he restrained the urge to glare at the sea of audience-seekers crowding the formal *throla*. Biting back a growl that threatened to erupt from him, he observed the spectators avidly witnessing the scandalous charges and complaints lodged against Princess Dohsan.

Stomach churning with bile caused by his forced self-restraint, he curled his fingers into fists when what he really wanted to do was throttle the aged, high-caste fem busy blackening the character of the *Chyya'va's* younger sister.

"I hesitate to grace this forward *drigini* by naming her a royal fem, despite her being your sister, Highness." The high-caste Lady pointed her accusing finger at Dohsan, twisting her face into an ingratiating grimace that he supposed she thought passed for a smile. "I personally caught the chit bare-breasted, her bold nipples buried circle-deep in my innocent son's *terat*...right in the *soalori* of my own home!"

'Dari snorted under his breath. The fem's son, Glenlaharo, was no boy. As a fully mature male, he had no business chasing—or allowing himself to be caught by—a pre-*pava* fem for *terat*-play.

"And I found your *soalori* to be surprisingly lovely...*really!*" The saucy princess rounded her eyes in fake earnestness. "The *surprising* part being that you decorated it yourself, or so Glenlaharo told me. Under those circumstances, the room is an...uh...*unexpected* blend of taste and comfort!"

'Dari grit his teeth, his anger segueing into helpless amusement.

By Deth, *how does she do that?* The young fem's brash and inappropriate comments always managed to pierce his stoic aloofness, dragging forth a reluctant smile.

He sighed. She was enjoying herself a tad too much for the seriousness of this situation.

He glanced at her from the corner of his eye. She reclined in her chair-of-state, lazily swinging one long bare leg. Her bright yellowy-green eyes danced with the delight garnered from baiting the prim elderly fem. Her unbound *tlinis*, grown lush and full in the time since he'd last seen her, bounced with her silent laughter. His jaw tightened as the unwelcome thought of Laharo's irreverent hands all over her firm, pert breasts plagued his mind.

A menacing feral growl brought him to full alert. His eyes flashed about the room, seeking danger, only to close in self-derision. The perpetrator was none other than himself. The thought of that upstart having Dohsan's bountiful flesh anywhere near his shriveled up *terat* brought out the beast in him.

How dare any qarm *put his hands on her? By Pythin's gate! Dohsan's* tlinis *belong to none but me...* Another growl rumbled deep in his chest as he gleefully imagined squeezing the life out of Glenlaharo.

As he stood at attention and fought to distance himself from the results of the princess's latest escapade, 'Dari realized the time had come to act upon his feelings before the chance passed forever.

For cycles, he had waited impatiently for Dohsan, stoically resisting her youngling teasing and flirting, eager for her to mature and come into her *pava* so he could claim her. Now that she was older and playing more serious games, what was he to do? He couldn't bring himself to stand by and watch while she expanded her flirtation to others.

By Deth, *no!*

His eyes narrowed in determination. He would wait no longer. Dohsan didn't know it yet—sitting there flashing her killer legs and deadly smile, unconcerned with the gravity of her recent escapades—but henceforth, any and all nipple-seating would be done by him or not at all. The time had come to claim the promise Dev had made him: his choice of a bride from among the Mars fem. His heart had chosen Dohsan long ago. Now he needed to put his flighty princess on notice.

"I cannot bear it...!"

And I cannot bear your shrill caterwauling another jern, *you ignorant* kritch! Her screechy tones shredded his nerves like *Metari* claws shredded flesh.

"*Chyya,* must I listen to my son's name being cheapened in the mouth of this slut?"

GanR'dari flinched. She really should have thought twice before insulting royalty. His were not the only eyes to widen at the fem's dangerous words.

In stunned disbelief, he watched the stupid fem dramatically clap both hands over her ears and eyes as if to block out the voice as well as the presence of one she had judged unworthy.

"Will you not command that rude, uncultured fem to cease speaking?"

'Dari had listened to enough. "You go too far, fem. How dare you cast aspersions upon a sib of the *Chyya'va?* You flirt with treason."

The stupid hag had moved from insults to treason. Before this fem sought to malign Dohsan, he had never thought he'd draw his sword against a helpless fem. Then again, he'd never had to endure the whiny voice and small-minded comments of this exasperating elderly noble vilifying the character of his beloved. "Noble or common, no one may malign a member of the royal house with impunity."

The fem's startled gaze flew to his face, widening with fear. No doubt she saw her fate in his cold expression.

If only he could actually *use* his weapon on her. The flat of his sword applied against her broad backside might not help her sour disposition, but it would go a long way toward soothing his savage anger. He growled in frustration at his inability to act upon his fantasies.

The elderly fem paled under the menacing scowl he directed her way, earning her a satisfied grunt. Her terror was just what he wanted to see. Perhaps if she were frightened enough, she'd stop her verbal attacks on Dohsan.

The fem's fearful reaction satisfied him on some primitive level and he cared not one iota about *her* so-called sensibilities. Not that she deserved any consideration—after all, her cruel words had put the flash of pain in the princess's eyes and he would tolerate no one inflicting such hurt on his chosen.

Dohsan may have hurriedly concealed her reaction, but he knew the pain had struck heart-deep. In the almost three cycles since they'd first met and clashed, he'd learned Princess Dohsan 'abret Glenbrevchanka prized her privacy. Her outgoing ways and playful antics were naught but carefully constructed camouflage, for she never willingly placed her emotions or personal business on public display.

Knowing her as he did, that fleeting glimpse of her inner turmoil distressed him. He felt a sharp wrench in his chest. Somehow, he connected emotionally for a few scant moments and her pain became his.

Overreacting to the sheen of tears in Dohsan's eyes, his fist tightened around his sword hilt. Pain pulsed between them. He ached for her and with her, wanted to bury his weapon in the soft, pudgy under-belly of the high-born fem. He rocked on the balls of his feet, his thoughts intent on murder, on removing the source of Dohsan's pain.

By Deth's balls, he would allow no one—least of all this insignificant kritch—*to hurt or harm his* Cherzda'va! He may not have claimed her yet, but she still belonged to him. He took care of his own…

The touch of *Chyya'va* Glennora's soft hand on his shocked him from thoughts of mayhem, freeing his mind while freezing him in place. Blazing eyes targeting their joined flesh, he registered her grasp on his hand, felt her silently insisting he hold to his duty. A fine tremor scissored through him, ice coating the flesh of his brow as he shakily lowered and sheathed his blade.

In the thick silence of averted bloodshed the sound of a harshly indrawn breath echoed. Shifting his maddened glare from Dohsan's tormentor, he turned his head and locked glances with the maker of that ragged sound.

Her wide-eyed look of astonishing *awareness* pleased him, further soothed his outraged ire. The last of his unreasoning rage drained away and gave place to new amusement as he relaxed; he was secure in the knowledge he had snagged her interest. She looked shocked. Smirking, he bit back a chuckle, liking the thought of her being shocked by his precipitous actions. He had many more future surprises planned for her.

A half-grin quirked his lips as he imagined the darkly sensual look that would distort her beautiful features while he licked at her dripping *nippa* and tongued her clit before carefully opening then entering her during their first mating. His *cherzda* bucked and swelled, responding strongly to his heated thoughts. With a decadent smile of pure sexual intent, he telegraphed her his intentions.

When her jaw dropped, he chuckled aloud, not the least bit averse to preening under her feminine response. Uncertainty mixed with disbelief was an expression he'd never seen on her sweet face. It looked good on her.

He knew she didn't know how to take him in his role as protector. After all, throughout most of their stormy relationship he had mainly been her accuser, not her champion. He had her guessing now, though she usually dished out as good as she got. Tamping down his giddy sense of anticipation, he looked forward to seeing what she would come up with to top his unexpected change in tactics.

At present, her retaliatory plans appeared non-existent. She seemed to be having difficulty breathing. The thin material of her shift did little to hide her lush contours and under his interested stare her shapely *tlinis* shook with her labored efforts to draw in air. Her stiffly erect nipples, jutting proudly forward, pushed against the sheer gown, beckoning his mouth and *terat*.

Forbidden visions of burying those long, juicy knots inside his contracting *terat* tormented him. His mouth watered. He gulped, swallowed thickly as his taboo thoughts sent searing desire flooding through every corner of his being.

His own breath snagged, caught in his chest. His *terat* stung and burned. His *cherzda* rose and saluted its mistress. Swollen and hard, it jutted skyward, a solid bar of aching, heat-seeking muscle that defied all attempts at control. The expanding girth of his erection distorted the austere lines of his court uniform, placing his excited state on display to all. Disgusted with this public, carnal reaction to a pre-*pava* fem, 'Dari cursed viciously under his breath, twitching at the folds of his tunic. Deciding a strategic retreat was in order; he took two steps sideways and sheltered his obvious assets behind the flared back of Nnora's throne. His arousal was for Dohsan's approving gaze, alone, not for salacious appraisal by the assembled masses.

Dohsan—the little opportunist—noticed his involuntary salutation and a wicked smile widened her lush mouth. She flashed him a teasing glance from under a sweep of thick lashes. Locking gazes with him, she swiped her tongue across her bottom lip, smearing a trail of glistening wetness along the pouting curve. Then, having made sure of his enthralled attention, she wiggled seductively, shifting her body so her breasts *jiggled* at him.

He stopped breathing altogether.

Silent laughter shook her body at his helpless response, setting all her feminine flesh to jouncing. She assessed his involuntary reaction to her mockery with dancing eyes.

Her deliberate, teasing motions pushed his passions close to the brink. Deploring his perverted weakness for this pre-*pava* temptress, he still could not stop mentally stripping her, imagining her spread out beneath him, taking his heat and hardness deep into her hot depths. Desire and disgust fought each other, burned in his gut. *Damn it! Was he no better than Glenlaharo?*

His desire turned to ashes. Dragging in a pained breath, he forced himself to break eye contact with her. Grimly, he wrestled his unruly libido to a halt, fought to regain control of his wayward lust. If he did not *get it together*—as Nnora often fondly said—he would lose himself in the treacherous sea of their mutually escalating arousal and succumb to his primal urgings to do something uncivilized in this most civilized hall.

The truly sad part about the whole situation was his total contentment at being held captive by her sultry gaze.

It took some time for him to rein in his lust and self-anger enough to get his mind back on his responsibilities. He immediately found cause to deplore his dedication to duty. Lady vaGhemmora had resumed her ranting.

Her haranguing had been going on at length and it struck him as odd that his *Chyya* and *Chyya'va* had patiently listened to her drawn-out blustering. Neither one had spoken up on their young relative's behalf during the fem's long-winded, mean-spirited tirade.

By Deth's Gate, why have Dev or Nnora said nothing in her defense? How can they remain silent through this kritch's escalating insults?

Heart aching for her, GanR'dari searched Dohsan's averted face, imagining how her sister's silence must hurt. Though he ached to go to her, he held back, knowing she would accept no comfort from him—especially not in the face of this crowd of witnesses.

He found it hard to do nothing confronted with her pain. He had poised himself to speak up on Dohsan's behalf despite her probable negative reaction, when he felt the restraining grip of Nnora's hand on his arm. Her voice—dripping with ice—rang out in the audience chamber.

"Lady vaGhemmora, your son is over twenty-nine cycles matured...is that not correct?"

'Dari blinked at that frosty anger. *So, our* Chyya'va *isn't as complacent as she let on... Good!*

A quick visual scan of the chamber showed he was not the only one to register Nnora's unusual level of fury. His gaze crossed that of his *Chyya's* and snapped back, belatedly noting the humor lurking in those dark depths.

Glendevtorvas had obviously decided his capable mate could deflate this fem's pretensions all by herself. The twinkling glint in his eyes invited his commander to share in the enjoyment of watching Nnora in action.

Winking at his ruler and friend, 'Dari settled back in anticipation. Obviously, contrary to his earlier doubts, Glennora had plainly taken exception to the insults heaped upon her baby sister. Lady vaGhemmora had no inkling of the storm about to overtake her.

"Well, yes, *Chyya'va!*"

'Dari grimaced. Her twittering response followed a high-pitched cackle that hurt his ears and scraped along his nerves. He'd never beheld a more pathetic sight than this elderly fem trying desperately to hold on to her non-existent youth. The silly hag must have practiced that giddy giggle a hundred times. He shook his head. She needed a lot more practice.

"However, he is an only child, a treasured heir—"

Another twitter.

"Despite his age, he has been very sheltered and..."

The fem's words petered out. Her practiced smile slid off her broad face as Nnora raised her hand, issuing an imperial command for silence.

"My sister, on the other hand, though as highly treasured, has never had the luxury of such sheltering. Barely sixteen and a quarter cycles, she lived through a war that decimated our colony's male population. She did not grow to maturity among *qarms,* so her exuberant determination to experiment can be understood and somewhat excused—"

GanR'dari bit back a guffaw at the disgruntled look marring Dohsan's expressive face. Obviously, in disagreement with Nnora's words, her mulish look registered her unhappiness. She fumed; her puckered eyebrows creased the buttery smooth skin of her brow as her full, inviting lips turned down. Seemed she didn't care for Nnora's assessment of her motives.

"Despite Dohsan's admittedly impressive figure," Nnora continued, "she remains pre-*pava* and is—by the laws of this planet—only a child. All we adults know that children will inevitably seek to explore their sexuality; however, I personally believe that any *mature qarm* who lends himself to participation in such explorations is reprehensible in the extreme. In fact, where I come from, we call those people *child* molesters—"

"Well, I *never*...!"

The horrified gasp interrupted her speech and the Chyya'va raised her chin, the look on her face promising dire results should the fem voice another outburst.

With a quickly buried smile, 'Dari silently applauded his star pupil. When he'd first met her, Nnora would never have said "boo" to a *greeve*. Now he proudly watched as she flawlessly deflated the pretentious fem.

"Lady vaGhemmora, the Crown finds your son's behavior indicative of low moral standards. One wonders where this *drigini*—we hesitate to gift him with the title of *qarm*, despite *you* being his mother—gained his manners."

'Dari braced himself, teeth clamping down hard on his bottom lip, hoping the sharp pain would help him control his welling mirth. It wouldn't be seemly for the commander of the Homeworld Forces to go rolling around the floor of the audience chamber, laughing his fool head off.

"Your *Chyya* and I are grateful you had the integrity to bring your son's low-bred incident to our attention. Everyone knows this is not the type of behavior we tolerate among our nobles. We applaud your fervor for decency, evidenced by your willingness to deliver up your own heir to corrective action. Obviously, seeing he is not here to represent his own behavior nor defend Dohsan in hers, your son has too much concern for his own hide, too little self-discipline and too much handy recreational material—"

'Dari added his own glare as Nnora flashed an "*I'll-deal-with-you-later*" glance toward her unrepentant sister.

Undaunted, Dohsan stuck out her tongue in retaliation, wagging it vigorously at her sister.

From the corner of his eye, he caught the languid flicker she sent in his own direction and his *cherzda* leaped. He sucked in a shaky breath as the muscles in his lower belly tightened. *Oh, the things he wanted to do with that flickering tongue of hers!*

"—as well as too much leisure time." Nnora finished cataloging the sins of the absent Glenlaharo. "Did I miss anything?"

"Nothing." Devtorvas's deep voice chimed in. He came to his feet. "I quite agree with your assessment, my dear, and believe we can easily take care of some of Glenlaharo's leisure time." He sauntered over to stand behind his mate, placing his hands on Nnora's shoulders. In front of the entire assemblage, he bent over, brushed his lips against his mate's in a blatant show of his full support and approval of his queen.

"To reward her zeal in bringing her own son's deviancy to our attention, we shall overlook his seditious misconduct this one time and grant the Ghemorra family the great honor of accepting their son into the royal guard. We can always use more warriors to police Rb'nTraq—"

Lady vaGhemorra's hands fluttered up to her throat. Her eyes bulged in terror as she frantically stared from one ruler to the other. A look of confused bewilderment blossomed and her mouth quivered as she moaned, unable to do aught but repeat the *Chyya's* words. "Po-police...? Rb'nTraq...? But...! *But that was not what I...!'*

Chyya Glendevtorvas quieted her with a regal lifting of his eyebrows and a coldly spoken command. "While I speak, fem...you do not."

Her eyes starting from her head, the fem gulped. The trembling fingers of both hands gripped the trailing panniers of her elaborate court gown. Her stiff neck bowed under the bluntly spoken reprimand. "For-forgive me, *Chyya*."

A calm smile turned Dev's lips up. "Forgiven, of course, Lady vaGhemmora."

With a dismissing nod in the fem's direction, he turned to his friend and second. "GanR'dari, you will see to it that the *qarm* is notified of his great honor at once. Have him escorted to orientation by first glowrise tomorrow. From there, he is all yours until he is transferred to Rb'nTraq. See that he learns the proper way to treat royalty...regardless the state of their maturity."

'Dari relaxed his lips into a smile wide enough to crease his cheeks as he bowed low to his *Chyya* and *Chyya'va*. "I shall indeed inform the fortunate *qarm* at once, my lieges. Er...that is, as soon as I see his Lady mother revived and escorted home."

Lips again quirking in amusement, he drew their attention to where the finally *quiet* high-caste fem had collapsed upon the decorative tiled floor.

Chapter Two

Dohsan tossed her screaming niece up into the air, ignoring her sister's half swallowed cry of trepidation. Glendevtoria squealed with delighted terror and hugged her aunt's neck tightly. "Mo, Auntie Doh! Mo!" Her little voice bounced about the walls, causing the toddler to shriek repeatedly with excitement.

"All right, my little star-shine girl... Hold on tight!" As she spoke, Dohsan twirled around in a tight circle until the smallest princess shut her eyes and leaned her head against her aunt's shoulder.

"Dizzy!"

Laughing, Dohsan tickled the tenacious toddler until she convulsed in her arms. "Aren't we both just as dizzy as we can be?"

She flung her niece high into the air and the two giggled together, their carefree voices echoing in the lofty chamber, the perfect acoustics magnifying their laughter a hundred times.

Dohsan loved these moments spent with her newest family member. The day's audience session had ended. All the toady-eaters and position-seekers were long gone. Just she, her sister and little Glendevtoria occupied the large, impressive *throla,* awaiting the arrival of the other unmated fem relocated from the Mars Colony.

Nnora had established quarterly meetings, requiring all the Mars colony fem—those free of the taint of poison introduced into the biosphere of Rb'qarm—of marriageable age to attend. Together, they discussed ways of decreasing the ongoing shortage of viable females, explored the possible social ramifications of the growing desperation among the marriageable males and sought resolutions—or at least, stopgaps—to the planet's dilemma.

The situation worsened daily, and the *Chyya'va* grew increasingly anxious to find some viable solution. Failing that, Nnora knew she needed to devise some fair, impartial way of distributing the too-few available fem among the impatient, sexually hungry males. Nnora had already taken the first step by informing all the fem they must first gain the *Chyya'va's* permission to marry before accepting a *qarm's* proposal—something that hadn't set well with any of the fem.

In response to the summons from her sister, Dohsan had contacted her brothers. They'd given her a ride home in their new *Lorme* and she had stayed just long enough to catch up on gossip with her mother before shuttling into the capital city.

Coming straight from her retreat in the remote, Jakwylla mountain range situated in the southernmost province, the culture shock had been intense. Used to interacting with *qarm* who knew their place and loved their cherished position in a fem-dominated society, the sight of hordes of unclaimed *qarm* accosting law-abiding fem trying to go about their daily chores was unsettling.

Having arrived at the palace too early for the meeting, Dohsan had spent some time investigating the worsening social climate. What she found hadn't been pretty. She had a lot to share with Nnora and the other fem, once their meeting commenced.

She hadn't been expecting to arrive in time to participate in her own character vilification ceremony, courtesy of the venomous Lady vaGhemmora. No sooner than she'd reached the palace, a guard had met her with the orders to attend Dev and Nnora in the throla. Not taking the time to change her clothes, she'd followed the guard to the public audience hall.

Shaking her head over that whole weird situation, Dohsan frowned, still puzzled over just what the fem had hoped to achieve with her ill-thought-out attack. A moment later, she figured it out. Throwing back her head, she laughed aloud.

Nnora glanced up from the sheaf of papers in her hands. "Share the joke?"

"I was just trying to figure out what Laharo's mama thought to gain with her attack against me and it dawned on me—" She had to break off or choke on her giggles. "—the idiot wanted you and Dev to force me into marriage with her son!" Dohsan whooped, doubling over in mirth.

"Took you long enough to get there!"

"You *knew* what she was about?"

Nnora's smile stretched her full lips and crinkled her dancing eyes. "Girl, she was so see-through her name should have been cellophane!"

"You sure strung me out long enough. How come you never got around to telling me?"

"The fact that I just witnessed you reaching the same conclusion proves I didn't need to bother."

About to blast her older sib for her high-handedness, Dohsan found herself distracted by two small hands framing her face and pressing against her cheeks to force her head around. "Pway wif me, Auntie Doh," her demanding niece ordered, "I wanna go *up!*"

Dohsan buried her nose in the soft crease of Toria's neck and inhaled deeply. Her heart lightened as she hugged her niece, enjoying the sweet baby smell rising off the tiny body. Oh, she wanted one of these!

"My Toria wants to go up, and so she shall!"

Her attention now fully centered on the bossy little princess in her arms, Dohsan cooed encouragement as she launched a wriggling Devtoria high and then snatched her out of the air at the last moment. She pretended to fumble and almost drop her before repeating the cycle in quick succession.

Listening to her niece shriek with laughter, she nostalgically thought back to a time when her own life had been secure and safe, filled with the simple thrills provided by loving parents. Lately, accusations and appearances to the contrary, any thrills had been few and far between.

"Dohsan, I swear you and Toria are going to be the death of me!"

The frantic note in Nnora's voice was hard to ignore as the *Chyya'va* of Rb'qarm and Rb'nTraq, hurried over to her younger sister. Reaching up, she snatched her giggling daughter before she could become airborne again. "Okay, young lady, playtime is over!"

A frown pulling her eyebrows together, Dohsan reluctantly surrendered her niece. She tried to play off the irritation she felt. "Get real, Nnora! It's not like I'm going to hurt my own niece. No matter how irresponsible you might think me, or how I might act in public or with others, Devtoria will always be safe with me. Besides being my niece, she is heir to your throne and deserving of my loyalty."

Her heart aching with envy, she watched her sister retreat with the giggling child. Arms wrapped about her torso, feeling empty and lonely, Dohsan told herself she'd better get over her unreasonable attitude.

Fighting back the tears that threatened, Dohsan swallowed her anger and jealousy as Nnora settled onto the comfortably padded throne to smile and coo at her first-born child. For the life of her, she couldn't understand her upside-down emotions. She watched mother and child play tickle-tummy and actually wanted to grab her niece and run away. *How crazy was that?* She would never dream of hurting Nnora, could never destroy her family by such an insane act.

On top of all else plaguing her lately had been the increasing need to cuddle a child born of her own body. Apparently, when her *pava* detonated, it had set other internal clocks to ticking...and she didn't think she could shut them down. Leastwise, nothing she'd tried so far had worked worth a damn.

Wanting a baby didn't bother her nearly as much as the fact that whenever she envisioned her future children, they all bore a striking resemblance to a certain haughty commander.

Dohsan scowled. *Why do I persist in wanting anything to do with Mr. Hoity-toity macho battle commander GanR'dari, beautiful as he is? He is entirely too macho, too busy being the hero. He probably isn't capable, let alone interested, in giving me what I truly need.*

Yet, how could she *not* want him? The male stood eight feet, four inches tall, every muscled inch bristling with power and masculine beauty. Blessed with shimmering green eyes that could melt her pussy with one possessive glare and a wide, mobile mouth with firm, full lips, he was her ideal of *qarm*hood.

The long, corded length of his arms beckoned her, bid her take comfort within his sheltering grasp. The wide expanse of his chest, the indented caves of his overly large *terat* tempted and teased her unmercifully. No male had ever been able to completely enclose her nipples within their *terat*. 'Dari's looked to be able to handle her long, thick nipples with room to spare.

Swallowing convulsively, she moaned, fantasizing about sinking her nipples into the deeply recessed interiors until her tightly puckered tips were engulfed beyond the circling rings of her areoles. A dollop of cream bubbled to the surface, coated her smooth, hairless mound with warm honey as she recalled the popular myth of how to judge the size of a *qarm's* sexual organs. Folklore said the depth of a *qarm's terat* indicated the length and thickness of his *cherzda*—if the sayings proved true, 'Dari's cock should be as thick as her wrist and almost as long as her forearm.

She shivered, thigh muscles tightening. Feeling wet and needy, she slid her legs against each other, shifting in an effort to relieve the building ache in her clit.

How could she *not* want 'Dari? She wanted to fuck him silly, to soothe and care for him... Okay, yes, sometimes she

simply wanted to *kill* the overbearing *qarm*. But mostly, she just
wanted *him*, wanted his attention, his approbation, his love.

Humph! Her best bet would be to fuck him until she'd had
her fill, then move on to a male who would be willing to be *Mr.*
Dohsan. Because no matter how she cast the future, there was
no way she could see GanR'dari willing to play lapdog for long.
Not even for her. And somewhere in the corner of her soul, she
wouldn't have him any other way.

She couldn't see a way to resolve this growing conflict,
couldn't find a path that would accommodate the both of them.
She couldn't make up her mind, couldn't decide what she really
wanted.

Whom was she kidding? She knew just what—or rather,
whom—she wanted. GanR'dari. She wanted 'Dari like a *Matari*
wanted flesh, craved him like a barren fem craved a *qarm's zhi.*

She wanted GanR'dari on her own terms, yet could she
tolerate or respect a male who allowed her to rule him in all
things? How long would it be before she tired of what she
deemed weakness and lost respect for the *qarm?*

Knowing herself to be a strong-willed fem, she knew she
required a strong-minded *qarm* to match her.

*Oh, Hel! I am damned if I do or if I do not! Insist on control
and lose my male, or grow to hate him for submitting to me?*

Sighing, she ended up where she started from, knowing she
should leave him alone and choose another to mate. Only one
thing stopped her from following her own good advice—her
dangerously growing needs.

"...I know you would never intentionally harm Toria, Doh-
si-do." Nnora's softly spoken words broke into the dizzying
cycle of her inner debate. "Unlike two *qarm* I *won't* mention,

I've also figured out the true intent behind your so-called wanton actions of the last few *Fael.* Though I think you and the other fem place yourselves in untold danger, I can't help but applaud your generosity of heart."

Her sister's gentle, understanding smile did much to soothe her agitated feelings. Still…

"So why did you snatch Devtoria from me as if I were a member of Deth's berserker legion?"

A self-depreciating laugh preceded Nnora's discomfited answer. "I never for a moment thought you capable of hurting her. I know how you love Toria, it's just—" Nnora's arms tightened fiercely about her baby. "She is such a miracle. I fear for her. She is almost the age I was when I lost my mother. It's not reasonable, I know, but I can't help the feelings of impending danger. If something should happen to me, I want Glendevtoria protected and cared for, not sent away and lost."

A sudden tightness in her chest stopped Dohsan from answering right away. Eyes growing moist, she shook her head, refuting her sister's worries, praying they were unfounded. "Nnora, nothing is going to happen to you."

"I know. But if it should, I want you to promise to watch over my daughter. Unlike my own childhood, I want hers to be filled with security and emotional surety. She should never have to wonder if her physical differences render her unlovable. I want her to grow up *knowing* her value as a person, knowing she is loved with every fiber of my being…and beautiful—so beautiful I can scarce believe I had anything to do with her being here."

"Let's not forget my *loving* contribution to her presence…and I hope some of those *being* fibers are available to your adoring mate."

Chyya Glendevtorvas sauntered into the room, his sparkling tangerine eyes glued to the faces of his mate and child. He waggled his eyebrows playfully. "I believe I had quite a lot to do with her being here." His smile fell away when he locked gazes with Nnora. "And I will personally see that nothing happens to you, so put away your fears, dearling."

"Oh, Dev, I love you so!"

Dohsan doubted the doting husband and father even saw her as he brushed past her to embrace Nnora and Glendevtoria. Their impassioned kiss had her shifting, bearing down in an effort to ease the twinge in her viciously throbbing clit. Usually Dev's and Nnora's loving relationship soothed her jangled nerves, reassured her all was right in her world. Lately, observing the heat and passion that arced between them like lightning served to arouse and madden her. She despaired of ever obtaining such a loving, understanding companion of her own, of being the other half of a *qarm's* soul.

"Good mid-rise, Dohsan." GanR'dari, following his typical custom, ghosted in behind his ruler and friend. Other than when he guarded the queen, the two *qarm* were inseparable.

She stiffened at his brusque greeting and the curt nod of his head. Just the sound of his voice started her rebellious *nippa* creaming, his heated gaze and knowing smirk serving to aggravate her arousal. With an indrawn breath, she cursed her responsive nipples and pulsating clit as the rich, evocative scent of her flowering—designed to draw potential mates to her side—wafted from her, waves of hormone-laden fragrance broadcasting her newly matured status to the two men.

"GanR'dari." She nodded stiffly—a regal inclination of her head—ignoring his suddenly glazed eyes and look of stunned enlightenment.

At least the terse greetings and formal nods they exchanged were better than their usual heated volleys. Or so she thought until the next words out of his mouth spoiled her good mood.

"So we have you to thank for that ugly scene in the *throla* today, baby-fem?"

Dohsan braced, resentful of his attack on her "ugly" behavior. So much for hoping today would be different than their usual encounters. She shrugged. "You've just received notice that I am no baby. Besides, parts of that incident were highly exaggerated."

"Really?" He ignored the first half of her response to address the latter. "I am curious to know which part that would be?"

Eyeing him cautiously, aware his smile did not reach his eyes, she said, "The most important part, of course."

"You *weren't* caught half-naked in her *soalori?* Your *tlinis weren't* buried circle-deep in her son's *terat?*" The last words were forced through clenched teeth.

His biting tones put her back up until she noted his starving gaze riveted on the afore-mentioned *tlinis.*

"Oh, I plead guilty to those parts...to an extent." Her sultry drawl accompanied an indolent roll of her shoulders. Intent on baiting him, on awakening and heightening *his* emerging needs, she continued, "My *tlinis* weren't buried circle-deep—his *terat* weren't that accommodating. I was referring to the part about her *soalori* being lovely. I exaggerated highly about that part."

"*Rejas!* Why will you take nothing seriously?"

"Don't you mean why don't I take *you* seriously? Last time I looked, that wasn't a crime. But I have been up in the mountains and away from court." She glanced over at Dev and Nnora, lips tilting as she spied their exasperated looks. "Either one of you recently declare it a crime not to take 'Dari seriously?"

She saw Nnora's lips curl up before she raised a hand to hide her amusement.

Dev's eyes twinkled as he shook his head. "Not yet. However, I, for one, find merit in the suggestion. 'Dari, shall I declare it law for one particular fem to take you seriously?"

A black frown marred his ruggedly handsome face as he spat his reply. "This is a serious matter and your teasing is not amusing. Should I care to engage her infantile attentions— *which I do not*—I would not require a royal edict to advance my cause."

Dohsan lowered her gaze, not wanting to see the pitying looks Devtorvas and her sister wore. 'Dari's reaction shocked them, but not her. She had grown used to being his verbal punching bag.

Why must he always go out of his way to inform the world he wants nothing to do with me?

Eyeing the commander coldly, she opened her mouth, determined to respond in like vitriolic manner until her angry gaze snagged on an interesting development.

He lied! He wanted her. Boy, did he want her!

She licked suddenly dry lips, eyes almost crossing as they locked with greedy attention on his prominent hard-on. Rising in a massive column of flesh, there was no hiding the mastodon jutting skyward from the juncture of his muscular thighs. Under her salivating stare, GanR'dari's cock swelled to an ultra-fem-pleasing size, faithfully delineated by the form-fitting cut of his palace dress uniform.

Oh, my! She definitely liked the new court style. It did a lot to showcase a male's...interest.

"Be grateful I do not take you seriously, Commander."

"Am I to shake in my battle boots, baby-fem?"

She looked up, met his eyes and found it impossible to look away.

"I think you might, *aged qarm*. I have become vaShafaran— a Keeper of the Ancient Paths. Any male I accept will bow in respect to the old ways...and to me."

"Surely you jest, Dohsan!"

Nnora's shocked outburst only added to the general feelings of isolation and discouragement Dohsan had been suffering lately. Having spoken with her sister at length on these matters, many times, she found it hard to believe her sister hadn't understood their recent conversations or had not taken her beliefs seriously enough to have given them further thought.

"You are skirting insanity, fem!" 'Dari's harsh words didn't hurt as much as Nnora's stinging censure because she never expected he would see the merit in her world view. She also knew he would realize how seriously her choice of life-path affected him and everyone around her. *Especially him.*

She opened her mouth to answer and found all her muscles frozen. Locked in place, she struggled, seeking to avoid the increasingly familiar yet unwelcome sensation of falling into trance.

Please, no! Not now. This is not the time to fall under vision—

Notwithstanding her wishes, the *seeing* engulfed her. She gasped, head spinning as her eyesight dimmed. Euphoria rushed through her as a kaleidoscope of scenes, scents and textures rolled over her, capturing her consciousness.

Glimpses of a possible future engulfed her, streamed before her in choppy pictures, fractured into stark, strobing flashes...

A shadow-shrouded room.

Glimpses of her own passion-contorted face.

Flashes of a male, half concealed by darkness.

Clumsy haste and intemperate hunger.

Masculine hands roughly cupping her breasts.

Loud sighs, breathless moans.

Hard fingers flexing, forcing engorged nipples into already spasming terat.

Swollen, itching nipples sinking into the suctioning mouths of the male's terat.

Urgent need spiraling out of control.

A million, million tiny pinpricks of delicious pain eating into her buried tips.

Strong, muscle-corded arms raising and shifting her.

Lowering and lifting her, working her nipples without mercy.

Muscled thighs moving between her legs, opening her.

A deft hand parting her slick folds, revealing her hot pink center.

Lustful, agonized moans.

Pava juices flowing hot and creamy, raining down on a rampant cherzda.

A shift, an upward thrust.

The heavy head slick between her outer lips, pressing against her nippa.

Sinking deep.

Surging.

Two bodies entwining, writhing in erotic bliss.

Frenzied cries shattering the silence of the quiet room.

Male triumph ringing out in the shadowed room.

Then muffled amusement.

"Quiet, baby-fem. If you wake the children, our love play will be over for the day..."

"...and I say again, no *qarm* worth his salt would allow a fem to rule over—*owww!* Damn-it-all, Nnora...that *hurt!*"

The tail end of Devtorvas's vehement statement, interrupted by his startled shout, snapped the threads of her vision.

She shuddered, trying to shake off her distraction. Clasping her arms about her waist, Dohsan allowed her body to slump against the wall as she closed her eyes and concentrated on breathing. Her pulse stuttered. Heaving lungs fought to supply needed air as she battled her way out of a dense sensual fog. The orgasmic feelings of the vision still careened through her, zinging through her veins like a thick sweet liqueur.

Thank the stars the flash had lasted but a few seconds. She could feel the weight of GanR'dari's intent stare but resisted the urge to turn and look at him. That way spelled disaster. Taking the big champion to the floor and humping his brains out was the last thing her sister and bond-brother needed to witness. She very much feared the possibility could become reality if she met his challenging gaze.

Picturing the event, she moaned softly. The muscles of her lower belly clenched tight with renewed desire. Her *pava* flowered, producing the sweet juice generated by her vision of the coupling she hoped would be in her near future. Feeling desperate, dying to experience that level of satiation right *now*, she struggled to achieve a measure of calm.

Harrumph! Damned useless attempt, that.

She squeezed her eyes tight, fearing she might resort to clawing through her outer layer of skin to get at the sexual irritation building underneath. Need slithered through her. Persistent, the crawling ache lurked just below the surface, shifting aimlessly from spot to tortured spot. Scalp, breasts, cunt—they all demanded satisfaction. Her scalp felt flushed and itchy. Her nipples *burned...* She ached to palm them, tweak the swollen tips between thumb and forefinger to assuage the need. Between her thighs, the nerves in her cunt sizzled and popped with aroused fury.

By the stars, she needed relief.

In the short time since entering *pava*, she had already learned that no amount of masturbating satisfied her escalating need for long. By sheer dint of will, she battled to ignore the rising floodtide, to gain control enough to address her bond-brother's prejudicial statement with a semblance of rational thought.

"You have forgotten your own history, my *Chyya.*" Dohsan kept her back to GanR'dari in order to focus on crossing wits with her brother-by-mating. "Inquire of your father, the historian. Ask *him* why the planet, Rb'nTraq originally revolted against the *Mother*-world. Ask how and why the war really began."

"I have heard those tales, as have we all." A choppy hand motion indicated Dev's intent to sweep away any consideration of her words. "They are only fables and legends generated by those crazy fem living alone in the mountains. They have long chosen to isolate themselves from the rest of the population. How could you consider any information garnered from them to be accurate? Or true, for that matter. You cannot truly believe fem once ruled our two planets?"

"On the contrary, I know it to be truth for historical records verify the ancient facts. Our colony also bears witness. Though we left the Mother World eons ago, we of the colony did not abandon or misplace our history. We retained our heritage, the old records—the ship's records that recorded the journeys of the outcasts—taught us all we needed to know. Our culture and our language remained pure, uncorrupted by time, unlike your own. When we lost Nnora's mother, we lost our queen, our *Chyya*. Father became regent, only, in the absence of a fem of the ruling line. We were so glad to find Nnora alive because it meant the royal line had not died out. She is the direct descendant of the ruler who left Rb'qarm those thousands of years ago."

Dev frowned. "Our language also remains unchanged since the ancient days."

The younger fem snorted. "Your language, like your history, is more distorted than you know."

"What do you mean by that, Dohsan? What proof do you have?" Nnora sounded intrigued.

"I, too, would hear proof. Facts, not just your opinion," Dev warned, dropping into the seat beside his wife. Only GanR'dari stood withdrawn, silent and brooding.

She looked at them, all three of them: Nnora, Dev and 'Dari. Three pairs of eyes trained on hers...question marks in one, skepticism in another and…what was the look in 'Dari's eyes? She could not fathom it.

Dohsan knew her sister was an information junkie and loved to learn new facts. Dev might not like what he would hear, but he was the one most likely to give her a fair hearing. He usually listened to her facts and judged them, not her. 'Dari was the X-factor. She had no way of knowing what went on behind his inscrutable eyes.

Before she could gather her thoughts, her niece held out her arms and barked an imperial command. "Mo!"

The little martinet's belief that nothing was more important than her playtime broke the tension and Dohsan laughed while she stooped to sweep her little love out of her daddy's arms.

"You all think you want me to tell you, to show you my proof, but I've just realized your minds are closed on this subject." She jounced Toria up and down, absently listening to her squeals of joy. "Like this babe, you have much yet to learn about our history and our true roles in our two worlds."

Slow, metered, *derisive* clapping sounded behind her. She froze. She would *not* turn, would not confront GanR'dari in his arrogance.

"Tell me, baby-fem—how are we to view this information you spout as anything but *gibberish?* Suddenly, *you* are to be hailed as the sage of the ages?"

Her arousal roared back, stronger than before, more relentless in scope. His show of disdain, his overbearing, *masculine* attitude had her aching to subdue him, to conquer his resistance.

To hell with this!

Dohsan pivoted slowly. She could feel the heat pouring off her, out of her.

A sense of her feminine power grew within her as she watched GanR'dari's peridot eyes widen, registering the molten message her hot gaze was sending.

She wrapped her arms tight about her baby niece and held on. Her loving grasp on Devtoria was the only thing stopping her from reaching out and grabbing the warrior. Twin desires warred within her. On one hand, she wanted to snatch and shake the hard-headed male. On the other, she yearned to take his lips and then his cock in a kiss aggressive enough to knock him to his knees.

Where had this emerging dominant streak come from? Over the last cycle, while gaining her maturity along with her second and greatest growth, she'd noticed an increasing inclination to exert her will over the slavering males that flocked about her in hopes of being considered as a possible mate. The willing submission of the sex-starved *qarms* only fed her newly gained dominant tendencies. It was so easy to influence them, to order their obedience. All, save GanR'dari, sought to do her will. He, alone, refused to submit, seemed resistant to all her charms and blandishments.

He was such an alpha-*qarm*.

Sometimes she wondered if perhaps she'd chosen him solely *because* of his continued resistance. Then she recalled the choice had been made cycles ago. Only lately had she come to doubt the wisdom of her decision. Not that she lacked faith in her ability to make GanR'dari accept her as mate...and on her terms. She did not mind that he would fight against surrendering to her. In fact, she looked forward to their coming battles, relishing the chance to pit her wits and resolve against the male who would have to prove himself her better, before she would accept him as her equal.

Concern that his self-respect might not survive her social dominance haunted her every moment. Despite the happy endings most of her visions had revealed, she put no faith in those portents. The waking dreams were merely windows upon many possible futures. In countless other visions, she had seen the two of them at sword's point...and at each other's throats. Those bleak future possibilities currently fueled recurring nightmares.

Despite her concerns, she could not resist taking the opportunity to secure his affections because, when it came right down to it, none other moved her, challenged her and made her function at the top of her abilities like 'Dari.

On top of that, his steadfast defiance aroused her more than another *qarm's terat*-play. His attitude brought out the huntress in her. The more he goaded her, pricked at her, the more she dreamed of taking him down, taming him, claiming him for all time. He was so *prime*...a worthy potential mate! Her *pava* slicked and contracted at the thought of sexually subduing all that brute strength and cunning intelligence.

She saw his nostrils flare; his eyes widened and snapped to meet her bold gaze. She tossed her hair back, making no effort to dampen her scent or hide her swelling nipples. She *wanted* him to know her for the mature fem she had become.

Smell my arousal. See my interest. Know I cream for you, ready myself for your insertion. I will mate with you!

She tossed the baby up one last time before carefully setting her down. Piling a mountain of toys before her niece to keep her occupied, she straightened and turned to confront the two disapproving *qarm* and her listening sister.

"You ask me on what I base my suppositions..." She thought a moment, carefully considering which word she could use to illustrate her point. "I will give you one example of how the language has been corrupted."

"Please do." Nnora smiled her encouragement.

"I cannot wait to hear this." GanR'dari crossed his arms over his chest and lifted his chin in her direction, signifying she should begin. She decided to ignore his little arrogant gesture.

"The most widely-spread error is the common rendering of the verb: va. You use it as *cherzda'va—belonging to my cock* and *Chyya'va—belonging to my ruler* and vaGlendevtorvas—*belonging to Glendevtorvas*. In its modern usage it is conjugated correctly, yet the *meaning* ascribed to it is erroneous."

She briefly met each gaze and saw she had their attention, her words held their interest.

"The correct meanings would be: *possessor of* my cock, *possessor of* my ruler and, *possessor of* Glendevtorvas." She cocked an eyebrow. "A slight difference, but a very *telling* one, don't you agree?"

Dohsan leaned down and kissed her small niece before glancing up at Nnora. "Forgive me if I don't stick around for your meeting, Nnora. I am so *not* in the mood right now."

She turned on her heel and stalked out, leaving behind one yelling toddler and three speechless adults.

Chapter Three

"Sires, if I may...?" GanR'dari gestured towards the doors swinging shut behind Dohsan, already striding towards them with focused determination.

Dev nodded quickly. "Of course, 'Dari. Catch her. She cannot be allowed to run about freely in her present state..."

"No, 'Dari, wait!"

Nnora's agitated voice caught him as he reached the door. He turned back in time to see Dev reach a hand toward his mate who shrugged the *Chyya* off, moving quickly to take up a position at the door.

"Don't you dare go after her, GanR'dari, I forbid it," Nnora bit off in between struggling out of Dev's careful grasp.

Devtorvas recaptured his fuming mate and wrapped his arms about her, ignoring further attempts to brush him off. He rocked her against his chest.

"She has flowered, Nnora. 'Dari and I both smelled the pheromones, as will every other *qarm* in the vicinity. There are some desperate, hungry males out there. It is best that GanR'dari catch up with her before it is too late. Besides, you and I know those two have been dancing toward this for over five of your Earth years."

GanR'dari flinched as he heard Nnora's despairing whisper, "But, she is my baby sister…"

"A baby no longer," Glendevtorvas pointed out dryly.

Grateful for Dev's intervention, 'Dari bowed low to his *Chyya'va*. "The two of us have been friends over three cycles now, Nnora. Trust that I will do nothing to harm our friendship. Nor will I hurt your sister. She is destined to be my mate."

Nnora stilled. "You might not wish or plan to hurt her, but you do so all too frequently."

He couldn't deny her accusations. "I am done waiting for her."

* * *

The afternoon light from the double suns flooded the day with a soft turquoise sheen and GanR'dari breathed deep of the clear, unpolluted air of his homeworld as he hurried after the princess. All about the lush, beautiful terrain of Rb'qarm sparkled under the twin glow of the mid-glow light, reminding him how much he loved his homeworld.

He had left once, following Glendevtorvas to Earth to claim his new queen, returning with joy at the end of the fruitful journey. His off world adventuring under his belt, so to speak, he had no desire ever to leave his homeland again.

Long strides eating up the distance, he entered the entry of the formal court gardens just in time to catch a flash of Dohsan's disappearing form exiting through the far gate. He hurried after her, his long legs making short work of the open corridors.

As he chased Dohsan, he pondered her radical worldviews. Much as he would like to dismiss her challenging words, deny their effect upon him at the deepest level, he could not. In the inner core of his being, the truth of her words resonated with a verity he could not gainsay. As surely as Nnora was the possessor of his *Chyya*, GanR'dari acknowledged that Dohsan possessed his very soul. More and more, it seemed like she always had.

* * *

"Dohsan! Wait!" He was beginning to get riled. He'd called her three times already and by Deth, he knew good and well she'd heard him.

She didn't stop moving, but pivoted on her heel and danced backwards before him. His eyes narrowed, drawn to the erotic display of her generous hips swaying before him as she rocked on her heels. Of a sudden, a memory came, blade sharp and gut-wrenching, of another time she had skipped backwards before him. In the corridors of the ship which brought them to Rb'qarm, she had taunted and teased him, had promised to rock his world, little knowing she had already made good on her threat.

"What the hell do you want, 'Dari?"

If the snarl had not told him she didn't feel in the mood to play, the black scowl on her face would have enlightened him. Well, so be it. His own mood was far from playful.

Reword that. He was definitely in the mood to engage in *fore*play and beyond, if she so desired.

Her rich scent wafted toward him on the sultry breeze. Heart kicking into overdrive, his nostrils flared as he inhaled deeply.

How did I miss her ripening? Does the girl I fell in love with still reside within this almost frightening package of feminine allure?

"You are no longer pre-*pava*." Try as he might, he could not prevent the censure from leaking through his words. Her sudden maturity felt almost like a betrayal.

"Well, *duh*, Sherlock!"

He growled. "Who is this Sherlock? Another *qarm* you have terat-fucked?"

Her eyes narrowed evilly, and his heart fell.

By the trials of Deth! Why is it I cannot manage just one peaceful meeting between us? I command the combined armies of two worlds and deal daily with hundreds of people from all walks of life. I have diplomacy down to an art, yet whenever I find myself around the fem I love, I lose all my vaunted savoir faire.

As if she read his thoughts, she asked plaintively, "Will I ever do something that you can approve of? Why is it whenever you see me, you attack me? Does your hatred for me run so deep?"

He grabbed her shoulders, needing to put his hands on her. "I do not know why I do so, baby-fem," he admitted, shaking his head. "I swear, I feel the highest regard for you. It is never my objective to upbraid you, but then you'll look at me, say something sassy and all my good intentions go out the door."

He turned her fully to him, entangling her eyes with his, reading her suspicions and misgivings in her captive yellow-green gaze. When he spoke again, his gruff voice betrayed his confused emotional state. "I am done playing games with you, Dohsan, done with waiting. You've known for cycles that I planned to claim you. Why did you not come to me when you achieved *pava?*" He shook her, emphasizing each word with a rumbling possessive growl. "And how in the name of all things holy could you give your breasts, *my tlinis*, to that belly-crawling *greeve*, Glenlaharo?"

He stared into her beautiful light eyes, wondering at her thoughts, her feelings. He searched her face, looking for some inkling she cared for him as he cared for her—deeply, obsessively, *helplessly.*

She tilted her head and stared back at him, her face still and neutral, deflecting his efforts at understanding her. Try as he might, he could read nothing in her measured stare. When had she grown up? Pre-*pava* play was one thing—easily dismissed, but flower-play held an entirely different connotation. Exactly *when* had she ceased being a girl at play and become a fem intent on... *what?*

"Why should you want to know? You care nothing for me—"

"Stop that! Of course I care, and I *really* want to know why you would withhold yourself from me yet share with others what I would hold sacred and—" He broke off, battling the wave of despair that threatened to engulf him.

"Perhaps the problem we have had all along is the fact that, for years, I have known that I planned to claim *you!* I gave you fair warning years ago. I staked my verbal claim on you then, and you went straight from witnessing my sister's mating signature, to sink Yorvala's overblown tits in your *terat.* Why did you choose Yorvala—the one fem who always hated me, who delighted in baiting me? Do you know how often she gloated in my hearing, gave us all a blow-by-blow account of how well you milked her?"

"Dohsan—"

Her head snapped up and she glared at him. He had no idea what to say. Deciding it was a good time to play dumb, he settled for saying nothing.

She dropped her chin, hiding her face from him. Her voice thickened. "You seated her and three others during the journey. You put their nipples in *my terat* and milked them dry." Giving way to her anger, she raised her fists and beat on his chest. Her blows were no light protests and he rocked back before catching his balance and her hands.

"You gave them what you denied to me." She twisted out of his reach, wrenching her hands out of his. Unreasoning anger tightened her chest when she realized he released her rather than let her bruise herself against his strength.

His eyes narrowed. "You were pre-*pava*. A *child!* What kind of pervert would I be to take advantage of a young girl's crush? It was bad enough that I wanted to do so. To act on my desires would have been dishonorable."

Her laughter was harsh. "Come off it, 'Dari. It wasn't a crush and I was never that naive. True, my body was immature and I couldn't get pregnant, couldn't give you children, thus proving my fertility. Still, I had emotions. I had feelings. And you trampled on them every day for almost two cycles. You are still trampling on them, now."

Shock roared through him. He hadn't known. "Dohsan—by the stars, baby-fem, I didn't..."

"I am more than a womb and a *nippa*, GanR'dari. Maybe you need to get up close and personal with those facts before you try to make a move on me."

"Believe me, I am more than aware of who and what you are. Though I will admit the sweet smell of your newly ripe *pava* is making my head reel." He inhaled deeply, drawing her exhilarating scent into his nostrils.

Her lip curled in disdain. "That's all you're interested in, isn't it?"

Advancing on him with fire in her eyes, she backed him up against the wall of the covered walkway. Letting her weight rest against him, she hiked her left leg over his thigh and drew the hem of her shift up to her waist, exposing her nakedness. Holding onto one of his arms for balance, she leaned back, widening her legs, revealing her smooth mound and the dripping flower between her thighs. Fanning her hand over her crotch and wafting her aroma towards his face, she taunted, "Get yourself a good whiff, *qarm*, because a whiff is all you'll *ever* get!"

Faster than thought, he grabbed her thigh, anchoring and supporting her as he spun her around, changing their positions. Holding her plastered against the ungiving wall, he pressed his body flush against hers. His pulse raced at the indescribable feel of her lush breasts flattened against his chest, scant *nicrons* away from his softening *terat*. With a shift and roll of his hips, he wedged his linen-covered cock between the lips of her naked *pava*. He thrust once, pushing up into her tight entrance, using his uniform as a cloth condom, which quickly became drenched with her heated moisture...and his own.

"Oh, I don't know about that, baby-fem," he growled, his labored breathing loud in his own ears as he battled to control his rampant lust.

By Deth! What am I thinking? To hold her here, exposed for the entire world to see, her breasts barely covered, thighs splayed, her dripping entrance stuffed with my cloth-covered cock. No matter how badly I wish it differently, I cannot take her in this public place.

This close, her potent smell dizzied him, made him light-headed. His softened terat throbbed in his chest, their pounding rhythm a demanding counterpoint to his racing pulse. His *cherzda* jerked against her, hardening and lengthening in her sultry heat. He pushed further in, forcing past the untried entrance to her *pava*, causing her swollen nether lips to part before his thick length. The wide head and over an inch of his *cherzda* pulsed insistently in the corridor just within the door of her sex. Her heat bathed the helmeted crown, twisting his gut in knots. If he didn't have her soon, he would go out of his mind.

"I swear your *pava* is burning me up. The head of my *cherzda* is ablaze in your honeyed juices!"

"Not enough!" she panted, trying to force his member to impale her deeper. "I need your cock higher up...further in." Her harsh breathing distorted her voice, made her words hoarse and indistinct. She bore down while rotating her hips, twisting his cock in the vise of her thighs and wedging more of his rigid shaft inside her tight depths.

The sharp pleasure/pain almost blew the top of his head off. Gritting his teeth, he rocked against her, teasing her with his shallow thrusts. "I love it when you use Earth terms for my *cherzda*. You make them sound so dirty and exciting."

For all their flirting, they had never kissed. Desperate to taste her, he captured her chin between steely fingers and took her mouth.

The world went away.

Her sweetness shocked his senses. Her tongue dueled with his, refusing to submit, giving and taking in a surging exchange of power. He drank deep, just now realizing how thirsty he had been for her taste, her love. With a moan, he thrust his tongue between her moist, full lips, striving to quench his thirst in her lush mouth.

"*Rojas*, baby-fem...you taste so damn sweet!" He groaned as he felt her fingers tugging on the hair at his nape. He obligingly lifted his head and met her dazed eyes. The pale yellowy-green pupils were dilated, the look in them vague. He continued to stare into her eyes as she slowly regained control of herself and focused her sharpened gaze on his face. To his delight, a heated wash of color swept up her cheeks, painting her skin a rosy hue.

Thinking she would feel compelled to slap him for his presumptuous actions, she surprised him again when she opened swollen, well-kissed lips and gruffly admitted, "I need to feel your *terat* tugging on my breasts, burning my nipples. Oh, Deth, 'Dari, seat me *now!*"

His cock surged harder and higher, swelling with lust and another emotion he feared to name. Rubbing her lips with one shaking finger, he leaned away, groaning at her racy words. "You beg so sweetly, baby-fem. If all the orders you issue are like that one, I'll have no objections obeying you. Unfortunately, this is one request I will have to disobey...for now."

Pulling further away, he reluctantly eased his *cherzda* out of her tight opening. His dampened cock-head felt cold and clammy as it exited her snug warmth and 'Dari wanted nothing more than to yank his tunic out of the way and slam back into her tight, welcoming center. He ran his fingers up the slit of her *pava*, lightly opening her, rubbing against the swollen lips. Her nectar poured out, drenching his fingers, threatening to overflow his palm. Eyes smoldering as he gazed into hers, he lapped her honeyed juices from the cup of his hand.

A hungry groan rumbled in his throat, vibrated his chest. Cursing the need, his hands regretfully smoothed over the bunched material of her shift. Fingers clinging, he slowly released the cloth, biting his lip as it gradually covered her delicious *pava*. His hands trembled in protest at the thought of having to ease her top up and over her straining breasts. 'Dari rested his forehead against hers, sucking in a fortifying breath.

"Why did you stop?" Her face blanched and her voice dropped. She lowered her chin, hiding from him. "Oh, gods, you don't want me—I am so ashamed!"

"Baby-fem, never think that! I want you more than life and I'm going to have you, just...not now. Not here, and not like this." He shuddered as he recalled how close he had come to taking her against the wall of the open portico.

"But, how can you leave me hurting this way? I *ache!*"

"*You* ache? I have a wood carving where my *cherzda* used to be, little-bit," he growled, sexual frustration shortening his temper. "In case you hadn't noticed, we've drawn a crowd. Unless you want to charge admission, I suggest we take this somewhere else...*fast.*"

Chapter Four

"Oh, great galloping galaxies!"

Dohsan cursed as arousal fled in the face of acute embarrassment. *Shiest, but there is nothing cute about this situation!* She checked the fall of her shift, frantic to conceal her blushing flesh from the interested gaze of over thirty slavering *qarms*. Snarling at the drooling males, practically daring them to comment on her disorderly dishabille, she straightened to her full height and turned on her unrepentant companion.

"Why the *frazing* hell didn't you say something before? I could just *kill* you," she hissed, seeing red as she tugged her sagging bodice over her heaving breasts. She pressed her palms against her still distended nipples, hoping the pressure would help to decrease their prominent size.

"Come on, Dohsan, be fair! I was occupied…and preoccupied, at that!"

"Humph! Some warrior you are, letting this large a crowd slip up on you unawares."

They both turned to assess the throng of agitated *qarms* just as one cocky fellow called out, "How about sharing that sweet morsel with the rest of us starving guys, my friend?"

"Yeah!" another hollered, "there looks to be plenty of her to go around."

"I want a taste of that juicy smelling *nippa!*"

"Did you see those thick nipples? I wouldn't mind sinking those into my *terat.* Probably have an inch left over!"

One *qarm* crudely rubbed his crotch, flicked his tunic back and revealed a massive *cherzda*, rampant with lust. He frantically pumped his sex as his eyes ate at her. She had never encountered such stark, open need.

"I'd give anything to feel a hot *pava* clasping my flesh instead of my own callused fist. I'd die for that!"

"*I'd kill for it!*" another growled, taking a menacing couple of steps forward.

Oh, shit on a shingle! We are frazing *screwed. Or at least, it appears* I'm *about to be!*

Without turning her head and barely moving her lips, Dohsan whispered, "I am unarmed and all you have is your sword. Can you take them?"

His hand on her shoulder, pushing her behind his bulk was her only answer as he took up a defensive stance before her.

"Gentle *Qarm*, hear me! I am GanR'dari 'abri GlenglanR'on, commander of the combined armed forces of Rb'nTraq and Rb'qarm, and the *Chyya's* own champion. This fem beside me is the princess Doh—"

One of the men cut him off, eyes gleaming, face distorted by lust. "That fem beside you is *flowering!* My *terat* have gone soft. *Do you know how long it has been since my* terat *softened or my* cherzda *rose...?"*

The plaintive note in the speaker's voice obviously echoed the emotions of the other males. Their expressions revealed hope and growing wonder as they all examined themselves and found signs of softening and quickening. Their voices rose in renewed clamor.

"I'm hard!"

"My terat *ache..."*

"By Deth, it's been too long—"

"Give her up!" one man shouted his voice harsh and threatening, implacable determination hardening the planes of his face. He pulled a knife—more like a short sword—from his thigh scabbard and advanced through the crowd to face GanR'dari in challenge.

Ice pooled in her belly as Dohsan listened to over twenty voices raised at once, all demanding her surrender, most voicing what they intended to do to her and with her. Her knees went wobbly. Fear turned her bowels to jelly and tears blurred her vision as she wondered if they would really rape her, fuck her against her will right out on the open street. Were the *qarm* that much out of control?

"Warrior, leave now and live. We only want the fem!"

A snarl rumbled in GanR'dari's throat, distorting his taunted response. "You are all insane—the lot of you—to even suggest such a thing!"

"We are not planning to hurt the fem, just fuck her..."

Chilling laughter arose all about, as the rogue *qarms* drew closer, every eye glued upon her fertile body. Dohsan fought to restrain her shudders, knowing the worst thing she could do in this explosive situation would be to show fear. But, oh, she was terrified—not for herself only, but for GanR'dari. She knew he would die before deserting her to this crowd of animalistic males. His next words proved her point.

"This many of you would cause my lady untold harm. Think you I would walk away, leaving her to your non-existent mercies? On the contrary, one irreverent hand laid upon her will result in a multitude of hurt, all of it yours."

The silken slide of steel skimming smooth leather sounded. GanR'dari's honed blade glinted in the late afternoon glow. One-handed, he spun the naked sword in a dizzying display of expert swordsmanship. He executed each precise, deadly movement so quickly; the eye saw only the afterimage of the light running in rivulets down the silvered steel.

"All who would taste death step forward..."

For a moment, nothing and no one moved. Even the wind died down. In the deafening silence, the song of GanR'dari's flashing sword hummed loudly, stirring a strong reaction within Dohsan.

Heart racing, pulse pounding, she stood entranced, pride and love flooding her senses, rushing through her blood like fluid lightning. Fear washed away by trust, she threw back her shoulders and stepped up beside her chosen mate, careful not to impede his sword arm. She knew, without a shadow of a doubt, that he would allow no one to harm her. In turn, she could not allow any of the desperate *qarm* to harm her beloved.

"There is no need for this, gentle *qarm*. In accordance with ancient tradition, and as a follower of the vaShafaran way, I declare a *Benlat I'Cherzda* quest. I invite you all to present yourselves at the palace two glowrise hence, where I will choose my preferred mate during the *Benlat I'Cherzda* ceremony."

The dark atmosphere changed drastically as the thirty-something crowd of *qarm* sent up a concerted shout of lustful anticipation. All save one.

"By Deth, I'll wait for no ceremony!" The knife-wielding *qarm* moved quickly, snatching Dohsan from her place at 'Dari's side. With a guttural roar, he clutched her close, one beefy forearm squeezing the breath from her, his huge palm clamping down on a breast.

GanR'dari voiced his wrath in a full-throated roar loud enough to shake the trees.

Heart pounding, pulse skittering in fear, Dohsan struggled against the lustful *qarm*, desperate to escape his grasp. Knowing she had to give 'Dari a clear path, she clawed at the hand groping her flesh. Calling upon her recent training, she worked her right hand, palm-upward, under the *qarm's* fist. Grabbing hold of his pinkie, she hauled back with all her strength. A snap sounded loudly and the *qarm's* grip gave way, allowing Dohsan to dance out of his reach.

A moment later, the agonized howl that split the air cut off abruptly as GanR'dari's sword flashed with murderous intent.

The thud of the *qarm's* disembodied head hitting the flagstones echoed gruesomely throughout the square. Fighting the urge to puke, Dohsan raised a shaking hand to her face, swiping at the splattered blood dripping into her eyes.

Blood-drenched sword held aloft and at the ready, GanR'dari stood with feet planted wide, eyes blazing and mouth stern.

"Who will be next?"

Chapter Five

His agitated footsteps rang on the flagstones, echoing off the chamber's thick stone walls as he paced before Dohsan, the *Chyya* and *Chyya'va*. "By Deth's balls, Dohsan, what were you thinking of?"

"Gee, I don't know, 'Dari. Saving your sorry life, maybe?"

Despite his plans to remain calm and non-confrontational, a blast of furnace-hot anger roared through him, igniting a new spike of agony to join the headache throbbing behind his burning eyes. The pain pulsed with every heartbeat, a measure of the hurt he suffered contemplating her actions, her lack of faith in his ability to see to her protection.

"I did not require your assistance then and I do not care for your sarcasm, now, fem!"

"Eat me!" Her eyes flashed, revealing her own anger with him. As usual, proof of her spirit, her courage in the face of danger flooded him with pride and admiration. Now, those feelings were swamped with the reminder of how close he'd come to losing her.

"That is second on my agenda, baby-fem. Right after I heat up your impudent bottom." Lust flared as her eyes widened in alarm and a delicious-looking flush of color bathed her cheeks.

"Not living likely, buster!" she gritted out, backing cautiously away from his menacing approach. "Not even when you're dead! You try that, I promise you'll have a fight on your hands."

"I'll relish seeing just how much *fight* you have within you."

She snarled, flashing her teeth as she flung about and headed out the room. "I'll be glad to show you. Stick around, chump, I'll be right back!"

The doors slammed against the outer walls, a testament to her strength. Each door weighed more than a hundred pounds.

Still angry and looking for a fight, 'Dari cursed, fists clenched at his side, eyes glued to the open portal. She'd left, not even willing to stay and defend herself against his accusations.

She was right not to trust me to see her safely out of danger. Even now, when she's gone through such trauma, I attack her—

Too disturbed to stand still, GanR'dari stormed back and forth across the broad expanse before the twin thrones in the vast *throla*, empty now except for him, Glendevtorvas and Glennora.

Nnora leaned forward, eyes glittering with determination. "I have repeatedly told you both that we are sitting on a powder keg, here. This event proves our people's condition is worsening. We *have* to do something about this situation or we will face events worse than the one you just came through, 'Dari."

"It was Dohsan's immature actions that sparked this present situation. If she had not—"

"Stop, 'Dari!" Nnora stood up and stamped over to stand toe-to-toe with her stubborn friend. "You just hold it right there. How dare you call my sister immature? She may be young, but she is far more enlightened to the problems facing our world than you and Dev seem to be. If you had any idea of what drives her, what motivates her—" She threw her hands up in the air. "*Men!*"

Devtorvas's barked laughter had both 'Dari and Nnora turning to frown at him. He waved his hands, dismissing their anger. "No need turning such fierce looks upon me. You two sound like squabbling siblings, the way you are going at each other. Both of you take a step back and come at this problem with more objectivity." He may have delivered his calm words as advice, but both knew a command when they heard one.

"I find it hard to be objective about the fem I love almost being force-fucked by a mob of *pava*-maddened *qarm* right before my face—" He broke off, unable to adequately express, even now, how frightened he had been.

"She could have died at their hands. If something had set that mob off again, there would have been nothing I could do to alter the outcome."

Frustrated, he whirled about and pounded his fists against the wall, a deep-throated roar of anger and tension ringing and echoing in the vast chamber.

The emotional storm quickly ran its course and he turning back to face his two friends. A little sheepishly, embarrassed by his outburst, he shook his head and tried again to explain, his words gruff and hesitant. "What would have happened if the other males had rushed me after I killed that first desperate soul? I would have done anything, bargained with Deth, himself, to save her, yet it wouldn't have been enough. What could I have done against that great a number? The realization that my inattention placed her in that kind of danger will be the theme of my future nightmares. I failed her and I never want to feel that helpless ever again."

"You have to let it go, 'Dari." Devtorvas cleared his throat; his voice gruff as he advised his long-time friend. "Hold on to the fact that you did not fail her, you saved her."

"That's not true, Dev. I was so engrossed in trying to bury my cock in her *pava*, that I paid no attention to our surroundings. You and I both would have the head of any raw recruit who pulled a no-brained stunt like that. I should have been alert and ready. Her life and safety depended on me being in control and today, my inattention nearly cost her dearly."

"You are too hard on yourself."

"No, *Chyya*, I am not. If anything, I am not hard enough." GanR'dari's voice hardened. "Saving Dohsan from herself is a glowrise to glowset undertaking, made more difficult because she will not modify her unruly behavior."

Rising anger dissipated the last lingering wisps of his melancholy. "As long as she continues to indulge in the kind of wild antics she was accused of today, she will continue to get into trouble. One day, it will be trouble I cannot handle."

A small hand landed in the middle of his chest with enough power to rock him back on his heels. He stared down at the aching area on his chest, and then raised his head until his disbelieving gaze focused on Nnora's angry expression. To say she looked spitting mad would have been an understatement.

"What was that for?" 'Dari rubbed his chest, slanting an indulgent glance toward his agitated queen.

"Do you have any idea of how asinine you sound? First of all, I do NOT need to hear you talking about sticking your mile long dong up my baby sister's vagina." She whispered the last word. "Furthermore, regardless of what you *think* went on in this *throla* earlier today, you couldn't be more wrong in your assessment of Dohsan's recent behavior."

Tears shimmered in his *Chyya'va's* iridescent neon-orange eyes, spilling over onto her pale cheeks. A pang of remorse hit 'Dari just before her fists landed against his chest with more force than before. Her blows landed uncomfortably close to his terat and he raised both hands to protect the sensitive area.

"Nnora, please don't cry!"

"I find it hard to believe you truly love Dohsan. You are always so quick to judge her, to find her lacking."

'Dari groaned. He hated that his words had caused his friend such distress. Still, how could she fault him, blame *him* because Dohsan acted as she did? Should he overlook the princess's high jinks and pretend everything was fine when it was not? *Hel no!*

"Look, I regret you are hurt by my words. I don't like seeing you so upset; however, you were there earlier, when I asked Dohsan if the accusations against her were legitimate and right now when I confronted her about her behavior this mid-glow."

"Yes, I heard her answer to you. It was flippant in the extreme. I also heard *how* you asked and I'll tell you this—" She shook her finger in his face before jabbing it repeatedly in his gut, punctuating every word with a poke of her stiffened digit. "If Devtorvas had been dumb enough to flaunt that arrogant attitude in *my* face, I would have answered him in the same way."

"Oww!" 'Dari caught Nnora's hand, halting the jabbing action of her forefinger. By Deth, the dainty fem had battle-steel-tipped nails. He searched her disgruntled face, trying to assess the depths of her anger. At a loss to understand why she remained so irate, he exchanged a confused glance with his friend and ruler. Devtorvas's shrug and blank expression told him he was on his own.

"How can you say I am arrogant when I have bent over backward accommodating your sister's adolescent whims?"

"First, she is no adolescent, as you now well know. Do you truly think she behaves as she does on a *whim?*" Nnora's mouth fell open. Her eyes narrowed. She glared at him, hands curling into claws at her side. "My God, Dohsan is right! You're worse than I thought!"

"Nnora, you have to admit this last complaint is the tenth or twelfth lodged in under a *Fael.* It seems your newly mature sister is intent upon being seated by as many *qarm* as she can accommodate in as short a time as possible."

"*Aarrrghhhh!* You two make me so crazy."

When the *Chyya'va* got that look on her face, the *Chyya* usually ended up sleeping in the barracks. Devtorvas was no fool and he quickly abandoned 'Dari to his own defense. "*Nippa,* we freely admit we are obviously too dense to understand what you seem to be trying to get across to us. May we skip the lecture and get straight to the part where 'Dari realizes the error of his ways? That way, he can deal with your sister's latest escapade, and we can get on with running our governments."

'Dari bit the inside of his cheek. It wouldn't do to laugh at one's king. He sighed. He didn't think less of Devtorvas for caving in. Banishment from your fem's bed was the worst punishment a *qarm* could imagine. Besides, no one ever believed his weak lies about missing the men when he showed up in the barracks looking like his favorite dog had turned and bit him.

Nnora shook her head, dejection dragging down the corners of her mouth. "Why can't you see what I see? What Dohsan sees? What all the Martian fem see?"

Devtorvas stood and wrapped his arms about her, cradling her back to his chest. "What I can see is that you are anxious over this and I would not have you distressed. Tell us what we are missing. We will listen with open hearts."

The calm cadence of his voice seemed to soothe her. She melted against him, turning her head into his shoulder, allowing him to support her. Raising her hands, she curled them around his thick forearms, cuddling up to her mate and purring in contentment.

GanR'dari blanked his expression. They didn't need to be privy to the tormenting envy that ate at him, welling up at times like these. He was a hungry *qarm*, starving for what Devtorvas and Nnora shared; a relationship that encompassed their entire beings. He wanted their shared heat and compassion, the same tenderness and torrid lust—all that and more—for himself and Dohsan.

Many times, he'd asked himself why he waited, why he had not claimed a mate from among the fertile fem of the Mars colony. Who would understand that his heart could be content with none but Dohsan, the sassy, vibrant hellion who challenged and intrigued him, who owned him body and soul? Much as he railed, ranted, and dragged his feet in denial, she had captured his heart in her immature hands a long time ago during a conversation in a starship's dim corridor.

"Dohsan isn't the only fem supposedly flitting from *qarm* to *qarm*," Nnora informed them, breaking into his introspection.

"Over a hundred of the un-mated Mars colony fem have been engaging in *terat*-play with the unattached males in their communities."

"*What?*"

"*Why?*"

Slanting a disbelieving look on her husband and friend, she drew away from Dev's embrace, planting her hands on her hips. "*Men!*"

'Dari sighed, exchanging a clueless glance with Glendevtorvas. In this, they were equals; males confronted with unfathomable feminine anger. "Now what have we done?"

She blew out an exasperated sigh. "What part of 'Our people are in a sexual crisis' don't you two understand? Yes, Lori has consented to stay and work on a cure, but who knows how long a breakthrough will take? My fellow colonists are aware of how desperate our men are. They are doing what they can to help. If engaging in *terat*-play generates hope and relieves some of the tensions underlying our society, then I say, 'Have at it!'"

"You *allowed* them to do this?" Devtorvas spun Nnora about to glare down into her defiant gaze.

"*Allowed?*" Nnora laughed. "These are grown women we are talking about, buddy. I don't *allow* them to do anything. I didn't, and still don't feel this is an area where I can dictate my will, but I certainly sympathize with their need to help. If I were unmated, I would be doing the same."

"Over my dead body," Devtorvas growled.

So, that was what Dohsan had been up to.

'Dari heaved a deep breath and released it on a resigned sigh. "If you knew what she was doing, why even listen to Lady vaGhemorra's viperous attack?"

Nnora lips turned up in a chilling smile. "In Earth vernacular, I was giving her enough rope to hang herself. She wanted a family connection with royalty and thought to force Dohsan into marriage with her son by generating scandal about her behavior. She failed to consider two things. First—" Nnora raised a finger, ticking off each point. "—Dohsan was pre-*pava* when she played with the vaGhemmora heir. Her son was clearly in the wrong, should anyone wish to pursue the matter legally. Second, and most importantly, no one forces Dohsan. That woman didn't realize the hell she courted by trying to maneuver an unwilling Dohsan into her family."

'Dari laughed ruefully. He could personally attest to Dohsan's stubbornness.

Now Nnora had hit him over the head with the true situation, he could plainly see how Dohsan would feel compelled to save the world...or at least, her portion of it.

He sighed. Good thing his appetite for a certain royal fem was huge. He'd soon be eating a substantial dish of contriteness before she got around to forgiving him...*if* she forgave him.

"'Dari, a word of advice—" Glendevtorvas came forward and slapped his friend on the arm. "My experience with a certain royal princess prompts me to issue a warning. Begin as you mean to go on. For some reason, these Mars-bred fem are used to ruling the roost as well as the kingdom. I suggest a firm hand..."

An indignant laugh bubbled in Nnora's throat as she playfully attacked her mate. "I can't believe you said that with a straight face, you rat!"

Dev grabbed his mate and nuzzled her neck, chuckling himself. "I love it when you talk Earther," he murmured licking the shell of her ear.

Anxious to get started on his apologies, GanR'dari excused himself from his romantically inclined rulers and prepared himself for the long trek to Dohsan's side. The distance to her quarters would be relatively short. He had also to bridge the galaxies-wide distance between their philosophies.

A gale force in the guise of Princess Dohsan swept through the open doors before he could reach them. They slammed again, this time into the jamb. A hollow thud echoed in the *throla* as the massive panels shuddered from the force used on them.

With an air of finality, Dohsan dropped the bar across the two doors, sealing the chamber from the outside world before turning to confront the three people occupying the room.

"So, you like Earther, Dev? How about this bit of colloquial English for you: You two motherfuckers are so full of shit a girl needs hip boots to wade through it. But that's okay, because I'm about to beat it out of at least one of you!"

Chapter Six

"Dohsan!" Nnora gasped. "What have I told you about your language? And why are you dressed like that?"

Dohsan tapped the hilt of her long weapon against her burnished breastplate. "I am going to war."

Wide gold armshield bands gleamed at wrists and forearms. Ornate leather greaves bound her upper arms. A matching shoulder protector rode her left neck, attached to the back and shoulder of the breastplate. A short leather skirt rode low on her hips, cut generously to provide ample movement. Knee-length boots and a girdle of linked discs—depicting her conquests— encircled the bare skin of her midriff, completing her outfit.

"Nnora, unless you want the flat of my sword against the flat of your bottom, I suggest you stay out of this."

Nnora's eyes narrowed and she drew herself up, straightened to her full height. Dohsan wasn't too impressed since she had towered over her older sister for years.

A full moment passed.

"Okay, I'm out." Nnora untangled herself from her mate and retreated from the field. She made herself comfortable far from the line of fire. "I'm kinda, sorta on your side, anyway so there's no need for posturing between us."

Dohsan nodded at her sister, spared her a brief smile. "Wise decision."

"Dohsan 'abret Glenbrevchanka, you forget whom you are speaking to," Dev cautioned, shaking his finger at her.

'Dari's incensed question cut across the *Chyya's* words, echoed loudly in the cavernous *throla*. "How *dare* you bring a naked blade into the presence of the *Chyya* and *Chyya'va?*"

She ignored 'Dari to address Dev. "No, *Chyya* Glendevtorvas 'abri Chyya Quasharel, I don't, but I *have* been so busy trying to impress your lunkhead of a commander that, for a short while, I had forgotten who *I* am."

Dohsan bowed and pointed her sword toward the *qarm* she intended to tame. "As for your question, I bring my bared weapon because I am here to challenge for ownership of the *Chyya's* champion."

'Dari's lips thinned. "And just who are you, that the *Chyya* would consider you worthy of crossing blades with his—"

"Silence, 'Dari!" Devtorvas waved his friend to stand down as he strode over to Dohsan. "This isn't about you and Dohsan right now. It's between her and me." A slight smile softening his lips, he faced her, brilliant tangerine eyes boring into hers, seeking answers from her. "If I am not mistaken, this royal fem is issuing a formal challenge. Is this so?"

"It is."

"By what right, other than insult, do you claim the right to demand my man of me?"

"By the ancient right belonging to a vaShafaran Prime. I renounce any claim of insult and declare the right of blood, strength and *pava*. I declare a *Benlat I'Cherzda* quest."

Devtorvas didn't quite manage to conceal his shock, though he did bite back his startled exclamation. "You have claimed the three most ancient rights and I cannot deny you. When would you have this match take place?"

"There are two witnesses present…yourself and your queen. Let the contest take place now, in this area before your throne."

A choked curse, broken off before it could be finished, reached her, pretty much revealed 'Dari's disgust of his involuntary involvement in the upcoming events.

Dohsan fought a smile. Knowing him, understanding his nature, she knew how he chafed at not having some say in an outcome that involved him.

She firmed her jaw along with her resolve. His upset didn't matter. Nothing mattered anymore, but laying claim to the *qarm* she had discovered she couldn't live without.

Her hand trembled on the hilt of her broadsword, remembering her fear when GanR'dari had faced the berserk *qarm*. One misstep, one other *qarm* losing control and joining ranks with the first, could have meant his life. At that moment, she'd known that, had 'Dari died, she'd have chosen to die with him.

"We need to set the limits of this challenge. First, no life threatening wounds are to be given."

"Agreed. It isn't my intention to injure him, after all."

Devtorvas ticked off another point. "The fight is not to last longer than three rounds—best out of three wins…and I will be the sole judge of what constitutes the winning point."

Dohsan stiffened. "How do I know you will be impartial?"

"I'll see to that!" Nnora promised, training a gimlet glare on her spouse. "If I don't believe he's been impartial, he'll find *me* indisposed for a week."

Devtorvas did not appear amused. "I have every intention of being fair. There is no need to threaten me, sweetness."

Nnora gave him a saccharine smile and blew him a kiss. "Just making sure my sister doesn't come up against any 'good-ole-boy' system, dearling."

"Don't I get a say in this?" 'Dari interrupted.

"No!" Dohsan, Devtorvas and Nnora all answered together.

Nnora crossed her arms. "You've messed up every chance you'd had so far. This time, let us handle it."

Dev placed one hand on his friend's shoulder. "I listened to what you said, earlier. That is why I'm taking this action, now."

"You have yet to say what I want to hear," Dohsan said quietly.

GanR'dari met her eyes, his electric green gaze intense and focused. Not taking his eyes off hers, he drew his sword and saluted her. "Then perhaps what you want to hear is, *en garde!*"

Dohsan laughed. "I love it when you talk Earther! When I've won you and have you spread out on my bed, remind me to teach you some other new words."

"Enough!" Dev took Nnora's hand and escorted her to their thrones. "Let us be clear. Should you win this contest, the *qarm*, GanR'dari 'abri GlenglanR'on becomes your mated possession. However, should my champion win this contest you become...what?"

"*My* mated possession," 'Dari demanded, "or I won't fight."

Dohsan inclined her head. Under her breath, she murmured, "I win in either case."

"It is agreed, then? Between you and 'Dari, no matter the outcome, neither Nnora nor I will interfere. Should you win, my commander is yours. Should you lose, he becomes your master. Royal or not..."

"It is agreed." Dohsan tossed her ponytail, flipping the bright red banner over her shoulder. "I for one will welcome your non-interference. I've always enjoyed *new* experiences."

Dev closed his eyes and shook his head. Nnora smothered a laugh against his shoulder.

"Then let the first round begin...now!"

* * *

She brought the fight to him. From the first, she kept the offensive, swinging effectively, wielding her sword with a strength he hadn't suspected she possessed. Time after time, her blows broke through his defenses, landing hard enough to dent his armor, easily winning the first round. There was no way Dev could have called it in his favor without looking like a fool.

His weak performance made him feel kind of foolish.

"What a nice, pretty suit of red armor, 'Dari. Sorry I've dented it up. Don't worry, though, I'll purchase a new suit for you."

"No, thank you. This one is doing the job. Why aren't *you* wearing one?"

She used a combination of lightning fast strikes and subtle attacks against him, delivering a flurry of blows with a fleetness he'd never encountered in another opponent. "My *tlinis* are protected. I haven't worn armor for over two cycles, having advanced beyond the need. Any blow you land will be one I've permitted."

'Dari grit his teeth, grimly determined to win this round. He faced off from the woman he loved, sword raised above his head. Legs braced, he prepared for her first advance, scanning her body for the telltale muscle twitch that always presaged the decision to *move*. "Damned arrogant, aren't you?"

She nodded toward Dev and himself. "I've learned from the best, thanks!"

'Dari dipped his sword and circled the tip, targeting the center of Dohsan's breastplate. With a yell, he moved a split *jern* after she did, rushing her as she brought her sword up in preparation of her attack.

Even with surprise and speed on his side, he failed to connect. He tried crowding her…she wasn't there; he pivoted to engage her from another angle, only to find she'd danced away. She didn't look or sound winded or tired. He was both, and he feared she could go on like this forever. He had to make his move now. Frustrated, he shouted, "Stand still, why don't you!"

"If you can't *keep* up, don't *step* up, old *qarm*!"

A blaze of shame and anger fueled his next moves, even as he found himself envying her for having the breath to tease him. He used his frustration and anger to give him the speed to catch her unawares and force her into an exchange of blows.

Steel rang. Their swords clashed. He pressed her hard. His breath came fast and uneven as he pushed her—pushed himself, more.

He *had* to land a blow. Soon…or he'd lose this second round and the match to her. Dohsan had agility and speed on her side. He had experience and strength… Given a choice right now, he'd pick some of that agility.

By Deth, she was light on her toes, volatile and fiery. Her hair flew about her as she twisted and danced, matching him every step, in every way. Hell, she looked good to him.

He didn't want to fight her, he wanted to fuck her right here, stake his claim on her with Dev and Nnora as witnesses. When this was over, he would bind her to him with every ceremony known to their people. She would never escape him.

He had the advantage close up. There was strength in her arms, but it didn't equal the strength he'd amassed during his years of defending the throne and fighting beside his *Chyya* on the many battlefields of Rb'qarm and Rb'nTraq.

Just before Dev called time for the round, he landed one telling blow.

His arm ached from the impact and he knew her *tlinis* had to be tingling from the vibrations resulting from the bite of his blade into her armored breastplate. Thank Deth that flimsy looking metal bra held up under his severe pounding.

"Hold! Round two goes to GanR'dari. The match now stands at one to one."

Heaving a sigh of relief, he warily disengaged and bowed, retreated to prepare for the next and final round. Dohsan stood her ground, a slight smile on her full lips. "Fortify yourself, 'Dari. I will not be so nice during this next round."

Chapter Seven

She felt good going into the last round. So far, she'd done everything she'd planned, making sure they both had one win to their credit. To judge by Nnora and Dev's expressions, neither suspected she'd engineered 'Dari's winning strike.

Her man was very proud. She didn't want him ashamed or belittled. He needed to be able to hold up his head in the future. Her next move would ensure he received all the sympathy needed to feel he had been at an unfair disadvantage.

"Are you both ready to begin again?"

"Wait." Dohsan faced the thrones. "The hit 'Dari landed has creased my armor. I am having difficulty breathing. May I have permission to remove the plate?"

Nnora giggled. "You want to fight bare-breasted, in the tradition of old Earth Amazons, huh?"

"How is my champion supposed to keep his mind on the fight?"

"That is not my problem. How am I supposed to breathe and fight in a dented breastplate?"

"Do not allow it, *Chyya!*" 'Dari stormed over to them, facial expression fierce. He grabbed Dohsan by the arm. "What are you thinking about? You are wearing little enough armor now. If you take that off, how will you protect yourself?"

Dohsan covered his hand with hers. "First, this match is supposed to be mid-level, no serious injuries. Make sure you don't strike to maim. Second, trust to my skill. I hold master's rank among the vaShafaran warriors. I haven't been bested in years."

"That's all well and good, but Dev is right. How am I supposed to keep my eyes on your sword? How would you like it if I chose to fight naked?"

Laughing, she let her gaze rove up and down his sweat-glistened body, let him see her enjoyment of that idea. "I would love it. I wouldn't have any problem keeping my eyes on your *sword!*"

'Dari shook his head, eyes dancing. "What am I going to do with you?"

She leaned over and licked a bead of sweat off his cheek, teasingly ran her tongue along the line of his jaw and chin. Drawing close enough to breathe in his distinctive smell, she whispered in his ear, "Fuck me. Until I melt all over your *cherzda,* until I scream!"

"That's going to happen regardless of which one of us wins," he promised, backing up and raising his sword.

"You better believe it." She danced away, unhooking the clasp of her embossed *tlini* armor and flinging it aside.

The *Chyya* looked between his champion and his bond-sister. "I take it this means you are now ready to resume."

"One more moment," 'Dari requested, lowering his sword and bowing to Dev.

"What now?" Nnora sighed, resting her chin on her elbow. "You both must hurry this along. While entertaining, I still would like to get back to our chambers before Devtoria goes to sleep."

"It is just... I think I should even the odds between us. If Dohsan will fight bare-breasted, I shall doff my own armor. I don't want it said I bested her due to being better protected."

"Good point, 'Dari. We will wait for you to remove your hauberk. Let me help you." Dev stepped down and came toward his friend, assisted him in taking off the heavy body armor. "There, that's done. Now, let's get this last round started. I am in agreement with Nnora. I don't want to miss my evening's play with Toria."

"I am ready." 'Dari retrieved his sword and faced Dohsan, a slight smile playing on his broad mouth. "Let us finish this business between us, love."

Dohsan raised her sword in answer. "You mock me, but one day you will call me that in all seriousness."

He didn't answer, just stepped into her space, forcing her to defend, rather than attack. He seemed to have caught his rhythm, matched her move for move. Parrying her thrusts, he met her swings with the flat of his sword, drove her back and back until she neared the far wall of the *throla*.

In sheer strength, he bested her, but again, he found he simply could not match her agility and quickness. Again and again, she slipped from his trap, brought the attack to him and skipped away.

She was having a grand time…until he tripped.

Swords engaged, pressed chest to chest, they grasped each other's off arm, fighting for the ascendancy. Using a trick learned in the Jakwylla, she twisted and came up under his arm, blocked his backswing with an upward thrust of her own.

With horror, she felt his foot slip on a rough patch of flooring. His arm slipped as he fought for balance, sword clattering discordantly as it fell to the ground.

"No, 'Dari!" Her swing initiated, she cried out, realizing she couldn't stop the stroke. Without his sword, 'Dari could not block the blow and she'd put all her might into it, believing he would be able to counter it.

With a cry of denial, she flipped in mid-air, flung her arm wide and released her sword, sending it flying from her hand. It struck the flagstones, the ringing of steel against rock loud in her ears as she dropped awkwardly from her desperate somersault.

The pain of her fall struck swiftly and she gasped, cradling an aching elbow. "Damn it!" she hissed, coming up on her knees, rocking back and forth. Tears flooded her eyes. She fought to stop them from falling.

A beloved hand came into her blurred line of vision. 'Dari reached down and helped her up, running his hands over every inch of her before gathering her into a tight hug. "You are hurt. What were you thinking, beloved?"

She winced when she straightened her elbow but didn't hesitate to return his embrace. Burying her head in his chest, she swallowed against the pain. "I had no choice. If you are hurt, it will never be by my hand!"

Without turning his head and breaking their gaze, he raised his voice so it reached the thrones. "I yield! Let this be over."

"No! I am the injured one. According to our agreement, the round should go to you."

Devtorvas stood and offered his hand to Nnora, raising her to her feet. Bending his head, they whispered furiously. Dohsan strained to catch an inkling of what they discussed so vehemently.

Silent at last, they clasped hands and approached the two combatants. "We have made a decision and it shall be final."

Still entwined, Dohsan and 'Dari faced the two rulers.

"Frankly, I don't understand everything about this vaShafaran sect you espouse, Dohsan, however I do know this— Nnora rules me in truth, allowing the opposite only in seeming. Looking back, I realize my father had the same relationship with my mother. We *qarm* might think ourselves in charge, but we only fool each other."

"In the end," Nnora interjected, "who rules doesn't matter. All that matters is who loves. You've both proved you love each other."

"So this is our ruling. This round is finished and declared tied. That makes the match a draw." He smiled.

"This places the ball back in your court. As agreed, neither Nnora nor I will interfere in your courtship. That means we will not side with either one of you. However, I do have one order. Your father arrives next week, so you need to reach some sort of agreement within the week."

"Yes, sir." 'Dari managed to salute without removing his arm from about Dohsan's waist.

"One more thing for you to consider, 'Dari… For what it's worth, Nnora's rule over me is not onerous. Being under her control has some mighty fine compensations."

"Dev?"

"Yes, Dohsan?"

"Thanks for the endorsement, but shouldn't you be heading back to the nursery? You don't want to miss GlenDevtoria's bedtime."

Nnora laughed aloud. "Oh, you are so cheeky! I think that's our cue to get lost, husband."

* * *

GanR'dari escorted Dohsan to her chambers and carefully closed the doors behind him.

She watched him lock the door, eyebrows rising in twin question marks. "Are you planning on staying with me?"

"Forever," he answered matter-of-factly. "Before forever begins, though, I've got something to say to you and a situation to clear up."

She sat on the side of her bed, leaned her weight back on her bent elbows. "I'm all ears."

"No, you're arrogant and overbearing, but no one could ever say you actually *listen.*"

Dohsan snapped upright, her indolent pose abandoned in favor of her indignant reaction. "You have some nerve insulting me, buddy!"

"You insult yourself, lessen your reputation by constantly reacting like a *betweener.* You are a grown fem, now. Time you started acting like one."

"If I'm not mistaken, you're about to treat me like one."

"Not before I mete out justified punishment. I cannot believe you put yourself forward to all those *qarm* this afternoon. What were you using for brain cells?"

"I can't believe you're still angry! Why can't you just be thankful we both managed to escape that mob uninjured?"

Baring his teeth in a caricature of a smile, GanR'dari narrowed the gap between them. The smell of her arousal bathed his hungry senses in liquid lust. Desire and anger rode him hard, glinted in his eyes. "*One* of us has *yet* to escape the event uninjured."

"You don't frighten me, GanR'dari 'abri GlenglanR'on! I am a princess of the blood royal. I just bested you in a fair fight. What do you think you can do to me?"

"Actually, the fight was declared a tie."

Dohsan planted her fists on her hips. "We both know better, though."

He smiled evilly. "True. Thanks to your underhanded machinations, though, no one *but* you and I know who the better swordsperson is."

Through narrowed eyes, he noted her rising excitement. His nostrils flared, drinking in the sharp spike of her honeyed fragrance. It wafted about him, richly fertile, life affirming...giving him an accurate measure of her true feelings. The rapid beat of her pulse at neck and breast, the unsteady warble of her voice gave added proof he had breached her vaunted control. He barely managed to swallow his triumphant shout.

Bet she hates those signs of weakness. I'll show her just how weak we both are in the face of our mutual bond...

"You asked what I could do to you. According to the command of our king, we are to resolve the issues of mating between us without bringing others into our dispute. Therefore, I guess the answer would be whatever I choose to, Princess Dohsan 'abret Glenbrevchanka. You are about to learn your *royal* blood has no significance between us. It will not protect you when just punishment is due." His gaze zeroed in on her throat, watched it move convulsively as she swallowed.

He captured her gaze and then deliberately let his eyes drop to chest level, let them cling there for long tarns before moving back up and watching her pulse throb hotly at neck and temple. When her nipples rose to tent her thin shift, a fierce, heady joy welled up within him. He thrilled at the knowledge that just his glance could move her and cause her to flower for him.

"Let me tell you the coming order of events. First, you *will* bare your bottom for me to administer just retribution. After that, I will—"

"'Dari, I could not bear the thought of seeing you killed or hurt."

"I know that, *cherzda'va*. You proved it beyond any doubt during that last round."

"Then where is my fault? I honestly don't see how you could label my trying to protect you wrong—"

Her look of perplexity softened his heart. The sincerity in her voice convinced him she truly didn't understand the rashness of her impulsive behavior, nor how insulted he had been by them.

"I'm glad your actions were motivated by a desire to help and not as an attempt to publicly flaunt what you consider to be your dominant status."

Her jaw tightened, eyes turned flinty. "If you *really* knew me, you would have known I would never make our personal interactions a subject of public observation."

Damn it, that smacked of truth, reminded him of a facet of her character he should have taken into consideration.

His chagrin knew no end. "Dohsan, you are right. I am so sor—"

"Never mind that now," she gritted out, waving his apology away. "Just tell me why my actions were so reprehensible in your eyes."

"Baby-fem, our government rests upon the shoulders of Devtorvas and Nnora but its protection also rests upon mine as *Chyya's* champion and commander of the Royal Armed Forces. The actions of those *qarms*—publicly accosting a fem as they did, tells us how close they are to turning rebel. The only authority those kinds of males understand is law backed by force. A weak champion infers a weak Throne, endangering the entire kingdom. Your declaration made me appear weak in the eyes of those men, today."

She nodded, lowering her eyes in self-disgust. "I can understand that. Believe me, that *wasn't* the message I meant to get across."

"I believe you. That is why your punishment will be tempered with pleasure."

"What gives you the right to punish me?" Frowning blackly, she backed up until her shoulders met the wall. "Perhaps I'll punish you!"

"When and if you feel the situation warrants it, baby-fem, you bring it on. You see—" slowly stalking her, he removed his tunic, baring his massive chest as he relentlessly closed the gap between them, "I have decided how we are going to work this domination thing…"

Her head snapped up, eyes narrowing. "Oh, yeah? *You've* decided, huh?"

"I have. Are you going to accept your punishment docilely? Or are we going to have our second fight?" He watched her carefully, noting the calculating look in her beautiful eyes.

"What makes you so sure you would win?"

"I would win because I'd be determined to do whatever was necessary while you've already proven you'd never do anything to hurt me."

"If I let you do this, are you going to hurt *me?*"

He chose to answer the real question behind her query. "Dohsan, you've proven you know me better than I know you by protecting my pride in front of your sister and my ruler. You have to know that I love you and will never *harm* you."

Loosing the ties at his waist, he allowed his pants to slide off his hips. His *cherzda* rose high and hard, all fifteen *nicrons* arching tight and throbbing. The sound of her choked off moan pleased him, further hardening his staff at the same time softening his heart.

"That doesn't mean I'm not going to heat up your cute ass for making yourself some sort of prize in that *Benlat-something* contest. Now, back to the question of who will rule in our mating—"

He could almost feel her wide-eyed, lustful stare burning him as he brought his body flush against hers. She didn't resist as he slowly divested her of the few items she wore, kissing and caressing each *nicron* of flesh as he uncovered it. Words were unnecessary between them, her heated gaze and rich flowering telling him everything he needed to know.

"This bonding is going to be a full partnership. You want domination. I can't argue that you've earned it, but I demand some control of my own."

His hands caressed her breasts, plumping the ripe curves, loving the resilient give of her feminine flesh under his demanding hands. "Give and take, baby, equally. That's what I'm offering, what you made possible for me to do without losing my honor or the respect of my king. So, if you feel motivated to give me an order in public, I'll obey you. In return, you had best be prepared to obey the ones I give you in private."

Her low, responsive groans had his balls drawing up, his *terat* dilating. His abdominal muscles contracted, causing his *cherzda* to jerk against her soft belly. He took her lips, his tongue voracious and demanding, parted hers to dip into the silky wet confines of her delicious mouth. His own moans rumbled from him as he ate at her, his hands roaming everywhere, touching everything.

Reverently, worshipfully, he palmed her *pava*, one adoring finger sliding through the slick fluids seeping from her swollen folds. Boldly, the finger advanced, eased its way past the tight ring of muscle at her entrance. Instantly, the incredible pressure and heat of her inner muscles clamping down upon his thick digit spun all rational thought out of his head. Reeling under the most powerful shaft of desire he'd ever endured, 'Dari dragged in a desperate gulp of oxygen and let it out with a harsh groan. The very air he breathed carried her essence, her unique flavor.

That quickly, for him, playtime ended.

Chapter Eight

The knee-weakening feel of his solitary finger was not enough. She needed more, needed his cock to fill her to overflowing. Ever since she'd had the thick head inside her virgin folds, she had wanted nothing more than to have him intimately stretching her, filling her full and flooding her with his seed.

She waited, breath stalled in her throat, for him to continue. Taking matters into her own hands, she bucked her hips, seeking more of him, trying to impale herself on his quiescent hand, only to have him retreat from her. Her long-held patience broke on a despairing wail. "'Dari!"

"Your scent is strong upon the air, baby-fem, telling me you hunger for me as much as my *terat* thirst for the first taste of your luscious *tlinis*. However, first things first..."

His mouth tightened as he eased his finger, then his hand from her clinging flesh. Her insides contracted, seeking the substance and heft that had just filled her. Its lack made her feel empty and lonely. She sighed, mourning the loss of his presence inside her.

She wanted to scream in frustration as he absently placed his finger between his lips, licking off her juices. He met her eyes and she saw the glimmer of lust in his disappear, replaced by implacable resolve.

"I must administer your punishment before pleasure, baby-fem." He had the nerve to smile, full lips quirking in amusement.

Her fingers, her palm, her hand itched to slap him. Hells bells, her entire body wanted to slap against his...*repeatedly*. He didn't fool her. His years as military commander had served him well in all walks of his life. He was used to battle. Now he battled her for sexual supremacy.

Yet, she could not deny her careless actions were deserving of punishment. Her brothers had warned her about the danger of venturing out on the streets. She had let her temper overcome her good sense and a *qarm* had died. It didn't matter that he had brought his demise upon himself. What mattered was her lack of responsible behavior. Had a fem under her command disregarded a valid warning and placed others in danger because of her lack of control, she'd have ordered *and* administered the fem's whipping, herself.

Dohsan squared her shoulders. A good leader accepted the consequences of her actions. She just hated to let 'Dari think he could orchestrate every step of this dance. He thought himself so smart. Every move he made, he planned far in advance. Though she wouldn't argue about the upcoming spanking, she would show him he could not predict her responses.

"Fine. Equality between us, I believe you said. So after my punishment, we will deal with yours." She almost laughed aloud at his arrested look. How had he thought this would work?

'Dari stiffened. His entire body screamed unease and wariness. "My punishment? What infraction do you hold against me?"

He hadn't taken her comment the way she meant it.

"You were derelict in your duty. You left me unsatisfied, earlier, and I will not tolerate that."

His face smoothed out, eyes flashed with humor. He nodded. "So be it."

"Now that's settled," Dohsan murmured, "how do you want me?"

His eyes blazed at her question and she glanced down to see his cock leaking *zhi* from the main opening at the tip and from the tiny slits along the circumference. She couldn't resist the opportunity to tease, "That badly, huh?"

Eyes sparking with lust, he ignored her dig to turn from her and sit on the side of her bed. He patted his thighs. "Come lie across my lap."

"How am I supposed to fit with that pole taking up all the room?" She eyed his bobbing cock and swallowed thickly, hungry to taste the thick confection that curled toward his stomach, the wide head higher than his belly button. The apertures circling the broad tip seeped *zhi*—the golden, slippery fluid that enhanced a fem's sexual enjoyment while it softened and relaxed the inner muscle of her *pava*.

His chuckle turned into a stomach-rippling laugh. Gods, he was beautiful...and soon to be all hers.

"Tuck my *cherzda* between your legs."

She flashed him a bright smile. "Gladly."

An exhilarating rush of fear-tinged excitement zinged through her, causing her to gasp for air as she advanced on her chosen mate. She found the situation both chilling and intriguing. Her heart tripped, her pulse thundered and her nipples hardened. Thick and excited, they accurately revealed her arousal, jutting forward as if to beg for the attention of his *terat.* A helpless whimper escaped her parted lips.

Standing before him, she chewed her inner cheek as she contemplated how to mount his thighs. His cock really did present an almost insurmountable obstacle. "I think it will be better if I do this in increments."

Kneeling at his left side, she slowly slid her torso forward. Making sure to brush his thighs with her hanging breasts, she eased up and over, allowing her body to drag over his tumescent erection. She paused, let her nipples dance over the head, then, bracing her hands on his sturdy thighs, she reared up and opened her legs, rubbing her naked mound against his hard length.

Beneath her belly, his muscles jumped—all of them—and she swore she felt his cock lengthen another *nicron* or two. Her body wept with joy at the thought of soon cradling all that masculine power and heat within her tight confines. Riding him would be an adventure she'd never want to end. All the excitement she'd need in life.

When she had dragged out the mounting as long as he would allow, she took his cock in hand and pressed it snugly between her thighs. The hot, hard bar branded the soft flesh of her inner thighs, so thick and heavy she had to strain to close her thighs about it. Her *pava* greeted him with a gush of sweet scent and she rode the pole of flesh, slicking it with her moisture.

"You finished?"

His dry tone did not upset her because she could feel his increased breathing all along her body. His tenseness and terse words betrayed his growing arousal. "If you have to ask, then I haven't begun."

The feel of his rough hands smoothing the skin of her bottom had her squirming and eager for more. Never had she thought to enjoy such dark games of discipline and dominance. She could not believe the titillation pouring through her, wrought by being in her present position.

"Feel free to holler..."

"Only when I come."

"Soon, I promise." His dark vow had her squirming and his hand flattened on her raised bottom in silent warning.

The first sharp smack caught her unawares. Her back bowed. His hand rested in the small of her back, focusing her, holding her, calming her. She held her breath before letting it flow out on a shaky stream. "You don't believe in warming up, do you?"

The second swat landed on the opposite cheek, branding her flesh with a stroke of fire. Her legs squeezed together as every muscle in her body tensed against the shock of pain, trapping his cock between her spasming thighs. She had no ready quip prepared this time. The heat slowly faded as she lay with her cheek cushioned against his hair-dusted leg, fighting the urge to cry. Pain and pleasure swirled together, so tightly entwined she couldn't distinguish one from the other.

Five more stinging slaps followed in quick succession. Each time, her thighs squeezed the thick cock surging between her legs, milking it strongly with her involuntary spasms. When she heard the sharp tortured groan sound above her head, she realized her captor suffered with her, as affected by this punishing as she was.

Hot liquid spilling from the slits along the head of his *cherzda* branded her flesh and the pain of the spanking mutated, changed into sparking, stinging pleasure as she concentrated on moving in such a way as to coax his cock into leaking more of his pre-ejaculate.

Her entire body shimmied under the hot lash of ecstasy. Her *pava* burned and pulsed, ached and wept as his strong hand slapped against her ass with just enough force to rock her dripping sex, her swollen, distended clitoris down on his rampant cock.

"Dohsan, this won't end until you lie still!"

She didn't want it to ever end. They both knew the punishment portion of the spanking had ended long ago.

"I cannot hold," she cried hoarsely. Her voice lowered, whispered words hovered on the edge of wonder. "I'm going to come!"

Suddenly, she felt herself flipped over. Her belly and thighs, covered with their mingled juices, grew chilled in the cool air of the chamber. Her nipples beaded in arousal, standing stiff and firm under his admiring gaze.

"By Deth, fem! Lift to me, I would taste your nipples!"

The growled demand made her weak with longing. She sprawled across his lap, his cock riding the small of her back as he bent his head and latched on to one upstanding nipple.

His mouth was not gentle. His lips tightened about the stiff, hard little knot, his tongue stabbed and prodded, teeth nipped before biting down just this side of pain, sending a frisson of crackling energy through her bloodstream. He raised his head, eyes burning as he looked into her half-closed eyes. "Your *tlinis* taste of sweet-ripened fruit. I could feast on you all day long..."

Bending and taking her other nipple between his teeth, he worried the tip.

She mewled, lost in the consuming flames of her *pava*, unable to articulate her needs. Arching her back, feeding him more of her aching flesh, she wordlessly demanded he accept the willing offering of her body.

Lightning exploded behind her eyelids as one masculine hand stroked boldly down her quivering belly and questing fingers opened her fleshy lips, using her own slick cream to ease his way into her heated depths. Two coated fingers slid up, twisted, pressing against a spot that had her lifting her hips and crying out, desperate to enhance the feelings spiraling through her. Legs shifting restlessly, she moaned a plea, "'Dari, seat my nipples...please...make me burn...'"

A gentle hand dropped to her hot bottom cheeks, soothing and petting the still heated flesh, his fingers tracing the marks he'd placed on her, his touch comforting and arousing at once. He turned and placed her on the bed, covering her with his body.

"You are very used to having your nipples seated, baby-fem. Under the circumstances, I think we will save that for another time."

The note of—hurt jealousy?—in his voice had her opening her eyes, examining his beloved features. In a face taut with barely controlled lust, his iridescent green eyes glittered brightly. Jaws tight, lips drawn back in a feral grimace, he reared over her, his massive chest hovering just above her reaching nipples. This close, she could see his *terat* dilating hungrily. She frowned. "If you fuck me without the seating, we cannot exchange the gift."

"I know." He lapped at an impudent nipple, opened his lips and sucked it up into his mouth, drawing hard on the tight point. "I've waited so long for you, love. I cannot bear the thought of sharing you just yet. I would delay our first child for a while longer."

She squirmed under the lashing of his tongue. "But it is not necessary to forgo your pleasure. I have studied the vaShafaran ways. There need not be a child, even with the sharing."

His mouth stilled on her breast. A moment later, he pushed himself up onto his outstretched arms, his bulky muscles easily holding his weight. A smile parted his lips as he bumped foreheads with her, dipped to take her mouth in a wild tangle of tongues and teeth.

Panting and gasping for air, they broke apart, only to re-engage again and again. He slid down on her, nuzzled her breasts, bringing his mouth into play. Nipping her flesh with lip-covered teeth, he licked a sizzling path between her sloping mounds and then returned to her nipples, sucking and tugging on them until they stood bright red and stiffly erect.

Catching her eye, he swallowed. "Know that from this moment on, your *tlinis* belong to me. My *terat* are the only ones that will milk you of your sweet gift. I will kill any *qarm* who dares usurp my place." He eased down upon her, lining her nipples up with his dilating *terat* and paused.

Don't stop! The anticipation will kill me.

Liquid fire seeped from her *pava*, coated the lips of her flowering center. Through her open mouth, she drew in unsteady gasps of air, arousal stealing her breath.

Who was doing all that whimpering?

"For Deth's sake, 'Dari...all your teasing is driving me insane!" Curling her hands around his forearms, she tugged sharply.

With a tortured groan, he let his arms collapse and fell on her, seating her nipples in one heated stroke.

His gift-producing enzymes attacked her buried nipples causing Dohsan to scream, as her breasts were flooded with burning pleasure. Her nipples pulsed under the stinging bites of complex proteins, her body convulsed as he drove her sensitive tips deeper into his clasping mouths.

Chills spilled across her chest, skittered down her arms and tingled in her belly. She lifted her arms and embraced his shoulders, anchored her fingers in the thick fall of his hair and tugged his mouth down to hers. She aggressively took his lips, dipping between them to tango with his tongue.

Opening her legs, she bent her knees, letting him settle heavily into the cradle of her splayed thighs. She wrapped her legs about his hips and arched into the heated bulk of his groin.

"I want you, now. Inside...hot, full and powerful. Join with me." The words rasped from her dry throat. She didn't care that they revealed her need, her desperation.

Snarling with impatience, he drew back, fisted his *cherzda* and aimed the huge head at her dripping entry.

Her pulse exploded, pounding like a wrecking ball at the wall of her chest. She squirmed, shimmying to help him align their sexes and threw back her head, crying out in triumph as he sank into her, his agate-hard length surging deep and sure.

Beneath her roving hands, powerful muscles in his lower body bunched, coiled and recoiled as his thighs spread her legs wider apart. His hips pistoned back and forth, driving his *cherzda* deep, withdrawing only to pound back into her, filling her and fulfilling her. He kept his eyes open, fused with hers as he fucked her with a focused determination that thrilled her to her soul.

Synchronizing his strokes with the milking of her nipples, he set up a mind-destroying rhythm that soon had her clinging to him in sexual greed, hungry for more of his masterful loving.

"Yes! That's what I want...fuck me hard, 'Dari...fuck me 'til I come..."

"Whose *tlinis* are these?" he ground out, pushing down on her captured tips, forcing part of her areolas into the churning mouths of his *terat.*

"Yours!"

"Whose *nippa* is this? Who is the only one you will come for?"

"It's yours, beloved, my *nippa* is yours. Let me come for you, only you! Please...*please...* 'Dari...make it *end!*"

She writhed on the low bed, wild sensations detonating in her breasts and loins, sparking in her veins like earthling firecrackers. Unable to identify the flooding stimuli as pain or bliss, agony or ecstasy, she hung suspended between the two, lost and found all at once. She exploded into eternity, held fast in the arms of her bonded mate.

Sated and happy, GanR'dari sprawled amid the rumpled sheets. Drenched in sweat, wrung out from their explosive, gritty sex, his chest heaved as he filled his starved lungs with air. Rolling his weary head to the right, he glanced over at her. "What exactly is a *Benlat I'Cherzda* quest?"

Gathering enough energy to lean up and give him a sleepy kiss, Dohsan chuckled. Snuggling against his bottom, she tugged the covers over them before slipping an arm around his waist to grip his sleeping *cherzda*. Settling down beside him, she kissed the back of his neck. "Two days from now, you'll find out more than you want to know..."

Chapter Nine

"Wake up, sleepy head. I have a spanking to administer before you report to work." A stinging slap to his bare flank accompanied her words.

'Dari jerked upright, eyes wide and unfocused, hand scrabbling for his sword. A bachelor on a world with few women, he was unaccustomed to waking with someone else in the room.

His mind sharpened and his eyes focused quickly enough when naked *tlinis*—attached to the most luscious body he'd seen in cycles—swayed into view. He couldn't resist taking one pebbled tip between his lips.

A soft feminine groan sounded above his head. Two hands bracketed his cheeks as he drew on the tasty nibblet.

"Aahh, 'Dari! You do that so well." Dohsan swayed forward, pulled by the tugging on her nipple and the drawing of his hands on her hips.

Bringing one knee up to rest on the mattress beside him, she leaned over and offered her other breast.

He gladly took advantage, switched his fervent attention to the other thick nubbin and gave it a serious tongue lapping. He pulled her closer, wrapped his arms about her waist and swung her down to the mattress. He rolled with her, came up over her, his mouth never releasing the morsel he'd captured.

Dohsan shifted her legs, opened them to cradle his hips between her thighs. Head thrown back, she lifted her torso, making herself more available to his mouth. "That feels incredible. The touch of your hand, your mouth—I've grown addicted to you."

'Dari pulled back enough to search her eyes, letting her plump tip pop free of his lips. He was always shocked whenever he encountered her openness. Another fem would have played coy, would have made him work to discover his worth in her eyes. Her willingness to expose herself to him was one of the things he loved about her.

"I love your scent. I'm dizzy with the aroma of your sweet *pava*. You smell of life, of hope, of family and home."

She ran a hand through the thick strands of his hair, her fingers tangling in the snags their night of tumultuous loving had placed there. Her beautiful smile lit up her face. "I like hearing you say that. Tell me more."

"What more would you hear…that I am through fighting you? That I do not want to live without you? All that is true."

She didn't stop stroking his hair. "I hear a 'but' in there."

"But, I don't know if I can live with you, the way you expect. If I do as you wish, I would have to renounce my loyalty to Glendevtorvas and Glennora."

"True."

"I don't know if I can do that. I've followed Dev for so long... He's my friend, as well as my *Chyya.*"

"I understand. No! I really do," she insisted, resting her head on his shoulder when he pulled away and sat up on the side of the bed.

"I know you do." He turned back to her, wrapped his arms about her naked body and holding on tightly. "Sometimes, I think you understand me better than I do myself. You knew I wouldn't be able to come to you without my pride intact, so you staged all that elaborate swordplay. We both know you could easily have bested me in the first few *jerns.*"

"I didn't want your pride. I didn't even want the win, just you. You are all I've ever wanted."

"And I want you, baby-fem. So why do I sense there is still a problem between us?"

"I need more than you by my side. I need to fulfill the role fate meant me to play. Our people are facing a major crisis and I plan to be at the forefront of finding the solution."

"And you can't be my mate and do that?"

"Oh, I can be your mate, but I refuse to be your *cherzda'va.* They are not one and the same."

'Dari's shoulders slumped in dejection at her seeming rejection. "Then what is to become of us? I love you, and want no other. You have spoiled me for anyone else."

"You must submit to the *Benlat 'I Cherzda.* Only when you have proved your loyalty and willingness to serve will I allow the bonding to take place between us."

"Then bring it on! I am ready to declare my love for you. Let all of Rb'qarm and Rb'nTraq know what you mean to me."

A slight smile turned her lips into an inverted bow. Placing her hands on his shoulders, she created a pocket of space between them. "You will gladly declare your love, but will you be as quick to declare yourself mated to a vaShafaran?"

He shrugged one shoulder and canted his head in an "I don't know" gesture. Pulling her back into a tight embrace, he nuzzled the soft flesh at the bend of her neck and shoulders. "I honestly do not know what your being vaShafaran entails, what your beliefs will demand of me. Before I can give you a balanced answer, I need to learn a lot more."

"A willingness to learn and an open mind is all I can ask."

"Will you teach me?"

"Everything. Gladly. But first, I will teach you about discipline."

He stiffened. After a moment's reflection, he relaxed with a chuckle. "You may be the better swordsperson, but I am stronger than you and more massively built. I doubt you could manage to hurt me with those tender hands of yours."

"Ah, but I never intend to hurt you. Besides, you're right about the relative strength. I'd only hurt myself if I tried to spank you. I have…something else in mind."

He quirked an eyebrow at her, not sure he trusted her devious mind when it came to cooking up torture schemes. He drew a laugh from her when he put both palms together in a prayerful attitude and begged, "Please try not to damage my tender sensibilities!"

Still chuckling, Dohsan gestured for him to lie on the bed. "Flat on your back, *qarm*, and stay put. I'll be right back."

Obedient to her command, 'Dari lay there, turning only his head to watch her sashay across the room, the full globes of her ass undulating gently as she walked. Salivating, he kept his eyes on her until she disappeared into the bathing facility.

Once she left his view, he allowed his eyes to drift shut and willed himself to be patient. In the silence, he caught the quiet snick of a cabinet opening and closing, then the soft pad of her feet as she returned to him.

Something small but dense dented the mattress by his shoulder and he turned his head toward it. Her words reached him before his eyes were fully open.

"Don't open your eyes. I want you to experience this with no distractions."

Immediately, 'Dari squeezed his eyes shut and returned his head to its original position. "All right, baby-fem, do your worst!"

One hand coasted down his chest, accompanied by a deep-throated purr. She dipped her forefinger into the deep well of one *terat* as she murmured, "Or, perhaps...my best, *sh'ta*. We shall soon see."

He lay beneath her questing hands, quiescent but far from peaceful. His *terat* stung and burned, more stimulated than they had been for a very long time. His *cherzda* throbbed and swelled, ever hopeful for a hot, snug channel to invade.

"My sister's foster-sister created a special potion for her.

"The instructions are easy: First, one brushes this potion on the skin and allows it to be absorbed. When wet with water or saliva, the doctored skin will tingle and burn. It is supposed to feel somewhat like our *tlinis* feel when covered with the enzymes inside your *terat*. I've always thought being seated felt like stinging, sparking fireworks. You'll have to tell me what it feels like to you."

'Dari groaned in anticipation. He'd heard fantastical tales of Nnora's magic potion, whispered in awestruck tones by a deliriously happy Dev. "Oh, yeah, do me, baby!"

A soft brush wafted almost weightlessly across his *terat*, dipped into the not-so-shallow depression and swirled around, coating every *nicron* of flesh with a viscous, spicy substance. The hot fragrance wafted about them, wreathing a spell of excitement, heightening their arousal.

"I smell your flowering, tangy and ripe on the air...the fragrance is making me hungry."

"You smell me and the potion. Lori put a lot of cinnamon, a *Terran* herb in it. Do not worry, I will feed your passions soon enough." Her calm words did nothing to soothe him as she continued painting his skin as she spoke.

She obviously intended to take her time torturing him, and he lay back, determined to take whatever she dished out. Gathering his resolve, he sought some distraction, something to keep his mind off grabbing her, throwing her under him and fucking her brains out.

"You're a mystic, aren't you? Earlier today, what I witnessed was you, having a vision. Isn't that true?"

The brush paused. "I call them 'seeings,' but yes, I am a third level mystic—yet another thing you must come to terms with."

"What did you see?"

She resumed painting. "Why do you want to know?"

'Dari shifted under her gently laid strokes, moaning as she carefully coated his *sirat* and *cherzda*. "Your face... I've never seen a more graphic rendering of pure lust. I hoped you'd seen a future where we are together."

Dohsan sighed. "I have seen many such futures…and many that showed us locked in mortal combat. *Seeings* do not reveal the future so much as show the possible results of treading a certain path. We do not write the future in stone, 'Dari, but in the sands of our changing and fluid decisions. A man with a bright future can make one wrong turn and blight his chances forever."

"I don't want to hear philosophy, Dohsan," he interrupted, fighting for the discipline to continue in blind stillness. Imbuing his voice with all the pleading he could manage, he begged, "Please tell me what you saw yesterday. I need to know what put that look on your face because I want to be the only one responsible for making you look like that."

Dohsan's hands cradled his cheeks, her breath fresh and flowery in his face. Kisses—delivered by lips soft as the snows of Veralla—touched down at forehead, cheeks and chin before honing in on his mouth. Her questing tongue met and greeted his, entangling in a slick, spicy interchange that set his hips pumping. "You are such a sweet *qarm*. I saw the two of us—our bodies entangled in sweaty sheets—joined and locked in love. I heard you caution me to silence lest we wake the children."

Knowing she'd seen them as a bonded couple, hearing that even one of their possible futures held the promise of children, brought tears to his eyes. "Will you ride me, Dohsan? Ride me, baby-fem. Put me out of my misery."

She laughed at his exaggeration. "Oh, *qarm*, we have yet to begin. Do not fret… I shall take diligent care of you."

"That is what I'm afraid of!"

Eyes still closed, he sensed Dohsan moving away from him. A whoosh of displaced air signaled her return.

"I am placing a *cherzda* inhibitor around this mighty staff, 'Dari."

His muscles locked in apprehension. "An inhibitor...? Why?"

"I don't want your *zhi* to seep out and wet the surrounding skin, yet. I don't think you could handle the sensations one on top of the other. We need to space them out carefully."

He tried to relax. "Please don't tighten it too much. Those things hurt!"

A stinging slap to his belly told him she didn't like hearing that.

"And just when have you had occasion to use an inhibitor?"

"When on patrol all the guards wear one. We usually put it on while limp to prevent an erection."

"Oh, well, in that case," she leaned over and placed an apologetic kiss on his flat stomach, "I'm sorry for the slap. I thought you'd used it to maintain an erection for longer than usual."

"Who has been available to play games like that with me, fem? I am not into *qarm* and we have had no viable fem for cycles. Even now, a flowering fem is worth her weight in Sirrilian silk."

"Lucky you, then, to have one of your own," she said, voice coming from the vicinity of his waist. Her fingers gripped his swollen *cherzda* firmly as she placed the ring around his turgid flesh and tightened it down. "Oh, my, don't you look delicious!"

"Thanks for the compliment," he grumbled, disgruntled over having yet to receive any hint of satisfaction. "If I could tempt you into *tasting...*"

"Oh, I intend to do just that, beloved."

She climbed on top of him, straddling his waist, her weight settling snug and comfortable upon him. She swept her hands up and down his chest, spread her fingers over his shoulders. "I thought I wanted you to keep your eyes closed, but now I believe you should open them. I want to see your reaction in your beautiful eyes."

Slowly, savoring each increment, 'Dari lifted his lashes to find Dohsan bent over him, her lips hovering only *nicrons* away from his.

A smile curved her generous mouth. "Do you know how I justified falling in love with you?"

Intrigued at the thought, he shook his head, hoping she intended to tell him what had inspired his greatest blessing. "No. Tell me."

"When I realized we had matching eyes. Growing up in a family where all the eyes were the same color but mine, I felt like a freak. Then I saw you and everything snapped into place. I just knew we belonged together. I know it was a stupid *'tweener* reasoning, but..."

"No, it wasn't stupid at all. It was very sweet and very true. We belong together."

"So you admit to being mine?"

"How could I belong to anyone else? Who else has yellow-green eyes?"

She laughed so hard, her head came to rest on his chest, her body rocked against his as she erupted in chuckles. His own mouth widened in a lighthearted grin as he gazed into her happy, carefree face. It was so rare that he saw her relaxed and playful. 'Dari realized the rambunctious *'tweener* he'd been drawn to all those cycles ago had matured into a caring, responsible fem. He would never understand why she'd chosen to fall in love with him.

She finally gained control over her rampant amusement and sat up, hands splayed on his chest. Her rounded bottom rested full on his surging cock as she circled his *terat* with both forefingers.

"I want you to suck my *tlinis*, 'Dari. Make them good and wet."

"I love your *tlinis*, baby. Bring them here…"

She leaned over and offered him her bounty, her full breasts swaying gently before him. His mouth opened eagerly and he took one pointed tip inside, drawing on it as if it constituted his only source of nourishment.

"Now the other one—" She tugged her flesh out of his grasping lips.

Reluctantly giving up his treasure, 'Dari rooted at her breast, blindly seeking the other nipple. Latching on, he drew it deep, pulling on it with the frantic rhythm of rising lust.

"Slurp on them, get them sopping wet."

He obeyed, glad for the opportunity to do what he'd been dying to do since awakening this glowrise.

Her voice sounded gruff when she issued her next commands. He smiled, sure his expertise had something to do with her eroding control. "Scoot up on the bed some. I want you half reclining when you seat my nipples."

It only took a moment for him to position himself according to her instructions. "Like this?"

"Perfect." She took a *tlini* in each hand and brought them to his *terat*, which had already softened in preparation. Squirming on his lap, she slowly inserted her long, thick nipples, both of them watching as they sank into the greedy wells of his suctioning mouths.

His hands came up, cupped her back and shoulders, and brought her closer to his undulating chest. Her fragrant scent wafted sharp and heavy on the air, signaling her spiraling arousal and sparking his own enzymes in response.

'Dari gasped.

Dohsan drew in a labored breath. "Do you begin to feel it?"

Something was wrong...different. All of a sudden, *he* was burning, tingling, as if a million, million tiny insects nibbled at his flesh! "By Deth's dark master, Dohsan, I burn!"

His body writhed beneath hers, desperate for relief, urgent in its demands for satiation. In the midst of his suffering he felt her hands removing the inhibitor, felt the hot, buttery heat of her feminine flesh engulfing the head of his *cherzda*.

"You're so big!" She gasped, trying to lower herself down his thick length. "Help me."

Hands eager, he sank his fingers in the generous curve of her bottom, flexed his hips and drove his cock up into the clinging depths of her *pava*.

A scream tore from her throat as she pressed down on him. He roared as he pressed up, seeking to embed every *nicron* of his aching flesh in her welcoming *nippa*.

She rode him hard, *tlinis* bouncing, her juices flowing in generous rivulets down his cock to coat his balls and the crack of his ass.

Knowing what to expect, he still wasn't ready when the tingling began. The pain was in the unusualness of the feelings. These nerve endings had never been stimulated in such a manner. The pleasure, in contrast to the slight pain, was off the scale. He had nothing to compare it with, didn't even have enough brainpower to concentrate enough to want to compare it. With a primal shout of need and love, 'Dari shuddered to climax, *terat* and *cherzda* convulsing in agonistic ecstasy.

Above him, Dohsan rode out his stormy movements, *pava* clasped tight around his massive cock. Her fingertips dug into his shoulders, her teeth worried the bend of his neck. Her knees, bent alongside his hips, trembled as her belly rippled, muscles moving strongly beneath the skin in an accompanying orgasm.

His *terat* still on fire, he milked her nipples, generating her gift. The life-giving substance poured from her, quickly absorbed by the tiny apertures embedded in his softened *terat*.

Head swimming from the rush, 'Dari wrapped his arms around Dohsan and flipped her to her back. "My turn."

Twisting his hips, he widened the space between her legs, sank deeper into her creamy channel. "Yesterday, I was tired from chasing after you, from fighting an insane *qarm* and from three rounds of combat. Yesterday, my strength was drained. This glowrise, I intend to give you the fucking you deserve..."

Setting up a heavy, pounding rhythm, he surged in and out of her clinging *pava*. "Use that mouth to excite me. Talk to me in Earther nasty."

Dohsan's smile showed all her teeth. "I collected a lot of the terms, you know."

He knew. Answering her with a grunt, he continued to pound into her. Digging his fingers into her full ass, he lifted her into his thrusts, hitting her womb with every stroke.

Dohsan's eyes glazed over. "Oh, yes, 'Dari! Yes! Fuck me! Slam your salami in my strawberry pie! Pound my pussy! Cram your cock in my cunt!"

His *sirat* tingled as they slapped against the soft flesh cleft her ass. Heat flowed down his back and lodged in his sacs as his body transmuted her gift into viable seed.

Pleasure swamped him, empowered him, weakened him and invigorated him as his hips blurred with the speed of his thrusts. Sweat dripped from his forehead, sheened his skin. Teeth clenched against the rising climax, he lowered his mouth to her ear. "Honor me. Don't kill my seed, but welcome it. Nourish and protect it. Accept my child...the only gift I can give you."

He thought he heard a vehement yes amid the howls and screams she emitted. He couldn't be too sure, though, due to the screaming and howling he was doing, himself.

* * *

"Where do you think you're going?"

'Dari looked up from fastening his tunic. He could feel his eyes sparking green fire as they drank in her glorious beauty. "Unfortunately, I have to escort your former beau to Rb'nTraq this glowrise. He's scheduled to begin training in the corps. I'll probably stay a couple of days to make sure he begins on the right foot."

Dohsan tilted her head, let her eyes rove over the fine figure he made in his form-fitting uniform. "I'd forgotten."

He came over to her, palmed her cheek. "I would love nothing more than to spend the day with you. Instead, I'll have to spend it thinking about you."

"Yep, you will. Open your tunic and drop your pants."

He dropped his jaw. "What? I don't have time…"

Dohsan shook her head. "'Dari, 'Dari…you didn't think I'd let you get away without having your punishment, did you?"

He sputtered. "I thought our earlier session was…"

"Oh, hell, no, buddy! I dare you to name one part of that lovemaking hurtful. Since you really haven't done anything seriously wrong, I simply decided to give you the pleasure before the punishment. Sorta reverse what you did to me."

"Dohsan—!"

"You can drop the tone, I'm not impressed. You can also drop the pants, as ordered. You don't have all day."

Fingers slow in obeying, 'Dari unlooped each knot of his court tunic from its ornate frog. Even slower, he undid the loops of his pants. "I did agree to this, didn't I?"

"You did."

Dohsan left the bed to stand before him. She placed both hands palm to palm and began a gentle rubbing that steadily increased until her hands blurred. The friction of her rubbing palms created a nimbus of glowing light around her fingers.

"*What the hel?*" 'Dari watched in fascination, his eyes clinging to her flying fingers.

Bringing her hands to his chest, she sank her fingers into his terat. He'd never softened so quickly and without the smell of the flowering. The tough skin shielding them seemed to melt at her touch. The heat, though intense, didn't burn…and it didn't fade when she removed her fingers.

"What are you doing to me?" He could barely get the words out past the choking excitement.

"This will ensure you think about me all day, lover."

Both hands came about his rising *cherzda*, imprinting their image in heat. One palm cupped his broad head, engulfing it in something more than warmth. Lastly, she brought both hands to his firm buttocks and squeezed, fingers digging in, burrowing until she touched and entered his anal sphincter with one slim fingertip.

He jumped back. His body shook uncontrollably. Flooded with unrelenting heat in his *terat*, cock and ass, he cursed duty and kingdom, wanting nothing more than to stay and relieve the un-dimming aches.

Becoming aware of Dohsan fastening his clothing for him, he growled his displeasure. Gritting his teeth, he snarled at her, "This is unfair!"

"Does it hurt?"

That gave him pause. "No-o, but—"

"Better hurry along to your assignment. It wouldn't do for the commander to be caught slacking."

Eyes narrowed, GanR'dari watched the evil woman he loved sashay on light toes into the bathing facility. She looked entirely too smug for his tastes.

"Think about me," she cooed, blowing him a kiss before waving closed the door between them.

Snatching up the rest of his equipment, he slung all the stuff in his duffle and stormed over to the inner door. Palming the panel, he found it locked against him and he split the air with curses foul enough to singe the ears of any civilized person.

By Deth, he wanted to kill her or fuck her…and not in any particular order. "You've made sure of that! You just better be here, naked and ready for me when I return tonight!"

He groaned as her tinkling laughter wafted through the door, along with the unique signature scent of her flowering *pava*.

The series continues in Lori's story, *Head Over Heels,* coming soon in e-book format from Loose Id.

Glossary of Words and Phrases

'abret—Daughter of...

'abri—Son of...

betweener (or 'tweener)—A fem between the un-awakened child and the flowering adult.

bret—Daughter

bri—Son

Cherzda—Male sexual organ; cock

Cherzda'va—Literally: Cock-riser or "my cock's possession"; colloquially: life-mate. The fems of the vaShuvar use the traditional usage of the "va" pronoun meaning "possessor" so the true translation of Cherzda'va would be "my cock's possessor."

Chyya—Ruler (king/queen) interchangeable between sexes.

Chyya'va—Literally: "my ruler's possession"; colloquially: co-ruler

Cycle—Rb'qarmshi/Rb'nTraqi year = 1.538 Earth years

Deth—A mythical figure of Rb'qarmshi pre-history. He was a trickster who challenged the gods and as punishment was given several impossible tasks to achieve. He was allowed to command the assistance only of those he had succeeded in tricking. Another famous character in Rb'qarmshi mythology was Hel, commander of Pythin's armies. While mighty in battle, Hel was gullible in the extreme. Deth constantly deceived him to the point they became almost constant companions. Common curses include: *By Deth's balls; By Deth's gate; By Deth and His minions; By Deth's pillars; Deth-brat; Hel and Deth.*

Doniom—Siesta, nap. The heat in the Jakwylla mountain ranges can become unbearable and the residents tend to retire inside during the hottest part of the day. Activities take place early morning and late afternoon into the evening.

Drigini—Low-bred, social climber.

Fael—Measurement of time. Closely resembles a month. 1 Fael=1.230 Earth months.

Fem—Female. A woman or girl.

Flower—A physical sign of feminine arousal. The female gives off a scent that attracts the male, causing his terat to soften.

Frazing—Inevitable, unavoidable with negative connotations.

Gifting—The act of the female's secreting the catalyst that activates the male sperm, rendering it viable.

Glen—The syllable at the beginning of the name that denotes a first-born child and heir.

Glowrise—Daybreak

Greeve—Native reptilian type creature of Rb'qarm that resembles an Earth snake.

Hurdles of Pythin—Rb'qarmshi god of war. The hurdles of Pythin refer to a task the god set the trickster Deth for stealing the commander of his armies.

Jern—Measurement of time which is equivalent to an Earth second.

Kritch—A bird whose shrieking call is so loudly irritating, the species has become endangered. People tend to kill the bird on sight.

Lorme—Shuttle craft that seats 20, powered by Riahc generators.

Metari—Densely furred wild and ferocious animal that ranges the high mountainous area of southern Rb'qarm.

Mid-rise—Corresponds with afternoon. The rising of the second sun that begins ascension just before the height of mid-day, which usually assures a warmer climate than the early morning.

mr'nok—Disaster

Nanobyte—Miniature computerized element capable of huge memory storage. An almost self-aware electronic unit.

Nanofyle—An interactive biological computer programming of a Nanobyte.

Nicron—A measure of distance equaling less than an inch, using standard Earth measurements.

Nippa—Coarse, crass term for a female's sex. Permissible as an endearment among mated pairs.

Pava—The Rb'qarmshi /Rb'nTraqi version of ovulation. A female undergoes this fertile cycle every three Earth years. Lasts for a duration of 1.5 Earth years.

Qarm—Male from Rb'qarm.

Rb'kylla plant—A plant that grows only on Rb'qarm. It is the only source of the feminine enzyme necessary to induce male potency.

Rb'qarm—Planet of Glendevtorvas's birth and considered the Home planet of the colonists on Mars.

Rb'qarmli—Language spoken by all Rb'qarmshi and Rb'nTraqi.

Rb'qarmshi—Belonging to or coming from the planet Rb'qarm.

Rb'nTraq—Planet colonized by Rb'qarm in the distant past. The inhabitants revolted against their parent planet and a civil war ensued that lasted over 200 years. The Rb'nTraqi recently lost the war.

Rb'nTraqi—Native of Rb'nTraq

Rejas—Technically, the name of the evil, hateful, demonic god of Rb'qarmshi theology. Loosely used as Hell! Damn! I'll be damned!

Riahc—Clean power source created by harnessing sub-atomic particles. Used to power generators and vessels.

Rojas—Technically, the name of the pure, loving, supportive god of Rb'qarmshi theology. Loosely used: Good lord! Heavens! Will you look at that!

Seating—The insertion of female breasts (or other body part) into the male terat.

Shiest—Shit (literal) crap, darn it (more colloquial)

Sh'ta—Warrior

Sirat—Testicles

Sirrilian—Having to do with the planet, Sirrilic. Sirrilic is a member world of the Trade Consortium.

Soalori—Formal greeting room in most upper-class Rb'qarm and Rb'nTraq houses.

Spratot—A winged predator that hunts the wild game of the high reaches. Much like a Terran hawk.

Terat—Male sexual organs situated below the nipples. These mouths are filled with muscles which milk the breasts of their mate or lover. The terat soften when aroused, and secrete an enzyme that causes the production of the female's gift (the activated fluid that triggers male fertility). The terat tissue then absorbs the fem's fluid, in turn producing activated sperm.

Throla—Royal audience chamber

Tlini(s)—Female breasts

Traq—Male from Rb'nTraq

Uzak—loosely translated: shit

vaShafaran—Possessor of the Ancient Path (literal).

Veralla—Planet in the Reticular system. Veralla's gravity is less than one-third of Earth norm with an extremely long winter. Through a scientific anomaly, the snow on Veralla is warm and flows in drifts, it doesn't fall. Younglings love to throw themselves into a bank of snow and wallow about in the warmth and softness.

Zhi—Male pre-cum that carries an enzyme that causes the interior walls of the female sex to become more elastic to accommodate the increased swelling of the male organ during orgasm.

Phrases

"Chyya! Hoden bra'qu...? Malau ne macinee?" Literally: "Ruler! Are you attacked? Is there need for my service?"

"Sh'tai, craal i nohtan'ka!" Loosely: "Warriors, a moment alone, please!"

Camille Anthony

Camille Anthony is a pseudonym for the author who lives in the beautifully wild Low Country of South Carolina. She is a transplant from Sunny California. A fertile imagination and a love of romance fuels her writing, which she has been doing since grade school. Her favorite stories are those of strong, honorable people—whatever the race, or planet of origin—who are driven by love and lust to find and hold that one special someone. She likes her heroines feisty, her heroes dominant and her passion red hot!

You can visit her on the Web at www.camilleanthony.com or e-mail her at camilleanthony@camilleanthony.com.

~*~

Other titles by Camille Anthony currently available from Loose Id:

Light on her Toes (e-book novella)

Werewulf Journals 1: Wild in the City (e-book only)

"Carte Blanche" in *Charming the Snake* with MaryJanice Davidson and Melissa Schroeder (soon to be released in e-book and print formats, Spring 2005)

Dancing on Air (coming in 2005 in e-book format)

Werewulf Journals 2: Trolling for Love (coming in 2005 in e-book format)

Read on for a tantalizing glimpse of
Ontarian Chronicles 1: Taken by the Storm
by
Cyndi Friberg
Available now in e-book format

Aspen, Colorado
Present Day

Holidays were hell for Charlotte Layton, and New Year's Eve was the worst of all. She was twenty-nine years old, financially secure, physically attractive—and utterly alone.

Knowing this night would hit hard, she'd retreated to her cabin near Aspen. Hidden in the majestic tranquility of the Colorado Rocky Mountains, this was the only place on Earth where she could find anything resembling peace.

After several hours of staring at the television in a sightless stupor, she decided to make a list. Lists helped her organize her thoughts and set priorities. She divided the notepad down the center and labeled the columns "pros" and "cons."

Taking a quick sip of coffee in between each entry, Charlotte quickly started to fill the page.

"Pros," she began. Hearing the entries helped her analyze them. "Large, reputable law firm. Lots of opportunity to advance. Their program to prepare me for the bar." With a chuckle, she added the word *exam*. This past year had been more than enough to prepare her for the bar.

Forcing her attention back to the notepad, she continued the list. "Moving my life in a new direction. Getting away from Victor's family."

The last one made her smile. It should be enough to solidify her decision, but she felt obligated to read the cons.

"Selling the house in Cherry Creek. Moving to a place where no one knows me." She paused, tapping her pencil against the edge of the kitchen table. Was that really a con? How would she ever get beyond this hopelessness when everything she did, everything she saw reminded her of Victor and Stephen?

Her wooden chair vibrated as the low rumble of thunder passed through the cabin. How bizarre. Didn't it have to be warm for a thunderstorm? Tossing down the pencil, but keeping the coffee mug, she walked to the window and glanced out into the darkness. All she could see through the clear winter night were trees and stars.

This cabin had always been her sanctuary. Even if she moved to Seattle, she intended to keep it. She returned to the kitchen table and the decision facing her. Picking up the pencil, she focused again on the cons. "Actually moving." That was always a pain. Even with movers, it could be a nightmare. "Exchanging sunshine for rain."

She tapped the pencil against the last entry, unable to speak the words. *Not being able to visit their graves.*

Grief slammed into her with physical force, and her coffee mug shattered. Screaming, Charlotte jumped back to avoid the flying shards and splatters of hot liquid.

What the heck just happened?

She ran for a dishcloth, quickly sopping up the rivulets of coffee. Stepping back, she surveyed the mess and couldn't believe her eyes. Pieces of ceramic lay scattered across the tabletop, but her gaze gravitated toward the notepad. Coffee had saturated the paper in a distinct pattern. A nearly perfect oval now accented the words "not being able to visit their graves."

Charlotte trembled. What was going on?

She'd been beyond tears for weeks. Part of her heart had been ripped from her chest with no warning, no anesthesia. Was madness setting in?

Grabbing the trashcan from under the sink, she swiped the table with the damp dishcloth. Ceramic fragments, notepad, even the pencil, went into the plastic bin.

Charlotte pulled on her leather jacket and hurried outside. *Breathe. Just take slow deep breaths.* She stared out across her sloping yard toward the rock formation that marked the edge of her property.

You're here to plan the future, not relive the past.

Moonlight glistened off patches of snow scattered across the hill beside the cabin. Tall pine trees cast long, spiky shadows, creating eerie shapes against the ground.

Relax. This is your haven. Nothing can hurt you here.

The crisp scent of pine mixed with chimney smoke. She inhaled again, comforted by the familiar smells. Cold mountain air stung her cheeks and made her nose tingle. She drew up her hood and buried her hands in her pockets.

It was time. If she didn't move on soon, the insidious cancer nibbling at her soul would consume her completely.

A loud explosion jarred Charlotte from her musing. She stumbled to the front of the porch, steadying herself against the railing. The earth shook and lightning branched across the sky.

"We don't have thunderstorms in December," she whispered.

Three more flashes followed in quick succession. The area glowed with eerie light.

She stood transfixed by the spectacle. How was this possible?

A sizzling bolt of lightning slashed in front of her face, driving her back a step. She screamed. The air vibrated with an electrical charge and thunder shook the earth.

What the hell is going on?

Smoke curled up into the moonlight beyond the ridge adjacent to her cabin. A moment later, flames leapt into the night sky. She flew into the cabin and searched frantically for her cell phone. Houses were scattered all over this mountain.

The nine-one-one operator asked the nature of her emergency.

"A tree was just struck by lightning. There's a fire."

After a long pause, the operator said, "You're calling from a cell phone. Please give me your exact location."

She relayed the information and glanced out the window. The fire had spread. "Hurry! It's really taking off."

"Are you sure it was lightning? It's much too cold—"

"For a thunderstorm," Charlotte finished for her. "I thought the same thing, but I saw it hit and the thunder shook my cabin."

The dispatcher insisted Charlotte hold the line until she heard sirens. Ending the call, Charlotte tossed the phone onto the small kitchen table and headed back outside.

The rock formation separated her cabin from the fire, but flames leapt from tree to tree. The rhythmic flash of strobes assured her that the firefighters were near. They would likely contain the blaze long before her cabin was in danger, but she wasn't taking any chances.

She turned, intending to scrounge for a hose, when an odd flash caught her eye. Something glinted at the base of the rock formation. Was the underbrush on fire? It hadn't snowed for several days, but it shouldn't be *that* dry.

Fear tumbled through her abdomen. One quick gust in the right direction, and her property could join this nightmare. Darting back into the cabin, she dumped the firewood out of its metal bucket and filled the bucket with water.

Smoke stung her eyes and made it difficult to see, but she moved as quickly as her sloppy burden would allow. She reached the rock formation and waved her hand back and forth, trying to disperse the smoke.

A soft moan emanated from the shadows. Oh, dear God, someone was out there. She set the bucket down, wishing she had grabbed a flashlight. Had someone been struck by lightning?

Or had they started the fire?

Suspicion drove her back a step. She couldn't just abandon someone if they needed help. Taking a deep breath, she started to call out to the firefighters.

Before the cry could pass her lips, some unseen force pulled her forward and buckled her knees. A strong hand clamped around her wrist and Charlotte screamed. She scuttled backward, but the hand held tightly to her wrist.

A man pulled himself from the bushes, using her resistance as leverage. She cried out again as more and more of him was revealed. His chest was wide, hairless, and bare to the frigid night air. Moonlight gleamed off his smooth, pale skin. A long, loose garment hung open from his shoulders to tangle about his legs. The sculpted contours of his chest and arms were offered no protection by the garment.

The man's other hand found Charlotte's upper arm, pulling her forward. Long black hair streamed all around him, disappearing into the leafy debris. She couldn't see his features, but it was obvious he had no intention of letting her go. She tugged against him frantically, her heart hammering in her chest.

He spoke rapidly, but she couldn't understand his words, could hardly hear him over the roaring in her ears. His voice snapped with authority and urgency. Trembling uncontrollably, she continued to resist.

The intensity in his tone suddenly faltered. He collapsed against the ground, dragging Charlotte with him. An exotic, spicy scent filled her nose as she sprawled across his chest. She lay there helplessly for a moment, inhaling the unusual scent; it made her dizzy and weak.

His hand grasped her hair painfully and pulled her face toward his. Charlotte tried to scream, but his mouth managed to find hers through the tangle of their hair.

It wasn't a kiss. She felt the cool pressure of his lips connecting with hers, but the contact wasn't tender or intimate. It was as if he were merely forming a seal between their bodies. For a long moment, he just held her there, molding his mouth to hers. She couldn't move. Was he paralyzing her somehow, or had her fear rendered her motionless?

Her skin tingled. Her muscles vibrated with a subtle pulsation. His mouth moved and the tingling became painful. She arched away from him, struggling to separate their mouths, but his hand tightened in her hair and his arm firmly encircled her back.

Charlotte panicked, writhing desperately to break his hold. He rolled over, dragging her beneath him and pinning her against the frozen ground. She felt heat gathering in the center of her abdomen, burning and building, until her whole body shook with tension. Then he drew it out of her, like sucking soda through a straw.

He finally tore his mouth from hers and Charlotte screamed. She shoved against his chest, but he was no longer solid. Her hands passed through him and she screamed again. He shimmered, wavering between substance and spirit for just a second, and then disintegrated entirely.

Scrambling to her feet, Charlotte searched the shadows in stunned disbelief. What, in the name of God, had just happened? She leaned forward, resting her hands on her knees. She gasped and panted, and lights danced before her eyes.

You're breathing too fast. Slow it down. Think. You need to think.

Someone was running toward her. She could hear their heavy footfall crashing and skidding across the uneven ground. Sucking in a shuddering breath, she scrambled for somewhere to hide, but her rescuer appeared too quickly.

He wore full firefighter regalia, complete with a masked helmet. The beam of his flashlight crossed her face. Charlotte squinted and averted her gaze.

"Are you all right, miss?" he asked, laying his gloved hand lightly on her arm. "We heard someone screaming."

He flipped up the transparent plate protecting his face, but she could barely make out his features in the shadows. He was well over six feet tall. She couldn't decide if his obvious brawn comforted or intimidated her.

"Is everything all right?" he asked again. "Are you injured?" The beam of his flashlight made a cursory pass over her body.

"I'm sorry," she said in a shaky voice. "I didn't mean to distract you from the fire."

He brought the flashlight up again, close to, but not directly in, her face. "What made you scream? Are you sure you're not injured?"

His eyes searched her face and Charlotte had to look away. How could she begin to explain what had just happened? "There was this... I saw..." She shook her head and crossed her arms over her chest, shaking helplessly.

"What is it?" He moved closer. "What frightened you? Why are you out here alone?"

"I'm not sure," she whispered. "I thought I saw..." She suddenly realized how insane she would sound if she attempted to explain the truth. She forced herself to smile, but drifted back a step.

He looked her over more carefully, ending his assessment with a chuckle. "You're not even wearing shoes." He shined the light on her wool-lined, leather slippers.

"I was trying to find my cat, but it got so smoky I couldn't see."

He didn't seem entirely convinced. "The cat will find its own way home; they always do. And we're here to deal with the fire. We've got a paramedic with our unit. I'd like him to take a look at you."

She shook her head. "Don't be ridiculous. There's nothing wrong with me, except a momentary lapse in judgment. You've got a fire to fight, and I'm going back to my cabin."

"We've got the fire contained. Thank God everything is frozen or we could have had a real mess on our hands. Which house is yours? I'll walk you home." He grinned, his white teeth a stark contrast to his sooty face. "Just in case you weren't imagining things."

"That's not necessary."

He pulled off his glove and extended his hand. "Sanders. Rod Sanders."

She shook his hand. "Charlotte Layton."

"See, now we're not strangers, so I can walk you home."

Relenting with an anemic smile, Charlotte started down the hill. "It will be a very short walk."

"Are you the one who called in the fire?" he asked, striding along beside her.

"Yes."

"Do you live here or did you come up for the ski season?"

That wasn't a professional question, but he seemed to be nice enough. If you couldn't trust a fireman, who could you trust? "The cabin is mine, but I live in Cherry Creek. And I'm not much of a skier."

"You up here all alone?"

"That's none of your business."

As they rounded the rock formation, the lights from her cabin made his flashlight unnecessary. He flipped it off with a soft chuckle.

"You're right. I apologize."

He sounded *mostly* sincere. She motioned toward the cabin. "Well, that's it. Thanks for seeing me home."

"Would you like me to check out the cabin?"

His persistent helpfulness had lost its charm. "No, thank you. I know my imagination just ran away with me."

"All right. Happy New Year."

"Happy New Year." She forced the words past her dry lips and stepped onto the porch.

He turned to go, then hesitated. "I'm on duty for the next four days. If you need anything, anything at all, just call the station."

"Thank you, Mr. Sanders." Was he flirting with her? It had been so long, she'd forgotten the signs.

She just wanted him to go away. Between the painful memories and her bizarre hallucination, Valium tempted her more right now than a strapping firefighter.

He finally left and she rushed into the cabin. With a sigh of relief, she leaned against the door. It hadn't happened. It couldn't have happened. How could it have happened?

As much as Charlotte tried to dismiss the incident as a stress-related hallucination, she *knew* it was real. She had touched the man, felt him press her into the ground, felt the pull of whatever he drained from her body.

A simple, rational explanation eluded her, dancing on the fringes of her consciousness like a mischievous sprite. But one thing was certain—it hadn't been her imagination.

~*~

"Ms. Friberg writes with humor, passion and rich detail, making *Taken by the Storm* a treat to read. For a story that will delight, entertain, and keep you on the edge of your seat, I highly recommend *Taken by the Storm* and award it RRT's Perfect 10."

—Terrie Figueroa, *Romance Reviews Today*

"*Taken by the Storm* had it all—tense action, suspense, erotic sex, humor and a wildly imaginative plot. I encourage everyone, especially fans of futuristic romance, to read Ms. Friberg's *Ontarian Chronicles 1: Taken by the Storm*, you won't be disappointed."

—Miaka Chase, *The Romance Studio*

Turn the page for an exciting excerpt from
The Reviewers International Organization Finalist for
Best Futuristic of 2004
For the Heart of Daria
by
Doreen DeSalvo
Available now in e-book format from Loose Id

The door slid open and the lights came on automatically. The woman gave a small whimper; no doubt her eyes were sore from the blast. "Dim lights by fifty percent." The lights dimmed.

He laid the woman on his bed, then went to the communication console. "Security."

No response.

"Security," he said again, louder.

"Yes, *Sarjah?*"

"There are two men on the dock approximately five measures from the ship. Take them into confinement."

"Yes, *Sarjah.* Shall we subdue them?"

What was the English word? He'd remembered it out on the dock. "Unconscious," he blurted. "They're already unconscious."

He glanced at the woman on his bed. She was stirring, but not with the jerky movements he'd seen after a severe disrupter blast. She'd be awake soon. His sweeping shot must have barely caught her. "Has the physician left the ship?"

"Yes, *Sarjah.* Are you injured?"

"No." And the woman wasn't seriously injured, either. Still... "Have him contact me when he returns."

Probably not until morning. Gray closed the connection and returned to the bed, staring down at the woman he'd rescued. Her skin was interesting, a combination of peach and beige that he'd rarely seen on Prendara, even among Earthers. Creamy skin. In the dry, sunny atmosphere of Prendara, that peachy skin would be dark with a tan. Only the native Prendarians stayed pale; their race had adapted, evolved, until their skin was naturally shielded from the harsh sun of their home planet.

The woman's mouth twisted as if in pain, and she struggled to sit up.

He sat next to her and laid a hand on her arm. She jerked away from him. "Alone," she mumbled. And then a horrified look crossed her face, no doubt because she couldn't speak. Or maybe because she couldn't open her eyes.

"You're safe now," he said. "Safe," he repeated, in case her hearing was affected by the blast.

Her expression relaxed, but she curled up on her side until she was a tight little ball. She still shivered.

Poor thing. He reached out to brush her long black hair off of her face, but stopped. Maybe she wouldn't want him to touch her. Her legs were trembling fiercely now, from either the blast or the cold. The docking chamber had been freezing, and her legs were bare.

Completely bare. His gaze wandered from the spiky shoes she wore up to her extremely short skirt. By the gods, her legs had no hair on them. What would all that creamy, bare flesh feel like?

No. He shouldn't be fantasizing about a woman who'd been attacked for sex. There wasn't even a word in Prendarian for what those men had tried to do to her.

He pulled one side of the thermo blanket over her, hiding those tantalizing legs. She sighed and burrowed down until her shoulders were covered. Maybe she really was cold.

Perhaps a gentle touch would calm her. No reason to resist. He reached out and brushed that long ebony hair back from her forehead.

She opened her eyes and gave a start when she saw him. But the expression in her eyes wasn't fear. She almost looked like… no, she couldn't recognize him. He'd never seen her before. Those huge, velvety brown eyes of hers wouldn't be easy to forget. They dominated her angular little face.

"I won't hurt you," he said softly. "Try to relax."

Her hand curled into a fist under her chin. "Thank…" Her brows drew together in a frown, and her eyes glistened with tears. She must be frightened by her helplessness, especially after those criminals had attacked her.

But she didn't seem to mind his presence, so he stroked her hair soothingly. "You won't be able to speak normally for a few minutes," he said, keeping his voice soft. "When you've recovered, you can make your claim to the Enforcers."

"No!" She struggled to sit up, but the tangled blanket and weakness from the disrupter blast kept her down.

"Relax. You're safe."

"No…" Her mouth twisted, but no more words came out. "No…no enf."

"No Enforcers?"

Her head jerked in an abrupt nod.

He frowned. The Enforcers must be contacted. They were responsible for gathering evidence against criminals like the two men who'd attacked her.

Her eyes were luminous, gazing at him steadily. She took a deep, shuddering breath. "Please," she said slowly, as if the word cost her strength. "No Enforcers."

She was recovering quickly. Already she could speak, even if her speech was slurred. But why didn't she want to give evidence to the Enforcers? Perhaps she knew those two criminals.

No. Even if she knew them, she surely wouldn't want to protect them from prosecution. Maybe she was afraid for herself.

Ah. Maybe she was an *unlicensed* prostitute. The Enforcers would trace her identity. They'd search her credentials, find no license, and confine her. No wonder she didn't want to talk to them. As an unlicensed prostitute, she'd be locked up like her attackers.

He'd never broken the law himself. Never even bent it. But he couldn't stand to see her look so agitated. And after all she'd been through, he wasn't going to cause her any more anguish.

"As you will," he said. "The Enforcers will collect the men who…" He didn't know the English word for what they'd tried to do to her. "The men who attacked you," he finished. "But you won't have to talk to the Enforcers if you don't want to."

She put her hand over his. Her skin felt warm. Prendarian women were cold, their body temperatures a couple of degrees below his. With so few Earth women on Prendara, he'd rarely felt warm flesh against his own.

"Thank you," she said.

He covered her warm, slender hand with his own. "You're welcome."

She smiled a little. "Who are you?"

"Gray." He didn't want her to know any more, didn't want her to know he was the privileged nephew of the Premier Leader. He wanted to be himself, for once.

"I'm Daria."

He'd never heard the name before, but it suited her. What was the polite response in English? Oh, yes. "It's nice to meet you."

Her smile widened. "So formal," she said, almost teasingly. "After all we've been through, I feel like we're old friends."

If she could smile like that after what had happened to her, she was clearly a resilient woman. Her speech sounded almost normal now, barely slurred. Her lips were full, her mouth too big for her narrow chin. What would it be like to kiss a woman whose mouth felt warm against his?

Gods, what kind of lunatic was he? After enduring that attack, she'd probably want to keep her distance from all men for at least a year. Including him. He pulled his hand away from hers and shifted his weight off the bed, then stood up.

Her smile faded. She reached out and grasped his hand. "Don't leave me."

He sat down again. "You need to rest."

"No, I need…"

Her face flushed with rosy color. Fascinating. Prendarian women, for all their paleness, rarely blushed.

"What do you need, Daria?" The strange name sounded lyrical.

She looked away from him. "I need some water. I'm thirsty."

Hardly a request worth blushing over. He kept a tension bottle next to the bed. He reached down, found it, and handed it to her.

She fumbled with the toggle. "I can't open it."

Strange that her fingers were still weak, considering how well she could speak. Disrupter blasts could have strange effects. He opened the toggle and handed the bottle back to her.

She rocked back and forth, struggling to sit up. Big brown eyes pleaded up at him. "Will you help me, please?"

He'd have to get a lot closer to support her. He gathered her in his arms, blanket and all, then sat on the bed with his back against the wall and her body cradled across his lap. He propped her head up on his shoulder. She fell back against him, resting limply in his arms.

He took the tension bottle in one hand, brought his arm around her, and lifted it to her mouth. "Can you nod when you're finished?"

"Yes."

She took a small sip, sucking water from the bottle. Then another. When she tipped her head back her hair brushed his cheek, smelling like some kind of exotic flower. Why had he assumed prostitutes would wear harsh perfume? This sweet-scented woman was nothing like he imagined a prostitute to be.

Lost in her fragrance, he almost missed her nod. He closed the toggle and dropped the bottle back onto the floor. He should leave her now.

Her hand came up and rested on his chest. "Thank you."

That gently stroking hand became the focus of every nerve ending in his body. If he didn't get her off his lap soon, he'd disgrace himself with a full arousal.

But another moment would do no harm. "You must be recovered now. Your fingers are wriggling."

Those tormenting fingers stopped. "I guess so." She sounded uncertain. "But I'm still cold."

He pulled the blanket closer, up over her shoulders. "Better?"

She nodded, teasing his chin with silky hair again, and nuzzled her cheek against his shoulder. Her mouth brushed his neck in an accidental kiss. "You feel so nice and warm," she murmured, lips moving against his skin.

Gods, those lips were hot. Unbidden, his root swelled against her hip. *Sanwar.* He didn't know the appropriate word to swear in English.

She shifted away a little, then back against him. Her hips moved, gently nudging his hardness. Though she stayed in his arms, she must have noticed his erection.

"I'm sorry." He loosened his hold on her. "I'm not always the master of myself."

"It's all right," she said, her voice husky. She snuggled even closer, her warm hand curling over his collarbone. "I'm still cold. You're warming me up." When she gave a little laugh, her breath rushed against his neck. "I guess we're both warming up. And I... I don't mind."

But he did. He very much did. Holding her like this, enjoying her body, when all she sought was warmth... This was not principled.

He lifted her and stood, then laid her gently down onto her back, cushioning her head, releasing her slowly. Reluctantly. When he let go of her completely, he very nearly bent his head and kissed her.

He stood up instead. "You need rest. I'll leave you in peace until morning."

"No! Gray, please don't leave me."

How could she look at him with such distress? He had to leave, for his own sanity. And for her own peace. He'd find a different woman—a willing woman—to share his pleasure. Or he'd ease his own needs. "No one will harm you. You're safe here."

"I know." Her voice seemed unhappy, and uneasiness still dimmed her expression.

"Do you need anything before I go?"

That rosy blush flooded her cheeks again. She bit her lower lip between little white teeth. "I need you to stay. I need you to hold me again."

That made no sense. "After what happened to you tonight, I'm surprised you want anyone to touch you." *Especially a man.*

Her blush spread, creeping down her neck, disappearing under the thermo blanket. How far did that rosy color go? He vaguely remembered her breasts as small, but firm. Was she blushing that far?

Sanwar, he had to quit thinking like this.

"Actually, I..." Her blush turned even more fiery, and her gaze dropped from his eyes to his chin. "I think I need to get back on the horse."

He understood the words, but they made no sense. Was she delirious? "Back on what horse?"

She gave a breathless, husky little laugh. The sound made his stomach tighten for some inexplicable reason. "You've never heard that expression?"

He shook his head. "I grew up on Prendara. My English is a bit..." What was the word? Something about metal...an ancient metal...iron. Ah, yes. "Rusty."

"Oh. Well, getting back on the horse..." She swallowed. "After you fall off a horse, they say you should get right back on, or else you'll always be afraid to...to ride."

Afraid to *ride?* Did she mean...did she want to have *sex* with him?

It seemed a gift from the gods. He'd been lusting after her, and now she was offering herself to him.

Offering herself out of fear.

No man of principle would take pleasure from a woman in her situation. And in his position, he was expected to have more principles than most.

Unfortunately.

"You have no cause for fear. Those men are in confinement."

She frowned, and her eyes grew misty. "You're turning me down." Her voice sounded brittle. As if he'd hurt her.

As if she really did want to lie with him.

He sat on the edge of the bed. "You were attacked less than an hour ago. It's difficult to believe that you want a man to touch you at all."

She gave him a sliver of a smile. "It's like I said... I want to get right back on the horse."

She sounded sincere. What did he know about sexual attacks? Nothing. All he knew was that Daria was asking him to lie with her...and he wanted rather desperately to do it. To join her in this bed, *his* bed, and show her more pleasure than she'd ever known from any of the callous men who paid for the use of her body.

Her fingers twined with his, spreading warmth through his hand. "Maybe I need someone to remind me that not all men are animals."

Now that he could believe.

"Maybe I just need *you,*" she murmured.

His breath caught. "You don't even know me."

Her fingers tightened on his, as if she'd never let go. "I know that you saved me."

"Anyone would have done the same."

She took a shuddering breath. "Plenty of men would have joined right in. Offered to hold me down. Taken a t-turn."

Praise the gods, he'd been there to save her.

"But not you." Her voice seemed softer now. Tender, like a lover's. "I can tell you're a really nice man."

He almost smiled. A *really nice man* wouldn't be thinking about tearing the blanket off of her and burying his face between those bare, hairless thighs. "Believe me, the world's full of nice men."

Her eyes shuttered, as if a veil hid her feelings. An expression she probably had a lot of practice using. "I don't meet many nice men."

In her occupation, it was no wonder. Lying in his bed, under his thermo blanket, gazing up at him through those long-lashed eyes...she looked so innocent. Innocent and warm. He could kiss those warm lips...run his hands over those long, smooth legs...bury his face—

"Please, Gray," she said softly. "Help me. Help me forget."

~*~

"Every once in a while, you get to read a story whose characters and scenes stay with you for a very long time. *For The Heart Of Daria* is a passionate, sensual, and very heartfelt story."

—Rocio Rosado, *Coffee Time Romance*

If you like your romances electrifyingly hot and out of this world, buy... *For the Heart of Daria* and lose yourself in an erotically stellar read.

—Lady Novelistic, Romance Junkies

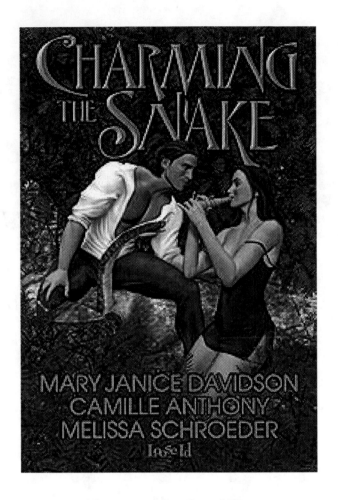

Celebrate St. Patrick's Day with a bit of blarney and a whole
lot of wicked fun...

Charming the Snake
MARYJANICE DAVIDSON
CAMILLE ANTHONY • MELISSA SCHROEDER

Coming Soon in E-book and Print

Printed in the United States
121566LV00002B/34/A

9 781596 320918